THAT FIRST
Montana
YEAR

by
DONNA L. SCOFIELD

THAT FIRST MONTANA YEAR BY DONNA L. SCOFIELD
Published by Heritage Beacon Fiction
an imprint of Lighthouse Publishing of the Carolinas
2333 Barton Oaks Dr., Raleigh, NC, 27614

ISBN: 978-1-971103-75-3
Copyright © 2015 by Donna L. Scofield
Cover design by Goran Tomic
Interior design by AtriTeX Technologies P Ltd

Available in print from your local bookstore, online, or from the publisher at:
www.lighthousepublishingofthecarolinas.com

For more information on this book and the author visit:
www.Donnahubbardscofield.com

Brought to you by the creative team at Lighthouse Publishing of the Carolinas:
Eddie Jones, Ann Tatlock, Jerri Menges, Brian Cross, Paige Boggs

Library of Congress Cataloging-in-Publication Data
Scofield, Donna L.
That First Montana Year / Donna L. Scofield 1st ed.

Printed in the United States of America

Praise for *That First Montana Year*

The dramatic opening of Donna Scofield's novel immediately draws me in. Carefully crafted details that depict the time and place lend authenticity to the plot. I care about the characters that come to life in an engaging story that combines realism with humor. I guarantee you that you will read That First Montana Year in one or two sittings.

~ Betty Van Ryder
Member of Washington State Council of Teachers of English
Served on national committee for National Council of
Teachers of English

Donna Scofield has written a wholesome inspirational and realistic Christian novel of hope set in Montana in the 1800s. Her powerful, fast-paced, can't-put-it-down novel is an emotional ride from the first page to the heart-rending conclusion.

~ Ms. Lynne Greene
Librarian, Davis High School, Yakima, WA
Professional freelance editor

You'll connect with the characters in this novel, and enjoy seeing them grow and change. If you like sweet romance with a dash of realism and historical accuracy, this book is for you.

~ Marilee Brothers
Author of The Unbidden Magic Series

A beautiful story, beautifully written. One of the most realistic historical novels I've ever read.

~**Rosanna Huffman**
Author of *Hand Me Down Husband*

That First Montana Year is a sweet, heart-tugging romance with characters and a story that follow you into the busy-ness of life. Quite engaging!

~ **Linnette R. Mullin**
Author of award-winning novel *Finding Beth*

Acknowledgments

This book was influenced by the unique beauty of Montana's Rocky Mountain Front, where the story takes place. The Homestead Village in the Museum of the Northern Great Plains in Fort Benton, Montana, was a wonderful source of information and inspiration. A special thank you to the kind people at the Choteau, Montana *Acantha* newspaper office, who located for me the out-of-print *History of Teton County*. It was invaluable.

Dedication

This book is dedicated to my husband, Russ,
my life and love partner for over sixty years, for his
constant support and encouragement.

Chapter 1

I didn't make it all the way to the privy before I lost my breakfast. I splattered the hollyhocks instead. That was when I knew that all the praying I'd been doing for the last two months was in vain.

How could I expect God to answer a prayer like that? How could I expect God to rescue me, to grant me a miracle when I'd done wrong? Will and I had both done wrong. Oh, yes, I'd repented afterward. I imagine Will had, too. He surely wouldn't have wanted this mess. I'd begged God for forgiveness, and promised never to let my desire lead me astray again. But now I knew I was going to pay for my sin.

When I heard Ma gasp, "B'Anne!" I knew my secret was out. I could have hidden it for another month at least, maybe two. Maybe by then I'd have figured out what to do. But it was too late now. Too late for a whole lot of things. I'd violated everything I'd been taught, and chosen to do wrong. Now my shame was exposed on the blossom of a hollyhock.

I rubbed the back of my hand across my mouth and turned to face Ma. It wasn't anger I saw on her face. It was sadness. I'd have felt much better if she'd been mad at me.

"Oh, B'Anne," Ma whispered, "you really are. I suspicioned it, but I didn't think it could be true."

I started to cry. "Please, Ma, don't tell Pa. Please don't."

"We have to, you know that. How do you think we'd keep something like this from your pa?" She shook her head, and her look hardened. "Who is it? Who's the father?"

I turned to the hollyhocks again, this time grateful for the bile that soured my mouth because it put off answering Ma. Of course, when I finished she was still standing there, now with her arms crossed. *Here comes the mad*, I thought.

"I … I'm not going to say." I wanted my voice to sound determined, but it trembled too much.

"We'll see about that!" Ma's voice was as steely as I'd wanted mine to be. She grabbed my arm and pulled me toward the back porch steps. "I imagine your father will change your mind, young lady!"

She sent Susie out to the field to fetch Pa, and within a few minutes I felt even guiltier than I had for the last two months. Ashamed, mortified, sick at heart as well as belly, I couldn't meet his eyes until he took my chin firmly and lifted it. In his eyes, I saw the same sadness I had seen in Ma's, but steely determination, too.

"Tell me who's responsible!" It was a command, not a question.

"It wouldn't do any good. He's long gone." I was crying hard. Pa wasn't one for hitting, but oh, how awful he could make a person feel. "He … he was a traveler, passing through to Des Moines. He was selling … selling clocks and such like to farmers, he said. I met him at the drugstore, and he bought me a strawberry phosphate. He was handsome. He said he would take me to Des Moines." I knew lying was another sin piled on top of the first one, but if there was any way out of bringing Will into this, I had to.

I hadn't thought I could feel any worse. But lying to my pa proved me wrong, and I knew it when I saw his disgust and sorrow, then suspicion. "You're lying," he said flatly. "I know my daughter. You may be in the family way, but you're not a harlot." The disgust returned. "Go to your room. I'll tend to you later."

As I headed up the stairs, I saw Tad run out the back door. *Even my big brother can't be in the same room with me*, I thought.

In the privacy of my bedroom, I cried until my throat was raw, and I couldn't breathe through my nose. I'd never felt so lonely and abandoned. Ever since I was a little girl, I'd been able to turn to God when I was troubled or frightened. Now it seemed like I couldn't. All my life Ma and Pa had taught me that God loved His children and would forgive them if they truly repented. Did I feel now like God wasn't with me because I hadn't truly repented? Had my repentance been the wrong kind … the save-your-own-skin kind?

I knelt by the side of my bed. I'd done it many times in the last two months, but this time it was different. "God, I know I've done wrong, and I'm truly sorry. I'm not asking you to rescue me. I'm begging you to forgive me, and to give me the strength to face this by myself, without hurting Ma and Pa any more than I already have. In Jesus' name, amen."

Then I got up and started pulling bloomers and shifts from my bureau drawers. I'd go to Aunt Isabel in Des Moines. For the last two months while I'd been trying to solve my problem in my mind, she was always the last, desperation answer. She'd take me in, and at least I could save my parents from embarrassment. I was glad this was the 1880s and not back in the dark ages when they could have sent me to a nunnery for misbehaving, or married me off to some cruel old man, like in the novels I read on the sly, knowing Pa and Ma would fiercely disapprove of them.

I was folding my nightgown when noise from downstairs made me hesitate, but I didn't stop. My Sunday church dress was hanging over my arm when Pa pounded on the bedroom door and roared, "Beatrice Anne, you get yourself downstairs! Now!"

I shoved the stack of clothes under the bed, took a deep breath and started down the stairs. There in the parlor stood my brother Tad, with a glower on his face that'd curdle cream. And standing beside him, his eye already swelling and a little trickle of dried blood below his nose, was Will, who used to be my sweetheart.

On a soft September evening eight months ago we'd gone for a walk down the lane, and he told me about beautiful Victoria from Boston, who'd come to visit relatives and captured his heart.

As we talked that night, I could tell he felt guilty and uncomfortable. What I felt was stunned and disbelieving. He'd been acting strange for the last few weeks … hadn't come out for Sunday supper like usual, didn't sit by me at church, didn't take me to the summer's last band concert in the square … but I'd told myself he was wrestling with problems. His mother had been hard at him to go to college back East and read law, and he didn't want to. He wanted to stay in Balsamview, our little Iowa town … with me. We'd even talked about someday, when the railroad went through, going up to Montana Territory and homesteading.

I'd known Will all my life. He and my brother were best friends. Although I was a year behind him in school, we had usually been in the same classroom. It wasn't until he held my hand for the first time that he stopped feeling like a brother.

"You and I weren't ever serious," he'd said sheepishly that long ago moonlit night. "It was just a … a childhood thing. We've been friends from the time we were little schoolmates."

I wanted to say, *And what about those kisses in the lane? What about how we were going to get married someday, soon as your ma gave up on you going to school back East?* But I wasn't going to be shamed in front of somebody I'd loved since I was eight years old. Although my heart felt like it had cracked into pieces in my chest, he'd never know it. I'd have my pride, at least.

So I'd managed a laugh, and said, "Was that worrying you? Don't be silly."

He'd glowed with relief, and I'd been able to hold back my tears until we said goodbye and I was safe in my bedroom. I knelt by my bed and prayed for Will to love me again. Later, when I could see that wasn't going to happen, I prayed for the grace to hold my head high when people looked at me with pity.

For a long time sadness washed over me every time I saw the back of his head in the pew ahead of me at church or glimpsed him in his father's store. But seeing him now it wasn't sadness I felt, it was anger and hatred.

"What are you doing here?" I snapped.

"Your brother paid me a visit. Why didn't you tell me, B'Anne? How do you think that makes me feel, being hauled out here to 'do right by you'?"

"I don't want you to 'do right by me.' I don't want anything from you. I don't want to ever see you again!"

I turned on Tad. "How did you know?" I demanded.

"I guessed." Tad studied the floor between his work boots carefully. "From the way you acted after that blizzard in February. From the way

Will started avoiding me about the same time. When you started running out to the privy every morning to throw up, I put two and two together."

"You picked a fine time to suddenly start noticing things!" I felt bad as soon as I said it because Tad was a good brother, and I saw I'd hurt his feelings. I was going to cry again, and I didn't want Will to see, so I turned to leave. But leaving wouldn't hide the fact that my actions apparently showed to everyone concerned.

Pa grabbed my arm. "You're not going anywhere," he said evenly. "Will, I think you have something to say."

Will stepped in front of me, swollen eye, bloody nose, and all. "B'Anne, I think we should get married. As soon as possible."

Well, I couldn't help it. I lost any calmness I had left. I threw myself at Pa, grabbed him around the neck, put my head on his shoulder, and howled like a baby. "Don't make me, Pa. Please don't make me. I'll go to some big city and get work; you won't have to be embarrassed by me. I can be a seamstress, or make hats, or work in a shoe factory. I could be a maid in some fancy lady's house." I looked up at the amazement on Pa's face. "I could … I could go live with Aunt Isabel in Des Moines. She'd help me. I know she would. After the baby's born she'd help me take care of it, and I'd find work."

Pa pried my arms from around his neck and stood me on my feet in front of him. "First off, there's no way you could support yourself and a baby. Second, we're not going to carry our problems to my sister. She's got enough of her own. And finally, the boy has to be given the chance to be a man. Accept his responsibility."

So that's all I was now … a responsibility. Not a woman to be loved, but a disgrace to be covered over by a marriage.

He gave me the sharp, looking-straight-into-your-heart gaze that brought sinners to the altar when he used it from the pulpit. "Most important, no grandchild of mine is going to be a bastard."

Will took my shoulder and turned me to face him. It was like I was one of those paper maché women in his pa's store, the kind they put dresses on, so ladies will buy them. People were just moving me here and there, wherever it suited them.

"I don't want to do it any more than you do, B'Anne," he said, "but it's what we've got to do. There's a child to think of. Surely working your life away in a shoe factory can't be better than marrying me."

I could tell I'd hurt his pride, but I didn't care. "Anything would be better than two people who don't love each other ... don't even *like* each other ... being tied together for the rest of their lives!"

I shrugged his hand off my shoulder and headed for the stairs. His voice followed me. "We might as well get it over with. How about day after tomorrow?"

Well, I thought despairingly, *it might be 1881 and they can't send me off to a nunnery, or marry me off to a cruel old man, but it looks like they can marry me off to a reluctant young man.*

Chapter 2

I'd hoped to be alone, but Ma followed me. She sat on the side of the bed and let me cry until I didn't have any tears left. Once the sobs turned to strangled sniffs, she wet the flannel washcloth in the pitcher on my nightstand and wiped my hot, wet face.

"Did he force you, B'Anne?" Her voice was calm and gentle. And, I think, hopeful.

"Not ... not really."

"What do you mean by 'not really'?"

Talking to Ma about this was awful. "Well ... we kissed a lot before I thought to stop him," I confessed. "And then I ... I didn't try very hard."

Ma sighed. "Oh, B'Anne, how could you?"

I'd been asking myself the question for two months, and I still didn't know the answer. I wasn't some wild floozy. I'd had good raising. Pa was a minister and Ma was the kind of woman that the Bible said was more precious than rubies. In all the time we'd been sweethearts, Will and I had never even considered not waiting for our wedding night. Oh, it had been hard sometimes, harder for Will than for me, I could tell, so I just didn't let things get started that would be hard to stop. How could I have let this happen, when we were no longer sweethearts? I didn't know the answer, so I didn't say anything to Ma's question.

"I thought he was almost engaged to that girl from Boston. So how'd this happen?"

"He was ... is. I don't know how it happened." How could I have let myself believe, even for a second, that he loved me again ... that he'd chosen me over Victoria?

"He's not engaged anymore," Ma said grimly.

"I know," I wailed, "and that's why he'll hate me all our lives." I buried my face in her lap. Oh, if I could be a little girl again, grieving about some imagined slight at school.

Ma stroked my damp hair as she had done then. "So that night you two spent in Ole Swenson's cabin, during the blizzard, was when it happened?"

"Yes, Ma. It was. Please, I don't want to talk about it anymore. I'm so ashamed. It happened, and I'm sorrier than you can know. I've disappointed you, and Pa, and shamed him something dreadful. Folks are going to talk so bad, about a minister's daughter having a shotgun wedding." I'd thought I didn't have any tears left, but here they came again.

Ma patted my shoulder, eased my head off her lap, and stood up. "You're right, B'Anne. You've shamed and disappointed us, and folks are going to gossip. You most certainly broke God's rule. But you didn't set out to hurt us on purpose. Least said, soonest mended, as my ma used to say." She pulled down the roller blind at the window and went to the door. "You rest now for a bit if you can." And she was gone.

My body rested, but my mind returned to that February blizzard.

It was a surprise storm. School let out early, and before I even got to the edge of town on old sway-backed Nell I knew I shouldn't have tried it. While I was struggling to make Nell face into the wind, Will's wagon pulled up alongside me. He told me to get in the buggy where it was warmer, and he'd take me home. He was on a delivery for his father out that way anyhow. Nell would find her way home.

I wanted to give Will a haughty refusal, but I was shivering, and my teeth were chattering. I'd been on my feet as much as on horseback, trying to force Nell on. My clothes were drenched with snow, and my mittens were full of the white powdery flakes. I climbed in the buggy.

Before we'd gone half a mile, I knew we weren't going to make it home. Every few yards Will stopped and cleared frozen moisture from the team's eyes and noses. "Look sharp out your side," he told me. "We should be close to Ole Swenson's cabin. He won't be there; I saw him get on the train to Chicago this morning, but he won't mind if we break in, under the circumstances." If the wind hadn't changed at just the right moment, we'd have missed the cabin. We didn't have to break in. Like most trusting farmers, Ole hadn't locked his door.

I lit a kerosene lamp and built a fire in the wood cookstove while Will unhitched his team and led them into Ole's stable, along with Nell, who had plunged along behind the buggy.

A search in Ole's pantry turned up only cornmeal, lard, and two withered, sprouting potatoes, so Will shoved his arms into the sleeves of his oilcloth slicker. "I was on my way out to Widow Oglethorpe's place with her monthly order," he told me. Taking the coil of rope hooked outside on the wall, he tied the loose end around his waist. "I'll get us some food from the buggy. While I'm gone, you change into something dry, or you'll end up with lung fever."

By the time he came back in with an armful of parcels, I was dressed in one of Ole's flannel shirts, which came to my knees. I simply couldn't force myself into a smelly pair of his gray long underwear, so I had wrapped a blanket around myself from the waist down. My wet clothes were draped over chairs by the stove to dry, with the bloomers and petticoat carefully covered by my dress and coat.

While the storm howled outside, we ate Widow Oglethorpe's tinned sardines and bacon that I cooked in the least-crusty skillet I could find. I peeled and fried the limp potatoes after the bacon was cooked, and we finished the meal with a tin of peaches, thanks to Widow Oglethorpe. When I handed Will his tin plate of food, our hands accidently touched, and I felt a jolt like lightning. Will's eyes met and held mine for a moment, and I couldn't help but wonder if he felt the same thing. Maybe Victoria's hold on him wasn't as strong as I thought. Then I pushed the idea out of my head. After all, they were practically betrothed. Will thanked God for the food, and we ate.

Afterward, we cleaned our dishes and huddled by the stove. Even with a healthy fire, the cabin was freezing cold. But the thing that chilled me to the bone was the prospect of making polite conversation all evening with Will. Back when we were friends we could talk forever, but now I couldn't think of anything that wouldn't sound awkward

"Ma and Pa are probably worried out of their minds."

"They probably think you spent the night in town, that old Burns saw the storm coming on and kept you at school, or sent you home with Opal or Annabelle," Will replied, "which is what he should have done."

The grandfather clock in the corner bonged seven times. Will pulled out his pocket watch and checked the time on it, then went to the clock and wound it. "I'll bet there are some checkers or dominoes or a cribbage board here someplace. Let's look around."

We found the cards and cribbage board, and in playing the game, our awkwardness faded away. At one point, I moved the wrong peg, and Will snatched my hand. "Hey, that one's mine." He didn't release my hand right away, and by the light of the kerosene lamp I saw a flush spread across his cheekbones, like the one I felt on my own. I pulled my hand away, and the game continued. I wondered if Will was as aware as I was of the closeness of our heads bent over the board. Before long the last remnants of tension faded, and we were laughing and teasing again the way we had in the pre-Victoria days. By the time the clock bonged nine times we were both beginning to yawn.

"Who sleeps where?" I asked.

"You can have the bed. I'll sleep on the floor."

"Oh, no. This filthy blanket I'm wearing is as close as I'm getting to Ole's bed. I shook the daylights out of it, but it still might have a few little friends left on it. I can't imagine lying on his mattress or putting my head on his pillow."

Will looked uncomfortable. "Me neither. But what …"

"I'll roll up in my blanket, with my clothes for a pillow, and sleep on this side of the stove. You can sleep over there." I pointed to the other side of the stove.

Will looked on Ole's bed for a blanket, then changed his mind. He dressed for the blizzard, tied the rope around his waist and went out, returning with a lap robe and the quilt that was always kept in the buggy for emergencies.

"That's not fair. I had to wrap up in a bed-buggy blanket while you had a nice clean quilt out there."

"I forgot." Will's voice was sheepish. "Really. I forgot." He offered me the quilt. "Here. We can trade."

"Never mind." I couldn't think of a way to remove the dirty gray blanket without Will seeing me dressed just in Ole's shirt.

"Here, then, take the lap robe, at least." He tucked it around my shoulders, and it seemed like his hands lingered there for a moment. A tiny hope flared inside me. Could he be wishing we were together, like we had been for so long?

We rolled up on opposite sides of the stove and were asleep in minutes. I figured God would forgive me for the brief little bedtime prayer, since I didn't have a bed to kneel by.

I woke up in the middle of the night because I was freezing. I pulled the ends of the blanket over me and felt around the floor in search of the lap robe that had slipped from my shoulders.

Another hand bumped mine. "It's all right," Will's sleepy voice said, "just cold." Now his hand touched my face, and he pulled me close. For a moment my body betrayed me, and I enjoyed the warmth of his arms. Then I put my hands on his chest and pushed. When his lips found mine, my body betrayed me again, and I kissed him back hungrily. My last sensible thought was embarrassment because my bloomers had still been too damp to put on before I went to sleep.

Afterward, turned on my side with my back to him, I cried.

"I'm sorry," Will whispered. "I'm so sorry, B'Anne, for hurting you, for … everything." He pulled me close and held me, his chest warming my back. He began stroking my bare shoulder. "We could do it again," he whispered. "It wouldn't hurt this time."

Amazed at my deceitful body, I turned to face him and put my arms around his neck. *He loves me again*, I told myself happily. He was right. It didn't hurt much the second time.

We lay there together until the room began to seem fiercely cold again, and then Will leaped up, added wood to the fire and scrambled back. He fell asleep almost immediately, but I lay awake for a long time, listening to the crackle of the fire. I knew we'd done wrong. In the Bible, and in life, good people waited until their union had been blessed by God before a man "knew" a woman. The Bible language was old-fashioned, but it fit. You "knew" each other in a special way like no other when you shared bodies. Yes, we'd done wrong by not waiting. But surely God would see that we truly loved each other and forgive us.

I lay in the dark, trying to make sense of the horrible, wonderful thing that had just happened. Did it change anything? Surely it must. Surely we couldn't go back to the way we'd been less than twelve hours ago.

But we did. In the morning, Will put more wood in the stove and crawled back beneath the covers. After a moment he said, "I guess this changes everything." His tone of voice revealed nothing.

He guesses *it changes everything? He's not sure?* Finally I broke the lengthening silence. "Not necessarily," I said, trying to hide the pain. "It doesn't have to change anything we don't want it to change. People might talk, but they'll never know for sure."*But God would know.* That burned in my heart like a branding iron. *God would know.*

People's talk didn't bother me as much as it once had. I'd spent months knowing that even my best friends were feeling sorry for me. Being an object of scandal might be a refreshing change from being an object of pity. "Close your eyes, please. I'm going to get dressed."

Obediently, Will turned his head and closed his eyes. My fingers were numb from cold and shaking with emotion, but I pulled on my bloomers and wrinkled clothes. I broke the ice on the enamel washbasin and splashed cold water on my face until I was sure my tears were under control. Then I said, "You can get up now."

I tidied Ole's cabin and then stood at the door, staring across the snow. Yes, we could make it home now. The snow was belly-deep on the horses, and it would be a difficult trip, but I knew Pa would be struggling toward us from home. And even if he wasn't, I'd crawl through the drifts rather than stay in the cabin with Will. I'd sinned. I'd cheapened myself beyond redemption and then foolishly told myself afterward that everything would turn out all right because Will had realized that he still loved me, had never really stopped loving me, had only lost sight of what we had because he was briefly infatuated with Victoria. I'd been wrong.

Now two months later, I knew I'd pay for it the rest of my life. How could I have been so foolish, thinking there was a happily ever after? More likely, I was in for a miserable ever after.

Chapter 3

Susie woke me from a sound sleep.

"Ma says to come downstairs now. Will and his pa are here." She tilted her head and gave me a long, level look. "You better wash your face first and comb your hair. And maybe change your dress. It's all wrinkly from sleeping in it." Susie was only eleven, but she was pretty smart.

"Tell them it'll be a few minutes."

Her face softened, and she patted my cheek. "It'll be all right, B'Anne." She re-wet the washcloth and handed it to me, and turned to the hooks on the wall, finding me a dress to change into. Susie wasn't just smart; she was sweet, too. Some of the girls I knew complained about their little sisters tagging along after them and tattling on them, but mine was special. She knew how to make me feel better.

I stared hopelessly in my wavy dresser mirror. My eyes were usually nothing to be ashamed of … large, and dark hazel. Now they were puffy, and my nose was red. My dark brown hair straggled out of its bun. Fair, clear skin had always been a good feature for me. Even when lots of girls' faces got all spotty, mine didn't. But now my face was so pale that the few freckles I did have showed up like fly specks on a white tablecloth, and the dark shadows under my eyes made me look old and sick. I'd lost weight from all the throwing up. I'd never been beautiful, like Victoria, but at least I'd been pretty. Now my cheekbones and chin looked sharper, like a fox. Well, I was still slender. For awhile, at least. I shuddered and turned away from the mirror.

A few minutes later, in a fresh dress, face washed, hair smoothed back, I went downstairs to face more humiliation. It wasn't as bad as I feared. At least Will's mother hadn't come along. She'd taken to her bed from the shock.

"She'll be fine," Mr. Carter said briefly. "Letty does that when things don't go her way." The look he gave me was sympathetic, not blaming.

Maybe everybody in the world didn't think it was my fault. We went into the parlor and Ma brought tea. Just like some social call. I didn't touch my tea, nor did Will.

"This is a hard thing," Will's father began. "I know you young folks don't want to get married. But it's the way it's going to be."

"What about Victoria?" I hated even saying the name, but I had to.

Will's answer was toneless, and he wasn't wasting words. "I mailed her a letter."

Mr. Carter cleared his throat and tried again. "I'm thinking it might be better for you to have a fresh start. Get away from all the talk, try to go back to a year ago, and pick up from there."

I don't know if Will was as disbelieving as I was. His face was closed. It told me nothing.

"I don't think that's possible, sir." Maybe crying myself out had helped. At least I was able to keep my voice from shaking.

Now Pa added his opinion. "B'Anne, hear us out. Mr. Carter's plan is a good one."

"My brother out in Montana Territory is alone, has no children of his own," Mr. Carter said. "He offered to help Will get a start out there earlier, before there was any thought of him going back East to school. I think it would be a good thing if Will took him up on it now. New country, new life, new start."

I remembered Will talking about it last year. He'd finished school, and was helping his pa in the store, waiting for me to finish. He'd been excited, thinking about having a farm of his own in Montana Territory. Then Victoria came to town. She was special … not a country girl. She was smart and flirty and fluttered her eyelashes till a person thought she was going blind. He fell for her like a ton of bricks. His ma saw her chance. Will had told me before how his ma had always planned for her boy to go to a fine college back East and read law, not be a small-town storekeeper like his pa.

It sure didn't take Will long to forget how he'd wanted to have a farm of his own when reading law meant living in the same city as Victoria.

Now my mind was whirling. Too many new things, too many decisions in too short a time. Common sense told me that, as dismal as the chances were for either of us to be happy, a fresh start would be better for us. We'd be in a place where nobody would know Will didn't choose to marry me but had to. When I went to the general store, I wouldn't wonder if friendly smiles were hiding pity or scorn.

Then I thought of having no one to answer my questions about having a baby, no one to share my dreams and worries. No best friend Minna. No girl cousins. Every woman wants her mother there when she has a baby, but for me, there'd be no Ma to help me through it when my baby was born.

No more sitting in the front row at church, knowing I had to be on my best behavior because the preacher's children should set an example. Often I was irritated about having to set an example, but always, the simple message Pa gave, and the familiar hymns, soothed my spirit. How can a body hear *What a Friend We Have in Jesus* and be annoyed? I pictured the loneliness of living on an isolated farm with a husband who resented me and would probably even resent the baby. I wanted to cry again, but I knew that if ever there was a time to be grown-up, this was it.

I pressed my lips together to stop their trembling and looked again at Will. I still couldn't read his stony, set face. I looked at Pa and Ma. Worried, sad, but trying to do what they thought best for me.

"All right," I said, my voice as expressionless as Will's face. "I'll go." Maybe being sent away *would* fix things.

Chapter 4

I never knew a person could get married so fast. Before my best friend Minna's wedding there were months of excited planning: fittings for the beautiful dress at the seamstress' shop; hemming more linens for her hope chest; sewing lace on new undergarments while she blushed a rosy pink; helping her and her ma decide what to serve at the wedding supper; choosing what to pack for their trip to Sioux City. There was an afternoon tea when her friends and relatives brought gifts for her new home.

My wedding was different. Instead of mailing fancy invitations, we sent Tad out with notes to Ma's two sisters, and to Minna and two other girls who had been my good friends since childhood.

Tad complained a bit about the errand, but in a joking way. "Will says that back East a man has invented a thing you can talk into where somebody miles away can hear and answer you back. If we had one of those contraptions, I could spend the day fishing, not delivering notes." The note said simply, "B'Anne and Will Carter are getting married day after tomorrow at ten o'clock in the morning, here at home, and leaving for Montana Territory immediately afterward. You're invited to the wedding." I'm sure Ma added a little explanation to her sisters. On Minna's and my friends' notes I wrote at the bottom, "Yes, things change. It's unexpected."

Then I went through my closet and bureau, packing my clothes. Ma had always made sure I had a couple of dresses as nice as we could afford cloth for, and she could sew, to wear to church on Sunday. Said she didn't want Pa looking down from the pulpit and seeing rag-tag children. I'd take those, of course, although I didn't know if Will would want to go to church with me. His family went to church … most everybody in town did … but I didn't think it was as heartfelt as it was for our family. Looking at my church dresses, I wondered if I could let out enough seams to be able to wear them in a few months. I knew I'd need sturdy, dark dresses on the wagon trip, and I'd need them after we got to Montana Territory, too. I'd be working hard, helping Will get a cabin built and a garden started. After we were settled, I'd be scrubbing clothes in a big kettle outside, and making soap, and weeding a garden.

I've never minded working hard. Once upon a time I imagined us working together, settling in our own little place. I'd pictured Will coming in from doing chores outside and putting his cold hands on my neck in the teasing way he had, or pulling me close for a quick hug before he headed to the washbasin to scrub up. It wouldn't be that way now. We'd work together when we had to, but most of the time we'd be in our own part of the world. He probably wouldn't want to be around me, reminding him of what he had to give up.

Packing for a trip would have been exciting. Packing to go away forever with someone you didn't even like anymore was the opposite. I felt as dull and dark as the work dresses I folded and put in the chest.

Ma was busy in the kitchen, setting out what she could spare in dishes, pots and pans and linens that I would need. When I looked in my half-filled hope chest, I had to blink back tears. Not much there to set up a home. About the same as the amount of hope in my heart.

That evening after supper Will came out to fetch me to his father's store. "Pa wants to outfit us, B'Anne," he explained. "This is the best time to do it. Tomorrow, he'll be helping me fix up the delivery wagon for the trip, putting on a canvas cover, greasing the axles, making sure it's in good shape for that many miles."

I hadn't moved to get my shawl, so he added impatiently, "Besides, Ma's still shut up in her bedroom. Makes this the best time to do it."

Ma must have seen the mutinous look on my face. "He's right, B'Anne. You need the help. Get your shawl and bonnet."

So we drove into town, not talking much. Halfway there I asked, "Is there a house for us to move into, or will we be staying with your uncle?"

"We'll stay with Uncle Hiram at first. But we need to take as much as we can to set up our own place. Pa says his brother probably isn't used to having folks around."

Oh, it gets better all the time. Now I'll have someone resenting me on the other end of the trip, too.

Mr. Carter's store was closed, but he was busy inside, piling boxes and bundles on the counter. "Here's what I've set out so far, B'Anne," he said. "Look it over and add what else you think you'll need."

"You shouldn't ... I wish I didn't have to ..." I began uncomfortably.

"Nonsense. I'd be spending money sending Will back East. Instead, I'm helping you two get started."

I went through the bundles, grateful that Will's mother wasn't there to make me feel even more awkward, like I was taking undeserved charity. There was a spider skillet to set on the coals for cooking on the trip, and two iron frying pans, a big kettle for boiling water, two saucepans and a coffeepot. He'd included serving utensils and mixing bowls, and a set of dishes, sturdy thick white ones.

Will had been prowling around the shelves, but now he spoke up. "Why don't you separate out what you'll need on the trip, and I can stow the rest away where it's harder to get at."

So I did. Mr. Carter added some dishtowels, baking tins, a couple of kerosene lamps, and a clock, and we moved on to food supplies. I separated some of the items out as Will had suggested, and Mr. Carter bundled up smaller amounts of the staples for use on the trip, so the larger containers would be untouched until we got to Montana.

I pictured the kitchen at home, trying to remember what was vital and what was just nice to have. After years of storekeeping, Will's pa was helpful there. He knew what women came in and bought regularly. He stacked up coffee, tea, sugar, salt, rice, beans, dried peas, flour, cornmeal, lard, saleratus, and yeast. Then he added dried fruit, a little wooden keg of smoked fish and one of salted beef. Tins of peaches and tomatoes, and even milk, came next. I eyed these cautiously. We never had store-canned food at home, but I guess I could learn to use it. I touched the little cloth bags that had already been laid out when we arrived. "What are these?" I asked.

"Spices, vanilla beans, cooking herbs, that kind of thing," Mr. Carter said with a smile. "Once you get settled, I'll bet you turn into a first-class cook."

I felt tears coming. He was such a kind, good man. I hoped Will would turn out to be more like his pa than his ma. "Thank you," I whispered. He patted my shoulder and moved to the dry goods side of the store.

"I'll put in the bacon and hams at the last minute, so we can figure out the best storage place in the wagon to keep them cooler," he said. "Now let's look for some cloth that'll serve your purpose."

I hesitated. Cloth was awfully dear. He pulled out a bolt of white outing flannel. "Diapers," he said briefly. A bolt of blue chambray followed. "Good for most anything." Then a bolt of red and white checked gingham and one of unbleached muslin. "Curtains, dresses, baby clothes, whatever."

It was full dark when we left, but the horse knew the way, and the lantern hanging on the front of the wagon shone dimly. When we stopped at the back porch, I climbed down quickly so it wouldn't look like I was expecting Will to help me, and ran inside.

Although it was late, Ma was still stacking things on the worktable in the kitchen. "We had a little bit of last summer's canning left down in the cellar, so I'm sending it along," she explained. "Strawberry preserves, bread and butter pickles, chow-chow, wild plum jam, piccalilli relish. It might be too late to plant a garden after you get there, and this'll make all the plain food taste better."

I looked at the wax-topped jars and little crocks and knew that every time I tasted those treats, I'd get homesick.

"Thank you, Ma," I murmured. I'd always wished we could live in a house by the church where Pa ministered, like most preachers' families did, but now I was grateful that he farmed as well, and that Ma thriftily preserved the crops for the family.

"I'm sending along that last batch of soap I made, too. I can make more after all this to-do is over with."

Ma picked up the sugar bowl sitting among the jars and crocks. Dainty, covered with little pink roses, it had always been my favorite thing in the house. "I think Granny Whitcomb would have wanted you to have this. She knew how you loved it."

"Are you sure you want me to take it?" My maternal grandmother and I had a special feeling for each other, from the time I was little. I would cherish the dish that had always sat in the middle of her table, then been passed on to her daughter. Still, I knew my ma loved it, too.

Ma nodded, and her voice was unsteady when she said, "I want you to have it. When you look at it, you can remember home." She put her arms around me when I started to cry. "It'll be all right, B'Anne," she whispered. "It'll work out. He's a good boy." I continued to cry, and she said, "Keep God in your heart and your home. Pray for strength and wisdom. God will help you."

She pulled a hankie from her apron pocket. I thought it was to wipe my eyes and reached for it. It was heavy. "There's three ten dollar pieces tied here," Ma explained. "I think you'll be happy, even if you have to work at it for awhile. But if worse comes to worst, it's enough to get you back home."

"But how ..." I began.

"Ever since Will took up with that girl from Boston, and I knew you wouldn't be marrying him, I've been putting most of my butter and egg money aside, saving up to send you to the teachers' college in Des Moines. Tad and your Pa put some in, too, and Tad went to the bank this afternoon and turned it into ten dollar pieces." She pressed the handkerchief firmly into my hand. "But this isn't for coming home when you have a big set-to, or you're so homesick you can't bear it. This is for something really bad, like Will takes to drink, or has other women, or doesn't provide for you and the baby." She paused for a moment. "Or beats you."

Disappointed as I was in Will, I couldn't imagine him beating me. But I took the hankie. "Thank you, Ma. I'll do my very best."

I went to sleep that night with it tucked under my pillow.

Chapter 5

Ma, Susie, and I spent the next morning cleaning the house and adding to the stack of things that would be packed into the wagon to go to Montana Territory. Ma chose two of the brightest patchwork quilts from her cedar cupboard, and we aired them out in the sunshine. "You should have brand-new ones," she worried, "but there's no time to finish even the half-done one in your hope chest."

I didn't mind taking the older ones. I could pick out patches from dresses Susie and Ma and I had worn, and Pa's and Tad's shirts. There were even a few from Granny's dresses and aprons. "I like these better than new quilts, Ma," I told her.

In midafternoon, Susie ran in from the porch where she'd been shaking rugs. "There's three buggies coming down the lane, Ma," she cried.

Ma whipped off her apron and smoothed the hair that had strayed out of its bun. "B'Anne, go change your dress. Quick!" she hissed. "And tidy your hair."

It was Aunt Sarah and her three daughters, Aunt Cora and her two daughters, my dear friend Minna and the two friends from school, Opal and Annabelle. Laden with baskets and parcels, they trooped into the house.

"Surprise!" Aunt Sarah cried. "It took some doing on short notice, but we're bringing you a party!"

Ma put the teakettle on while her sisters arranged the goodies on the table … little sandwiches, chess tarts, and sugar cookies. My cousins and the three friends from school surrounded me with hugs and squealed congratulations.

I hesitated. It would be so easy to pretend this was like every other wedding party of excited girls. Finally, I shook my head. "You all know why I'm getting married," I said flatly. "I don't think congratulations are in order."

Rose, my favorite cousin, spoke just as seriously as I had. "Yes, we know, B'Anne, but we love you. One way or another, you're getting married. And you're having a party, like it or not."

Well, I'd been honest. At least there were no false pretenses. I swallowed hard. "I appreciate your party. I'll remember it always."

There was a brand new patchwork quilt that my two aunts and five cousins had managed to put together after they got our note. "The top was already pieced," Aunt Sarah said modestly. "We just all got together and quilted it."

"Until midnight," my cousin Betsy added.

There were other surprises: a china teapot from Mr. Carter's store, one I'd admired for a long time but never expected to have. Minna had been with me once when I remarked how pretty it was, and she remembered. Opal gave me a fancy pickle dish, cut-glass. Annabelle gave me a vase, blue as the bachelor buttons that grow on the prairie. Practical Aunt Sarah brought two goose-down pillows. Aunt Cora, not so practical, gave me a framed picture of Jesus watching over two children crossing a rickety bridge. My, the stores in town must have been busy that morning.

My cousins gave me embroidered pillowcases and tea towels that I knew came from their own hope chests.

Alice said airily, "We've got plenty of time to re-stock them; none of us are getting married soon."

We all laughed when her older sister Elvira snapped, "Speak for yourself, little sister. Some of us are going to have to sew a mite faster than others!"

Cousin Rose handed me a soft bundle wrapped up in an embroidered tablecloth that I'd seen in her hope chest. I gasped at the contents. Pretty undergarments and a nightgown trimmed with ribbon and lace. She patted my hand when I turned to her in amazement. "You know we've been getting ready for me to go to the church college in Minnesota," she said. "There's plenty of time to get ready all over again before September, and I want you to have these things. There's something else, too, but it's just a loan."

She led me up to my bedroom, with all the girls traipsing behind, and had me try on the prettiest dress I'd ever seen. It was dusty pink crepe de chine, with long, full sleeves. The collar and tight cuffs were of hand-tatted lace, and the bodice was rows of finely stitched tucks.

"I want you to wear it for your wedding," Rose said. "I'd give it to you, but I'm selfish. I love it too much to let it go. It's for recitals and such at Concordia. So I tell myself you'd probably not have any place to wear it on a Montana homestead, anyhow."

"You're right," I agreed. "There wouldn't be. But I'd love to wear it tomorrow." I realized with a shock that I hadn't even paid any mind to what I'd wear for my wedding. Now I wouldn't have to. How lucky I was that Rose was so talented she'd need a fancy dress when she played in concerts and recitals at college.

We ate our treats and drank our tea. I gave thank-you's and got kisses and hugs in return, and everybody straggled out to the buggies, except Lorinda, my oldest cousin. While the rest of her family waited in the buggy, Lorinda brought out a parcel she'd stuck under the table when she first came in.

"I didn't want you to open this in front of the other girls," she told me. "There'll come a time when it takes more than wearing your apron high to hide your belly. Here are two shirtwaists Ma made me when I was carrying Bobby. They're big and blousy, and when you wear them over a skirt you don't button, it covers up the gap just fine." She opened the parcel to show me the shirtwaists and two dresses folded under them. "These are ugly as sin," she said matter-of-factly, "but they're comfortable there at the last."

She was right about them being ugly. They looked more like Mother Hubbard nightgowns than dresses, except they were calico instead of flannel. "What ...what if you need them again?" I asked.

"Oh, I'll need them again. But not soon." She knocked on the tabletop for luck. "Just mail them back when you're through with them."

I hugged her again. "Thank you, Lorinda. And thank you for not giving them to me in front of the other girls."

Ma and I tidied up the room. As she shook the tablecloth over the back porch rail so the chickens could eat the crumbs, she was shaking her head, still surprised. "That Sarah. She's the only person I know who could get such a nice party together in less than a day's time."

Will drove up just before supper. "I need everything you're taking," he said. "Pa and I have the wagon ready to load. We'll be able to head for Montana as soon as the deed's done tomorrow."

As soon as the deed's done. He can't even say the word *wedding*. I turned my back on him, too mad to talk, and marched upstairs and pointed out my trunk, packed and ready to go. Will and Tad carried it down, and my hope chest, now stuffed instead of half-empty. Ma sent Tad to the cellar for baskets to hold more miscellaneous items and food she was sending. I had already wrapped Granny's sugar bowl and the breakable gifts from the party in my new tea towels and stored them safely in the hope chest.

Will seemed a little jollier than he'd been for the last two days. He acted like he didn't even know he'd hurt my feelings, which made me wonder how thick-headed a man could be and still live. He complained in a joking way. "How much plunder are you taking, B'Anne? We've only got two horses, you know."

"As much as I need," I told him in what Ma said later was a snippy way. I couldn't help being snippy; I was still upset about those "deed is done" words. "I'm going to a place I've never seen, to a job I've never done. I'm taking everything I can." Then, in a milder voice, "My aunts and cousins and some friends from school brought me a little party this afternoon, and some nice presents." He was looking at me with a pleasant expression on his face, so I added, "Rose loaned me a pretty dress to wear tomorrow."

I wondered about that pleasant expression. Maybe he wasn't as dumb as I thought and had finally caught on that he'd said something wrong, although I doubted he even knew what it was.

He even tried a smile when he said, "That's nice. My arms are too long for my jacket sleeves, but Pa took it to Miz Browning first thing today, and she says she can have them lengthened by tomorrow morning."

"Is your ma coming?"

He looked uncomfortable. "No, I don't think so." Then he brightened a little. "But my two sisters are. And Pa, of course."

Will started to climb into the wagon, then turned and said, "Pa sent a telegram to Uncle Hiram. He won't get it until the next time he goes into Choteau; that's the town where he gets his supplies. So we can't expect an answer before we leave, but I'm sure he'll be glad to see us."

My face must have shown my dismay because he said quickly, "It'll be all right, B'Anne. He meant it when he made the offer earlier. Pa says Uncle Hiram doesn't chew his cabbage twice."

"I hope you're right." Maybe the man thought a thing over good before he spoke, and then didn't change his mind, but I hoped having a pregnant wife tag along with his nephew didn't cool his hospitality.

After Will drove back to town, we sat down to a quiet supper. Instead of just having leftovers from noon dinner, Ma had made potato soup, the food I always wanted when I was sick. She'd baked cornbread to go with it. As she took the big iron skillet out of the oven, she reminded me, "Always bake your cornbread in the iron skillet, B'Anne. It makes it nice and crusty on the bottom and cooks it better all the way through."

Pa said the blessing, and we started to eat, but it was hard to swallow over the big lump in my throat. This was the last supper I'd have around this table. Tomorrow morning we'd probably have a snatched, hurried breakfast, so this might even be the last *meal* we'd all share. But I knew Ma had made the soup especially for me, so I swallowed the lump.

At bedtime, we knelt down by our chairs like always, and Pa led family prayer. I couldn't wait for the words of comfort. Had I ever really listened to Pa's words before, when he prayed? I surely needed them now.

"Lord, please bless the two young people," he prayed. "Let their sad start turn into something better. Protect them on their trip, and watch over them as they start a home in Montana." He was silent for a moment, and when he started again his voice was kind of quivery. "Lord, keep our girl B'Anne under your wing. She takes our love with her." Then he gave his usual "Thank you for all our blessings, help the sick and afflicted, in Jesus' name, amen," and we rose.

Pa was usually a very reserved man, so it meant a lot to me when he stopped me as I headed for the stairs. He pulled me into his arms, held me tight for a moment, then kissed me on my forehead and let me go. He opened the drawer of the bureau where Ma stored table linens and pulled out a Bible. Handing it to me, he said, "Take this to your new home, B'Anne, and let it guide you. And know that your ma and I will always love you."

I opened the book to the fore-leaf. There, on the line that was supposed to hold the owner's name, Pa had written:

"Given to Beatrice Anne Hopewell by her mother and father on April 25, 1881."

Now I had two gifts for the future from my parents ... a family Bible and three ten-dollar pieces. I hoped they didn't cancel each other out.

Chapter 6

We were up before sunrise on my wedding day. We always had morning prayers at breakfast, but I didn't wait for that. "Dear Lord," I whispered, "I thank you for your protection. Please help me make it through this day. And please help Will and me to make the best of this marriage, for the sake of our baby. Please help me be the kind of wife I should be." At the very end I added, "Please soften Will's heart, so he stops hating me. In Jesus' name, amen."

Downstairs, breakfast was a rush … I didn't even bother. And we scattered to the chores Ma assigned. Then she chased the men out, and I bathed in the galvanized tub in front of the stove. I dried my hair on the back porch steps as the sun came up.

After we emptied the tub on the currant bushes and put the kitchen to rights again, Tad brought in armfuls of forsythia and wild blue iris, and I arranged them in baskets. Susie polished the parlor furniture with beeswax, although she complained she'd just done it yesterday morning. At Ma's direction, Pa and Tad carried her sewing machine out to the back porch. "It's my wedding gift to you, B'Anne," she said. "Will can just find room for it. You'll need it more than I will for awhile. I've been wanting a new one, anyhow."

It was the first I'd heard of her wanting a new one. "Ma, I can't take your machine."

"Yes, you can," she replied firmly. "You're going to hem diapers and make baby clothes, and curtains for your cabin."

Ma was right, but I still felt bad … like I was being rewarded for sinning. I could tell her mind was made up, though. When Ma's mind was made up, nothing stood in her way.

When I went upstairs to change out of my old work dress, Ma was frosting the lemon sponge cake she'd made the evening before, and Susie was filling the big coffeepot we used for church dinners.

Minna and her husband arrived early, and she hurried upstairs to my bedroom before I'd even gotten out of my old calico.

"Somebody's supposed to help the bride get dressed," she scolded.

"Oh, Minna, I'm not a bride. I'm a girl getting married because she has to."

"Shush," Minna said firmly. "You and Will loved each other before. You will again. Now get that old thing off. Because like it or not, you *are* a bride today."

She laced me into the stays that Ma was forever scolding me for not wearing and cinched it up so tight it felt like my stomach was mashed into my backbone. Then I put on the fancy new camisole and bloomers Rose had given me, and the full petticoat that went with the dress, so it stood out nice and swirly. Minna heated the curling iron in the kerosene lamp chimney while she arranged my dark brown hair in a fancy bun on top of my head. Then she curled the tendrils she'd left out by my ears and temples, and a few on the back of my neck. She stood back and looked me over.

"You're too pale."

"That's because I threw up just before you got here," I explained. "At least that's over, and I won't have to run to the privy during the fancy words."

Minna dug into her reticule and pulled out a little pot of colored stuff. She dabbed a tiny bit on each cheek and rubbed it all around until it looked natural. Then she did the same for my lips.

"Pa's going to have a fit to see me painted up," I said. "First in the family way and then a painted lady. What will he say?"

"It's so natural looking, he won't even notice." She went to the door and called down, "Susie, bring me some kitchen matches."

Susie stood there and watched in amazement as Minna lit the matches, blew them out and let them cool, then carefully penciled the sooty ends over my eyebrows. She did the same thing with my eyelashes while I cringed, afraid I'd get a match in the eye and be blinded.

I didn't let myself look in the mirror until she was all done. The fancy hair made me look taller and older, not like a scared little girl. The darkened eyelashes made my hazel eyes look bigger and brighter. The rosy stuff made my skin look not so sallow, and my chin and cheekbones not so sharp. I didn't look nearly as much like a cornered fox as I had a couple of days ago.

"Oh, mercy," my little sister said, "you look beautiful, B'Anne."

"Don't you ever try this," I warned her. "Pa will tan your hide." Maybe he should have tanned my hide more often, and I wouldn't be this way. No, I couldn't blame Pa. This was all my own doing.

I heard buggies in the lane, and voices in the parlor. Soft music from the pump organ drifted up, and I knew Rose had arrived. My hands were like ice, and a huge lump had formed in my throat. In the hurry of all the preparation I'd managed to forget what it all meant— marriage to a man who didn't want me, a baby he didn't want. I blinked back tears, afraid I'd end up with soot all over my face, and everyone would know I was painted up. I didn't want to do this. I *couldn't* do this. Then Tad hurried into my room, all brushed and important in his Sunday suit. He thrust a bouquet of flowers at me. "Will's here. He brought these for you."

It was white lilacs and pink tulips, with a bow of pink ribbon tied around them. "I saw him when I went to the store yesterday afternoon and told him your dress was pink," Minna whispered. "He said his sister picked the flowers from her garden."

Good friend Minna. Will probably hadn't even thought about flowers until she told him. Still, it was a nice thing for him to do, and it gave me the courage I needed to go through with it.

"Wait to come down until the music starts playing loud," Minna warned, as she, Tad, and Susie went downstairs.

When Rose really clomped down on those familiar chords, I left my room and came down the stairs. But I didn't do the mincy, slow walk that brides do in church weddings. I just walked down the stairs like an ordinary person.

The parlor was pretty full for a wedding that was put together in two days. My aunts and their husbands and all my cousins were there, as well as Minna and her husband and my two good friends from school, with their beaus. Will's two sisters and their families had come. The oldest one looked prissy and cold; probably shared her ma's feelings about Will marrying me. The other one smiled at me and tilted her head in a little "hello" signal.

Will, his pa and Tad were standing on one side of the parlor window. Miz Browning had done a good job on Will's jacket. I hoped he was through growing because those sleeves probably couldn't be altered again. The sleeves came down a little past his wrist, just as they should. Will was a tall boy. I was no little china doll, but my head barely came past his shoulder. I had a bitter memory of seeing Victoria and Will coming out of the store one day last summer. She was so tiny her head didn't even come up to his shoulder, and she was tilting it way back to look up at him with those batting eyelashes. He had her hand tucked inside his elbow protectively. She had a tiny little parasol, and her blond hair seemed to glitter in the sun.

Now, all these months later, I pushed the memory out of my mind and stole a quick look at Will's face. He looked like a man at a funeral, not a wedding, with his clenched jaw and rigid shoulders. I wondered if, like me, he was fighting the urge to run out the front door and not stop until he reached the county line.

Ma, Susie and Minna were on the other side of the window. Pa stood with his back to the window and the family Bible open in his hands. Will stepped out to stand in front of Pa and I joined him, holding my flowers in both hands. He reached over and put one of my hands in the crook of his elbow. I guess I should have done that myself, but I didn't think to. I wasn't comfortable touching him in such a forward way, no matter what had happened that night in the blizzard.

I sucked in my breath and stood up straight, wanting to look my best for this thrown-together wedding. I'd taken one last glance in my mirror before starting downstairs. The borrowed dress was flattering, puffing up my bosom where it needed puffing and showing my slim waist. Minna had done wonders with my thick brown hair, and her face paint made me look like a pretty girl, not a frightened child. But I'd never be as pretty as Victoria.

Then Pa began in his deep, meaningful voice, and my frivolous thoughts melted away. I listened and tried to take his words to heart, but they didn't seem to apply to Will and me. "Till death do us part" sounded more like a threat than a vow. Till death do us part, with someone who doesn't love me. Pa skipped the "you may kiss the bride" part that some folks had in weddings and some not. It didn't seem awkward to leave it out. Probably not as awkward as two chunks of ice bumping their lips together.

Afterward, there was Ma's lemon sponge cake and coffee, and opening some more gifts. Will's two sisters did well by him. The older, prissy one gave us a big kerosene lamp with roses painted on its round chimney. The nice one brought a basin and ewer to go on a bedroom bureau. It was painted with flowers, too, and there were two soft flannel washcloths and some pretty soap in the basin.

Tad and Will wrestled Ma's sewing machine into the wagon while I carefully wrapped the new breakables in linens from the hope chest and tucked them into what I hoped were safe nooks and corners. Then I went upstairs and changed from the borrowed pink dress to my Sunday gray serge skirt and striped shirtwaist.

Pa met me at the bottom of the stairs. "B'Anne, I need the Bible we gave you, to enter your marriage."

Without too much trouble, Will retrieved it from my hope chest. Pa sat down at his big desk in the corner of the parlor, dipped his pen in the inkwell, and carefully filled out the information without a blot or blemish. I looked down at the words written in Pa's firm hand: "Beatrice Anne Hopewell and William Barton Carter were united in holy wedlock on April 26, 1881, in Balsamview, Iowa, by Rev. Jacob Hopewell."

I swallowed hard as I read the statement. Somehow seeing the words there in my Bible made getting married more real than the wedding itself. Pa's finger pointed to the blank lines under what he'd written. "Here's where you'll list your children." I nodded, and Will did too.

"Yes, sir. And we'll keep the book safe." I think he was as impressed with the solemnity of the moment as I was.

Pa gave the book to Will, took my hand and pressed it over Will's so we were holding the Bible together under Pa's work-hardened fingers. "God bless you both," he whispered, and we turned to leave.

Everybody gathered around the wagon to see us off. Aunt Sarah hurried to her buggy and came back with a big basket. "This is so you won't have to cook for a little while," she explained. Oh, how I was going to miss these relatives that I'd never really appreciated before.

Suddenly Ma said, "Wait. Don't go yet. I forgot something." She brought a stoneware crock from the kitchen and handed it to me to tuck under the wagon seat. "They help with the sickness if you eat one first thing in the morning," she whispered. I lifted the lid, and the scent of her spicy gingersnaps drifted out. Ma must have made them in the middle of the night while I was sleeping.

"Oh, Ma," I whimpered. "I miss you already."

"Get a stiff back, girl. You can do it." She hugged me hard and then pushed me toward Will, who handed me up in the wagon like a gentleman should.

I waved until we rounded the bend and I couldn't see them any longer. Of course, I hadn't been able to see them through the tears for the last few minutes, anyhow.

Will handed me his big white handkerchief, quickly looking away again. I could imagine how I looked, red nose, swollen eyes. Probably I'd washed the soot off my eyelashes and down my cheeks. The pink pomade, too. "Well, it's done," he said. "Four days ago I never dreamed I'd be married and headed for Montana Territory."

I couldn't tell if he was just expressing surprise and looking ahead to an adventure halfway hopefully, or if he was bitter. Myself, I was feeling sad and lonely, and afraid. I was looking ahead, but not at all hopefully. "Me, either," I muttered. "I guess if you do wrong, you pay for it."

There was no wondering about his feelings when he replied, "I don't know if the crime was worth a life sentence, though." I don't think he had any idea how much those words hurt me.

Will turned the wagon on the main road heading west, and we rode on in silence.

Chapter 7

The sun was going down before we finally found a good spot to camp for the night, near a creek and with fallen tree branches for firewood. Will tethered the horses to graze and built a fire while I got out Aunt Sarah's basket. I boiled water for tea and filled our tin plates with fried chicken, ham biscuits, and baked beans. We ate in silence as the prairie turned from green to gray, and then black. Frogs from the creek set up their racket, and the mosquitoes found us, in spite of our smoky fire.

I cleaned our few dishes in the water I'd heated, and while Will checked on the animals, I found a bush to hide behind for a toilet. Back at the wagon, I washed and put on my nightgown. I crawled to the mattress in the middle of the wagon and pulled the quilt up to my chin, wondering what was expected of me. We'd barely spoken all afternoon. Surely Will wouldn't demand his husbandly rights.

But he did. When he joined me on the mattress, he rolled over and took me, matter-of-fact, quick, hard, wordless. He wasn't cruel, just uncaring.

Afterward, we lay there in silence for a long time. I could tell by his breathing that he was awake. I didn't think I'd ever sleep again. All I could think was years and years of this, the rest of my life. Work hard all day, cook and clean for him, and at night … this. I wanted to cry, but I didn't want Will to hear me. *Not that he'd mind*, I thought bitterly, *unless it kept him awake.*

I crawled to the head of the wagon and prepared to climb down. "Where you going?" Will asked.

"Toilet."

"Better put on shoes. Could be snakes out there."

I felt around for my shoes and slipped into them. I went farther than the bush this time. I wanted to be out of Will's hearing. I sat on the ground, wrapped my arms around my knees, and sobbed until my throat was raw.

There was no bed to kneel beside, but if I'd ever needed prayer it was now. Pa had taught us the proper way to pray when we were little children. I remember sitting on his knee while he explained, "God is your Heavenly Father. He keeps you safe and gives you everything in your life. You must always thank Him. Don't just ask for things, like a spoiled young'un at the store, wanting a licorice stick."

"Dear God, thank You for my family. I love them and will surely miss them," I whispered. I had to swallow hard before I could go on. "Please help me to be a good wife to Will so things might get better between us. Please soften Will's heart to me, and please help us make the kind of home for our baby that Pa and Ma made for me. In Jesus' name, amen."

When I returned to the wagon, I saw Will standing there in the moonlight, leaning against the wagon. "You were gone a long time," he said. "Began to think maybe a coyote got you."

It was all too much. I'd just prayed to be a good wife, but I couldn't seem to stop the bitter words boiling out of my mouth. "That'd make things easier, wouldn't it? I don't think I'd even care, except a coyote's not big enough to do the job right."

I tried to choke back the sobs, clenched my body until my teeth hurt, but they burst out anyhow. "Will, we can't do this," I cried. "*I* can't do this. Please, please let me go. We got married. Our folks can't tell us what to do now. Just take me to the nearest train station. I'll go to my aunt in Des Moines. You won't have to be bothered with me, or with the baby, I promise. We'll … we'll get a divorce … people do that sometimes nowadays … and you can marry Victoria." My voice had started out quiet and desperate, and gotten louder and higher as I went on. At the end, I was sobbing again.

Will stepped away from the wagon and put his hands on my shoulders. "Shh, shh. Calm down." He sighed deeply. "We need to talk. Not mad talk, just talk." He pulled forward one of the boxes we'd sat on at suppertime and plunked me down on it. Then he poked the fire up and put a couple of dry branches on it, and balanced the water pot on rocks so one side was over the fire. I had a feeling he was inventing things to do, to gain time.

Finally, he pulled the other box forward and sat down across from me, almost knee to knee. "I'm sorry. I shouldn't have done that. I suppose a man's got a right to his wife, but not that way like she's some girl he paid for."

He was right. That was just the way I'd felt, only I couldn't identify the feeling until he put it into words. Didn't know anything about women that men bought, I guess.

"I won't do that again, I promise." He leaned forward and touched my knee. "I'm not a bad person. I wasn't raised to act like that. My family's not as religious as yours, but we're decent people and we try to do what's right. I know what I just did isn't what God would want a husband to do."

As the fire blazed, I was able to see his face, and it looked like he meant it. There was no hardness there now. I said, "Even if you don't treat me like that again, this isn't going to work."

"Not if we keep on this way," Will agreed.

"And no matter how we try to make things work, you aren't going to be able to forgive me for costing you Victoria."

He looked away, into the darkness beyond the wagon, and then back to me. "It's time to be honest. I was beginning to have some doubts about Victoria. Ma pushed so hard for me to ask her to marry me, and the harder she pushed the more I wondered." He heaved a deep sigh, which sounded like it had come from the soles of his feet. "She was pretty and smart, and she knew how to tease a fellow till he about went crazy. When she visited here, she made me feel like I was a big, important man. But when she went back home and started writing letters, then I began to worry."

He picked up a stick and stirred the fire, not meeting my eyes. "All she talked about was parties, and dances, and ball gowns, and important people she'd been to visit. I began to wonder what we'd talk about if we got married. And if I'd be able to afford maids and ball gowns and the fancy kind of house she grew up in. And if we had anything in common at all."

I stared at him. Well, here was one thing I didn't have to worry about any longer. Maybe we still didn't like each other and didn't want to be married, but at least I didn't have to feel like I'd ruined his life.

"That night ... that night at Ole's cabin, I'd just got another of those letters from her. Shallow, frilly, vain. So I wasn't really half-asleep when it happened. I was lying there wondering if Victoria was a mistake, and remembering the good times you and I used to have."

I wanted to slap him silly and had to tamp down my anger before I was able to speak. Still, my voice wasn't even and level, like a wife's should be. I spat words out at him like bullets. "You could have said or done something different the next day, so I didn't feel so dirty and used."

"I know. I was embarrassed, and ashamed, and didn't want to look like I had come crawling back to you." He shrugged, then continued, "And I hadn't completely decided about Victoria yet."

"Well, that was big of you, to try me out so you could make up your mind!" I jumped up from my box, wanting to leave but having no place to go.

Will grabbed my arm. "Wait. That makes it sound worse than it really was." He took a deep breath and tried again. "It wasn't like that. It wasn't a thing I decided. It just ... happened. You were there close to me, and your hair smelled pretty, and your skin felt soft. I just wanted you real bad, and I didn't try to stop myself."

"What made ... tonight ... happen?" I needed to know which was the real Will: the boy I used to love, or the man who took me selfishly.

"I guess I was mad," he said sheepishly. "When we first drove off, I said something, intending to start talking like normal people, and you answered me back bitter. I figured you should be relieved the whole thing was settled, like I was, and willing to start fresh. But it seemed like you were still mad ... probably always would be. So I spent the whole rest of the afternoon feeling sorry for myself that I'd done the right thing and didn't get any credit for it, I guess."

He hung his head; I couldn't see his expression now. "I guess I decided if I weren't appreciated, I'd at least get my money's worth. I'm sorry. I'm ashamed now."

We sat in silence for a long time, surrounded by the prairie night noises ... wind through the grass, the munching of the horses as they grazed, frogs croaking from the creek. I didn't know what to say. We still didn't love each other, still didn't want to be married, but we didn't seem to hate each other now. And we were still going to have a baby. That hadn't changed.

"Maybe we can start over. Not pretending things we don't feel, but at least not hating each other." I didn't want to offer and be rebuffed, but I knew I had to make a forward step to match his.

"Yes," he said eagerly, "that's what I was thinking. There are a lot of things we both like; that hasn't changed. I'm still happy to have a farm of my own in Montana ... *our* own, I mean. And you're still the girl who could take on a life that might be hard, and do your best." He looked at me quickly. "I didn't mean that to sound like I was buying a workhorse or something like that."

I was surprised to find a little laugh bubbling out. "Well, at least you haven't checked my teeth or asked the last owner about my disposition."

"Oh, I know all about your disposition. We've been friends a long time." Will was laughing now, too. "But I'm still willing to take you to Montana."

I wondered if he felt as relieved as I did. Maybe so. But I wasn't ready for the awkwardness of sharing that mattress with him again just yet. "There's some cocoa powder and tinned milk that's not hard to get to," I offered. "Shall I make us some hot chocolate?"

"That sounds good." He followed me to the back of the wagon, and I started to climb up so I could reach into where I thought the cocoa was.

"Wait," he said. "I made this for you." He snapped up two hooks, and the back of the wagon let down on chains to make a work table. Then he reached inside and pulled out a wooden box, and set it on the ground by the workspace. "There," he said. "Step up on the box. Just the right height to be handy for you."

I felt a lump in my throat. He had done this to make my work easier when I'd been busy hating him. Of course, I thought he'd been hating me, too, but still … "That was very nice of you, Will. Thank you."

We sat by the fire and sipped our hot chocolate. "Remember when we did this as youngsters?"

"Yes, B'Anne, I do. Your ma made the best cocoa in the county."

"Do you think we'll be able to get a stove for our cabin?" I asked. "I know it was too heavy to haul in the wagon."

Will blew on his cup. "If there's not one easy to locate, Pa's going to send one up by boat to Fort Benton. That's a Montana Territory town on the Missouri River. Shouldn't be too hard to get it from there to Choteau." He took a sip. "Been talk about getting a train through to Choteau. They've already got the rail to some of the other parts of Montana Territory, but not that far north yet. Probably because it wasn't as necessary, with steamboats coming up the river to Fort Benton." He grinned at me, a little awkwardly. "Pa thought of sending us up by steamboat, but he figured we needed the long trip in the wagon to calm us down some. Might even mean we'd get to Montana on speaking terms."

"Guess he's a pretty smart man, isn't he?" After a moment I added, "I wish your ma didn't hate me so much, Will. I know it must be hard for you."

"Not really. When Ma gets her head set, she can't tolerate anyone standing in her way. That's one reason we're better off moving to Montana. She might not ever like you, but at least she can't make your life miserable."

A gust of wind stirred the fire and flapped the canvas of the wagon. Far off, a coyote yipped that sad wail that makes the hair on the back of your neck stand up. We sat silently but it didn't feel awkward, as if I had to fill the quiet with words. It felt like the old Will was sitting there with me, the boy I'd known as long as I could remember.

We'd made a beginning in our life, but I knew there'd be bumps and mudholes along the path. All I could do was hope we'd not find the road too rough to follow. I fell asleep that night praying … alone … missing Pa's prayers, but grateful for the small seed of hope Will and I had sown over cups of cocoa.

Chapter 8

I woke up with that familiar sickness in my stomach, threw off the quilt and scrambled to the front of the wagon. I didn't feel like I was going to throw up right that moment, but I knew it would come soon. I found Ma's crock of gingersnap cookies under the seat and pulled two out. Just the smell of them helped a little. To be on the safe side, I crawled down from the wagon and sat on one of the boxes by last night's cold fire. Now at least I'd be able to make it into the bushes before I disgraced myself.

I took a bite of the hard cookie and let it melt in my mouth while I thought about the events of last night. Maybe we could make this work, after all. I surely felt more hopeful than I had this time yesterday morning, getting ready for my wedding. I heard Will climb from the wagon and wondered if he was thinking about the same things I was.

"Morning," he said cheerfully, and scraped through last night's fire for live embers. There weren't any, so he gathered twigs and started a new one, and filled the water kettle from the creek.

I thought maybe I'd make it without throwing up this morning, when suddenly there it was again. I lurched into the bushes. What a thing to do on the first morning after you're married. I was embarrassed for Will to see this and hoped he was still busy at the fire. Then he touched my shoulder. "Here," he said, handing me a wet rag and a dipper of cold water. I rinsed my mouth, washed my face, and we started back to the wagon.

"Does that happen every morning?"

"Once in awhile it skips a day. But it should stop soon, Ma said. I hope she's right."

The fire was blazing nicely by now, and I warmed my hands by it before climbing in the wagon to get dressed. I folded my good skirt and shirtwaist and put them away, and pulled on a sturdy calico dress. From outside Will called, "Should I start coffee?"

What would Ma think of me letting my husband make his own coffee? Worse still, what would *Will's* ma think? I felt a little guilty, but the fact that he offered to turn his hand to woman's work put a smile in my heart. It'd be easier to get used to never hearing fancy words from Will if I remembered that sometimes actions speak louder than words. So when I answered him, I tried to put enough warmth into my voice to let him know I appreciated it.

"Thank you, Will. Tea's the only thing that stays in my stomach in the mornings, but I'd be glad to make you some coffee."

"No, I'll make it. I like it strong enough to strain through my teeth."

One more thing to remember: Will liked his coffee strong.

Breakfast was from Aunt Sarah's basket, with just Ma's gingersnaps for me, and we were underway as the sun came up.

That first day set the pattern for our journey. Before long, it seemed like we'd been rolling across the prairie forever. I sometimes got out and walked to break the monotony, and sometimes I drove the team while Will walked. After Aunt Sarah's basket was emptied, I cooked breakfast on the morning fire, usually side meat, with cornbread or sometimes biscuits baked in the Dutch oven, set in the coals. For the first week, I started cooking the meal, and Will finished it while I threw up in the bushes. Then the sickness stopped.

I tried to use the morning fire to fix something we could eat cold at noon, too. We always stopped at that point for an hour or so to let the horses rest and graze. We passed quite a few farms in the first part of the trip. Often we'd buy milk, eggs or butter from the housewife, just enough to use up before they went bad. After awhile the farms were few and far between, so we couldn't buy those staples, but Will was able to bring down a rabbit or a brace of prairie chickens during the day when needed. In the evenings, I cooked a good hot meal from our supplies, or from whatever Will had shot. Sitting by the warm fire in the evening's chill, hearing the creek gurgle and frogs rumble, the food tasted better than a banquet.

For days the view was the same ... flat prairie and waving grass. Then desolate prairie, with lots of rocks and not much waving grass.

Some days we talked about the future.

"I hope Choteau's not like this," Will said, as the dust rolled up behind us, "so dry and barren. I guess a person could get used to it if they could make a living farming. Folks must, or Uncle Hiram wouldn't have stayed on, and there wouldn't be a little town. But it'd feel a lot more like home with trees and creeks, like Iowa."

"Ma says you can put down roots and be happy wherever you are, as long as you're with your family." I snuck a sideways glance at his face, and dared to add, "I'm hoping we can be a family." I hungered to hear Will say something sweet and magical, like in the old-timey love songs.

He just nodded and said, "We will be."

Some days we didn't talk much. Will's face would seem closed and withdrawn to me. I was afraid he was thinking about Victoria in Boston. No matter what he had said that night by the fire, there had to be some feelings left ... probably regret. If he was drawn to her beauty, the memory must linger, and there was nothing I could do about that.

Or he might be worrying about the future, picturing hard work and failure. If I thought that was what was troubling him, I'd try to cheer him up. I'd make a cautious start: "I wish the horses could go faster. I can hardly wait to get started ... find the land, plant a garden, get a little place built." If he perked up and responded, the climate got better. If he didn't, it was a long, quiet day, with my worries buzzing around in my head like blowflies looking for a place to land.

"I think we're in Montana Territory now," Will said one morning when we'd been on the trail about two and a half weeks. Then, evidently seeing the excitement on my face, he added quickly, "*Southeast* Montana. Still a long way to go."

The weather had been unseasonably hot for the last few days, so we were pleased to see a cloud bank rolling in. The cool, fresh breeze lifted our spirits like a glass of lemonade in the sweltering summertime.

Soon, though, it was more than a fresh breeze. Wailing gusts of wind rattled the canvas wagon cover. Thunder rolled overhead and lightning sizzled from the sky. The horses shied and whinnied in terror.

"We've got to get to shelter!" Will shouted over the howl of the wind, peering through the curtains of rain as he struggled to control the team. "We passed a gully a little way back. We can get out of the wind there. It'll have to do."

He forced the horses to turn and when we reached the gully, they scrambled and slid down the slope, the wagon careening behind them.

"Get under the wagon!"

I hurried to obey. I was soaked by the time I got under, but at least the wagon protected me from the wind. A few feet away, I could see Will's legs as he stood between the horses, trying to calm them.

A nearby flash left that sharp lightning smell. On hands and knees, I scrambled to the front end and stuck my head out. "Will, get under cover!" I screamed.

"Can't," he shouted back. "They're about to go crazy!"

I crawled out to help him. Surely two bodies could hold the horses better than one.

"Get back under the wagon!" he bellowed. "Do you want to get killed?"

Well, of course I didn't want to get killed. I didn't want him to get killed, either. But this didn't seem to be the time to argue. As I scurried under the wagon, a huge gust shrieked past us. With a ripping sound, the canvas wagon cover billowed and soared up and away.

"Oh, no," I heard Will groan, barely audible through the wind and rain. "Watch it," he yelled. "We'll have to find it."

I followed the white cover with my eyes until I lost it in a flash of lightning.

The wind, thunder, and lightning stopped almost at the same time, but the rain poured down in a deluge. The horses were still spooked, so Will continued to stand between them, holding their halters while water ran off his hat brim. I listened to the downpour pounding the grass around me and pictured the supplies and bedding just above my head being soaked.

"Come out, B'Anne, we've got to get higher." Will's voice was hoarse and sounded exhausted. As I crawled out, what had been a dry gully turned into a fast-running creek. Will pulled and talked the horses up the slope. Handing the reins to me, he said, "They're calmer now. Hang onto them for a minute." He climbed into the wagon and got our big cooking pot and two buckets, and set them on the ground to catch the rain. Then he unhitched the horses and led them over to a big rock. Beckoning for me to follow, he slumped down on the rock, still holding the reins.

"We can't get much wetter than we are already, but sitting on the rock's probably more comfortable than the soggy ground. Maybe the rain will wash the mud off us."

I joined him, and we sat side by side on the rock in the pouring rain. Will shifted the reins to his other hand and put his arm around my shoulders. "Well, I thought things were going a little bit too smooth."

I nodded. "I've heard of gully-washers. Now I know what the word means."

When the rain slackened, Will tethered Gracie to a stake. Then he saddled Gus. Pulling out the bundle of kindling we always kept in the wagon for the next fire, he piled it on the ground and dug a hole. We gathered brush from under the sage bushes, where it had been protected from the rain, and he chopped off lower branches that had stayed a little dryer. He started a fire in the hole, slowly and carefully adding brush until it took hold.

"I'm going after the wagon cover. We can't do without it." He added another sage branch as he talked. "I hope I'll be back by dark, but if I'm not, the fire will guide me in. Probably be a good idea to light the kerosene lanterns, too, and set them up on the rock."

I wanted to sound brave, but I'm afraid my voice quavered. "Let me come with you, Will. I can help you look."

He shook his head. "We can't leave the wagon untended. I'll load the gun before I go, but you won't need it. We haven't seen any other folks for quite awhile."

"What about coyotes or wolves?"

"The fire will keep them off, if there are any around."

He coiled a big loop of rope around the saddle horn to tie around the cover to make it easier to carry and got ready to climb into the saddle. I must have looked as pitiful as I felt because he put his arms around me for a minute. "You'll be all right, B'Anne. I'll be right back.

And remember, you couldn't come with me, anyhow. You can't ride horseback when you're in the family way. You just hunker down and wait for me." Then he set off in the direction of where we'd last seen the wagon cover.

Well, I hunkered down for a little while, adding tears to the general wetness. The rain stopped completely, and the traitor sun beamed down like nothing bad had ever happened, and raised steam off the wet prairie. I looked at my little stack of sagebrush branches, took the hatchet and attacked the lower branches around me until the stack was big enough to last through the whole night if it had to. But I surely hoped it didn't have to. We'd learned that sage makes a quick, hot fire, but it doesn't hold like wood does, so I had to have a pretty big stack before I stopped.

I climbed up in the wagon and threw down our wet bedding, and spread it over bushes in the sun. Most of the water had run out the seams of the wagon bed, but I mopped up the corners that were still wet. Thank the good Lord Will's pa had packed the flour, cornmeal and sugar in metal tins. I spread out the canvas ground cover we'd brought along in case we had to sleep on the ground, and laid our wet food supplies on it to dry.

The sun moved slowly to the west, and still no Will. I cut some more branches, turned the drying bedding and supplies. I thought about bringing some water up from the gully, but it was fast drying up, and what was left was muddy, so I was glad Will had thought to catch the rainwater.

When twilight started to creep in, I raked some of the embers to one side and put the Dutch oven over them. Then I baked a skillet of cornbread. I'd cook bacon at the last minute, when I spotted Will.

I lit the kerosene lanterns and put them on the rock. How I wished I had a higher place to put them, so Will would be sure to see their light. I climbed up to the wagon seat so I could see farther over the prairie, without the fire blinding me, and knelt to pray. Yes, I thanked God, but mostly I prayed for Will's safety. Wet food and damaged goods weren't important, but Will was.

The night birds tuned up their voices. Out at the edge of the darkness I saw nighthawks and owls swoop and snatch their supper as it scurried through the grass. Coyotes wailed, far enough away to not scare me yet. I made sure the gun was beside me, just in case.

Still no Will.

What if something had happened to him? What if the horse had stepped in a gopher hole and fallen on him? What if he'd strayed into some canyon and couldn't see the fire or lanterns? What if I never saw him again?

I was wiping my tears with my sleeve when I realized that I wasn't frightened for myself. I could always hitch Gracie to the wagon and follow the track back the way we'd come. This horrible empty feeling was because I was imagining a life without Will.

Gracie nickered and I heard an answer from the darkness. I jumped down, grabbed a lantern and stumbled toward the sound. There came Gus, with a big white bundle on his back.

"Will?" I called out.

"I got it!" he yelled triumphantly. "Had to go halfway back to Iowa, but I got it!"

He swung off the horse and came to meet me. I put down the lantern and ran toward him. We met in the middle, arms tight around each other.

After a moment, Will lifted his head. "You're crying," he exclaimed. "You didn't need to be that scared, B'Anne. You were safe."

I buried my head on his shoulder. "I wasn't scared for me ... I was scared for you." Then I babbled out all the dangers I'd imagined, ending with Will being eaten by a coyote.

Even though he had to be exhausted, Will started laughing. "B'Anne, if there were ever a coyote big enough to eat a human being, it'd be in some traveling medicine show."

I wiped my face on my damp skirt-tail as we walked to the wagon. I fried the bacon and opened a tin of milk to make gravy to go over the cornbread, while Will walked around with the lantern, admiring the way I'd spread things out to dry.

We spent two days at that campsite drying out our belongings and waiting for the prairie to firm up again, so we wouldn't be slogging through mud. Will took the buckets and rode ahead to the creek we'd been following before the storm, so I could do a laundry, as long as we were stopped anyhow. He nailed the canvas cover back on the wagon, and then we were on our way again.

One afternoon, a dark smudge appeared on the horizon, and within a few days we could see that it was faraway mountains.

"I'm glad we're not going all the way to Oregon," Will said. "They don't look like anything I'd want to cross in a wagon."

Soon the grass was thicker again, and beyond the foothills that were our destination, the jagged, snow-covered Rockies jutted into the sky, their peaks wearing shawls of misty clouds draped on their shoulders.

"Do you think it'll be colder in Choteau since it's close to the foothills?" I asked. "Is it good garden country?"

"I think it's good for growing. It's not right up against the mountains. Pa says it's called the Rocky Mountain Front. He came out quite a few years ago to visit Uncle Hiram. Pa said Choteau was still prairie, but beginning to get some little hills and valleys. More trees there than on the prairie. Sounds like folks would be able to have good gardens. Shorter growing season, though." A long pause, then "I sure hope he remembered right."

Seeing those faraway mountains made the end of our trip seem closer. I was getting anxious to be in a house again ... but a house of our own, not just staying with Will's Uncle Hiram.

A wave of homesickness washed over me. It wasn't as bad as it would have been if Will and I still hated each other, but sometimes that lonely feeling snuck in unexpected.

We were friends now ... more than friends in the night under the patchwork quilt, with the dying fire making a glow outside the canvas.

I was happier than I'd expected to be when we set out from Iowa, but I was careful. I didn't take it for granted that this would last forever. Even under the patchwork quilt, Will had never said "I love you." The first time he'd reached for me, about a week after that awful wedding night, he was awkward and careful. I could tell he wanted to be sure I didn't think it was going to be like that again. And it wasn't. He was gentle and considerate. After a few nights, it gave me pleasure, too. I'd always heard that this was a distasteful thing women had to put up with because their husbands wanted it, so I was surprised. Then I remembered how Minna had blushed and smiled when they got back from their wedding trip, like she had a secret she wasn't ready to tell me. That sly minx.

Will seemed to enjoy it a lot, which pleased me. Maybe it would make being married seem like not such a burden when he had this to look forward to. But I was careful to not ask too much of him. I didn't wait to be helped down from the wagon. Soon enough, the time would come when he'd *have* to help me. As long as I was able-bodied, he didn't have to.

My mind would rest easier if I didn't have to wonder what the future would be like. Much as he enjoyed the nighttime thing, what would happen when I was big and awkward, and he couldn't have that pleasure? Would he remember back to Victoria, and resent me again? What would happen if Montana turned out to be a disappointment, if we worked like dogs without success, and I didn't have enough supplies to make good meals, and my clothes got old and ragged? Would he wish he were still free, not stuck on a homestead with someone he didn't love?

One afternoon in the middle of my worrying, Will stopped the wagon and reached behind the seat for his rifle. Handing me the reins, he jumped down. "Follow the ruts for awhile," he said as he headed out onto the prairie. "A rabbit just hopped across the trail into the grass. With any luck, we can have it for supper."

A few minutes later, I heard a shot. I slowed the horses until they were moseying along. I didn't feel comfortable alone out here on the big, wide, empty plain. There was such a lonesome feeling, the sky a huge bowl overhead, the land stretching far as the eye could see without another human being in sight, and the wind sounding mournful, bending the grass and lifting it again. When Will came loping up to the wagon, I was as relieved as if he'd been gone for days, not minutes.

We let the horses graze while he cleaned the rabbit, and I fixed a bowl of salt water for it to soak in. Might take out some of the gaminess; might even make it a little tender, although past experience told me that was a slim chance. These jackrabbits had muscles like racehorses, Will said.

When we stopped that evening, I browned the meat in the spider pan and then added a little water so it'd simmer until we were too hungry to wait any longer. I added a big pinch of sage and some wild onions we'd found by the creek when we stopped at noon, and baked biscuits in the Dutch oven.

The sun disappeared behind the Rockies long before we perched on wooden boxes to eat stewed rabbit and sop up the gravy with biscuits. Nighthawks spiraled and swooped in the darkening sky over the prairie. The soft sigh of wind through grass sounded like some strange, sad music, but the matter-of-fact chomping of the horses took away that foolish notion.

Will took another biscuit and spooned gravy over it. "Good supper," he said approvingly. Jerking his head toward the hungrily feeding horses, he said, "I hope Gus and Gracie get a bellyful of grass tonight. They're going to need it tomorrow." He took a bite and chewed the tough meat energetically, finally swallowing it with a mouthful of coffee. "Did you notice we started climbing this afternoon?"

"Finally." I rearranged the food on my plate with listless little pushes of my two-tined fork. I was sick of rabbit and prairie hen, even of antelope. I was sick to *death* of bacon, ham and salt pork that was just this side of rancid. I wanted something green.

"I'm always going to start an early garden, like Ma does," I said.

We had never spoken of "always," of any future more distant than the coming seedtime and harvest. It saddened me that we never talked about the baby I carried. A baby deserves parents who look forward to its birth. My cousin Lorinda had feather-stitched hems in tiny gowns and confided, with a cozy smile in her voice, "Arthur's hoping for a boy, of course. Wants to name him James, after his father … Arthur's father, that is … the baby's grandpa." A few stitches in silence, then, "Arthur says our sons are going to be more than farmers. Well, maybe the first one can be a farmer, to inherit the place and take care of us when we're old, but the rest are going to get a good education, Arthur says. Even the girls."

I was pretty sure *my* baby's father thought of his child as strictly a duty. Or maybe a punishment. To compensate, I sometimes patted the stomach that was beginning to show a tiny bulge when I undressed to put on my nightgown. *I love you, baby,* I would send in thought. And I would picture a tow-headed boy scattering corn for the chickens, or a little girl in pinafore and pigtails standing on a chair to cut out sugar cookies.

"Want me to get your shawl?" Will asked. "Seems colder tonight; probably because we're higher up, closer to the mountains."

"No, I'm fine." I longed to dump my uneaten supper in the grass but knew I must try a few more bites, at least. "There's still some apple butter left in that little crock if you want some on your biscuit."

"Apple butter would taste pretty good." Will got up to get the crock. "You want some?"

"Yes, just a dab on my biscuit." Apple butter had, at least, been fresh at one time.

Will shoved a clump of sagebrush branches into the fire, and the crackling of the flames blended with the yipping night song of coyotes and the rush of wind through the prairie grass. The air was getting chillier by the minute. We finished supper quickly, and I washed dishes in the pot of water that had been heating at the edge of the fire, while Will re-tethered the horses in fresh grass closer to the wagon.

When Will joined me on our straw tick, he pulled me against his chest and sank quickly into sleep, still holding me in his arms.

Half-asleep, I tried to decide whether this was a good course of events. Did it mean I meant more to him than satisfying a quick hunger? Or was it, maybe that he was already growing tired of the only thing I had to offer?

The wind flapped the canvas wagon cover, and the eerie cry of coyotes made a little shiver run up my spine. I nestled closer to Will's warmth. Maybe I'd better just be content with what I had.

The next day, and the next, and for what seemed like forever, we moved toward mountains that never seemed to get any closer.

"I'll bet it'll only be a few years before folks don't have to make this long trip by wagon," Will said, gesturing out toward the seemingly endless prairie. "Here it is 1881, and there's railroad all the way out to Oregon, but not up north where we're going. Guess the Missouri River does the job instead of a train. Surely won't be much longer, though."

"Well, I'd like to be on a train right now. Sure would feel better than this wagon seat."

The skin on my face felt tight from the sun and wind, and I wished too late that I'd followed Ma's advice and worn a sunbonnet. My lips were so dry and blistery that the little pot of glycerin and rosewater didn't do any good. My back ached from the constant jostling of the wagon.

One of Will's silent afternoons came when I was feeling lower than I had since that awful wedding night. I snuck a sideways look at his set jaw as we lurched and rumbled across the prairie. It was all I could do to keep from grabbing his sunburned ear, jerking his head around to face me, and telling him just exactly what I truly thought about leaving everybody I loved behind and traveling across Purgatory to what might be Hell, for all I knew.

My fingers were tingling with what I wanted to do; I could just feel the satisfaction of grabbing his ear. But I pressed my lips together and stared at the mountains again. Surely they were closer today. They had to be. Who cared where we were headed for? At least I'd be able to climb down from this cursed wagon.

Chapter 9

We pulled into Choteau on June 2, in the midafternoon. I'd never been so glad to see storefronts and wooden sidewalks in my life. Choteau wasn't a big town, but it was the end of the journey, and as far as I was concerned, the general store provided all the civilization I needed. The Rockies looming over Choteau's shoulder made it seem all the more a welcoming haven.

"Look." Will gestured toward the sign hanging outside a two-story white house next to the general store, "There's a doctor. And a dry goods store, as well as the general store."

"And two saloons." I echoed the opinions I'd grown up with. My folks disapproved of liquor.

"You sound just like your mother," Will said with a chuckle, "and a lot like mine."

I changed the subject quickly. "How far from town is your Uncle Hiram's place?"

"About five miles, Pa said." Will pulled gently on the reins and angled the horses to a stop in front of the general store. "We'll ask some questions here, and then head out. Should be able to get there by dark."

I looked down at my wrinkled dress. I wanted to go inside the store, even if it was just to admire the stocked shelves. It'd been a long time since we'd even waved or exchanged a few words with people we met in other wagons. But I didn't want to embarrass Will or myself with my appearance. "I think I'll just wait here in the wagon."

"Don't be silly. We need to get some supplies to take out with us." Will saw me trying to brush the wrinkles from my skirt. "Is that why you don't want to go in? You look fine." He nodded toward a woman walking down the board sidewalk in faded calico and a sunbonnet. "See? Let's go."

We bought some butter, eggs, and a jug of milk. "I doubt if Uncle Hiram keeps a milk cow," Will explained. "Living alone, he probably wouldn't want to be bothered with feeding and milking."

The storekeeper explained how to get to Hiram Carter's place, and we started out again. It wasn't a road we were following, just a wagon trail. The afternoon was beautiful; warm but with a soft breeze bending the tall grass. Unlike the desolate expanse of prairie we had traveled through, this grass was lush and green. The endless flatness had been replaced with gentle little hills and hollows. There were clumps of wild roses here and there, and down by the creek, willow and cottonwood trees. Meadowlarks trilled their song over the waving grass.

"This is pretty country," I said. "It's more like Iowa than all that dry land we passed through."

"Pa said it's because there's more rain closer to the mountains."

After awhile, the trail dwindled down to just a pair of wheel tracks, and then we topped a gentle rise and saw Uncle Hiram's place on the prairie below. It looked good to me, after living for more than a month in a wagon. There was a sturdy log cabin, a barn, a fenced enclosure, and a couple more small outbuildings.

My heart started to beat a little faster. Had Will's uncle received the telegram? What if he didn't even know we were coming, and we showed up on his doorstep? He'd never married; what if he didn't like women and resented me? He could be a stubborn, woman-hating old bachelor for all I knew.

I suddenly pictured the cluttered cabin of the old bachelor Ole, where this whole misadventure started when our baby was conceived that night of the blizzard. Remembering Ole's filthy bedding and the empty tin cans he kept all over the place to spit tobacco in, my stomach gave a little lurch of nausea.

"Is your uncle a … a nice man?" I probably should have asked that question about eight hundred miles ago.

"Don't know," Will answered cheerfully. "Never met him."

"What?" My mouth dropped open in shock. "Your pa sent us out to somebody you've never even met?"

"When we talked about it, Pa told me Uncle Hiram was probably lonesome for kinfolk. I'm the only boy in the family. Pa says when I was born Uncle Hiram sent a twenty-dollar gold piece for me. He sent a letter, too, telling Pa to raise me up good and strong, so when I was grown I could come out to Montana and be a rancher." Will gave me a little grin and added, "Pa said Ma put the gold piece in the bank, but she burned the letter in the kitchen stove."

I was so flummoxed I couldn't speak for a moment. Then I said, "So all we know is your uncle did something so bad that your mother cut him out of the family. But we don't know what that bad thing was. Blood's thicker than water, so your pa still loves him. When you were born, he sent a gold piece and an invitation to come out to see him if they raised you strong enough." I felt like snatching the reins and turning the wagon back in the direction we'd come from. Instead, I gave a long sigh and tried to make my voice calm. "Well, I sure hope they raised you strong enough, and that he hasn't changed his mind in the last eighteen years. And I hope the bad thing he did wasn't killing somebody."

"It'll all work out, B'Anne, and we'll only be there for a little while, till we get our own cabin up. We can sleep in the wagon so we don't get in his way. We'll be able to tell if he doesn't want us. If that's the case, we'll just find our piece of land and camp on it till we get a cabin built."

Will's face looked a lot more serious than it had a few minutes ago, so I dropped the subject. Besides, what good would it do to worry about it now? It wouldn't change anything. As Ma would have said, we'd made our bed and now we had to lie in it.

When we drove up, Will tied the horses to the corral fence and helped me down. I let him help me this time, feeling so unsure of myself I was afraid I might stumble. We walked up onto the little porch and Will called out, "Hallo the house! Uncle Hiram, it's Will."

An older man, a little bent and bow-legged but looking a lot like Will's pa, came around the corner of the house. "Howdy. Got your telegram when I went into town last week, so I figured you'd be driving in any day." He shook Will's hand, and Will introduced him to me.

The old man gave me a long looking-over. "You're both pretty young to be married. Hope you're tough enough to make it. Time will tell."

It wasn't a very warm welcome, but at least he hadn't sent us away. He led us inside. "We don't have enough daylight left to show you the place I have in mind, but we can head over there first thing in the morning. We don't want to waste any time. It's a prime piece, and nobody's claimed it yet. Homesteading's been a little slower this far north, but now that there's talk of the railroad coming in, it's going to pick up mighty fast." He gestured to the wash-stand in the corner. "You probably want to wash up. The necessary's out back. Supper's ready in a little bit."

I offered to help.

"It's just stew. Nothing left to do."

Twilight crept in as we ate. Uncle Hiram lit the kerosene lamp and shut the door. "Cools off pretty quick at night," he said. "Gets mighty hot in the summertime, but the nights aren't too bad. We get a few when it doesn't cool off, but not many."

I insisted on washing the dishes while Will and his uncle talked about farming and cattle, and the family back in Iowa. Afterward, Hiram lit a kerosene lantern for us to take out to the wagon. "Your pa followed up the telegram with a letter. I know you've got a rough start ahead of you. Let's hope you both got enough starch in your backbone to see it through." He swung his level gaze to me. "'Specially you, missy. Homesteading's harder on women. If they're fond of frills and furbelows, it's extra hard." He handed the lantern to Will and closed the door behind us.

Out in our wagon, I said, "I don't think he likes me, Will. He seemed glad enough to see you, but I felt in the way."

"I'm sure he doesn't dislike you, B'Anne. He just doesn't have any fancy parlor manners. That's probably why Ma doesn't like him. You worry too much."

"Well, maybe you don't worry *enough*. The only time he talked to me was just as we were leaving."

"It'd be better if you wait until you really have something to worry about before you start in. We've got to get up early in the morning. Good night." He didn't even kiss me. Well, what did I expect? I guess Will didn't have any parlor manners either. Must run in the family.

Next morning we rode across a stretch of green prairie, crossed the creek, and walked the horses up and down some gradual rises until we came to the piece of land Uncle Hiram had in mind. He was right. It was a pretty place. There was a perfect home site atop a small knoll that angled down to a creek. There were even a couple of cottonwood trees to provide shade. The creek banks and a slope off to the west were wooded, a pleasant surprise after the prairie.

Uncle Hiram gestured toward the knoll. "Since there's trees there, I don't think you'd have to dig very deep for a well. And you've got a good clean creek to carry water from till you get one dug." He turned slowly, looking across the land in all directions. "I almost claimed here instead of where I am, but since I had wheat in mind, I wanted flat land. If you're thinking cattle, this would be the perfect place. But if you're thinking wheat, we'd better look farther."

I pictured a cozy little house on that knoll, with a big garden stretching down to the creek. My mind put a rail fence and a barn on that flat stretch to the east, with a milk cow and young steer inside. Pretty soon I had a chicken roost and pigsty attached to the side of the barn, with Rhode Island Red hens pecking in the grass, plump pigs headed for bacon, and a pond dug for the ducks and geese that would give me down for pillows.

Will's eyes met mine. "I'm seeing cattle all over this grass. We could raise all the hay we need in those meadows on the other side of the knoll. Uncle Hiram says we could drive the beef to Choteau every fall to sell."

I smiled. We weren't seeing the same scene, but we were both happy with the place.

We drove to Choteau that day and filed a claim.

Chapter 10

Well, now we had a piece of land, but that was all. We had to build a shelter to live in, a place that met the homesteading requirements. They weren't much.

The three of us were sitting at Uncle Hiram's table after supper, drinking coffee so strong I was surprised it didn't melt the spoon. I let my mind stray for a minute, wondering if all old bachelors were like Will's uncle … meaning they made a big pot of coffee and just kept reheating it until it was finally gone.

"If we put up the minimum the government asks for, there'd be enough money left to buy some calves right away and have them decent enough size to live through the winter," Will explained to me. "Then the next fall we could sell them, and buy more. But it means we'll be living in a pretty rough house. More like a shack, really."

I'd seen a few of those shacks on the way. They were awful. But if we built a decent house now, we wouldn't have anything to live on for a long time. I remembered what Will had said about me being the kind of girl who could make the best of homesteading, unlike Victoria.

"We don't need anything fancy. We just need to keep warm in the winter." I thought I detected approval on Uncle Hiram's face, but I couldn't be sure. All those deep sun wrinkles made his skin look like the inside of Pa's buffalo coat.

So we planned to build simple. Uncle Hiram helped Will determine what supplies he'd need to buy.

"Don't stint on the windows," he advised. "I did, in my first shack, and it was so dark and dismal I like to went crazy that first winter." He stroked his bristly chin. "And although you want to build cheap, don't go for just tar paper. The wind cuts right through it. I had to sleep in my buffalo coat and break the ice in the water bucket every morning. The next summer I built this cabin."

Will nodded to show he understood, and Uncle Hiram continued. "You can put up a good sturdy place, say fourteen feet by sixteen. Then when the money's more settled, you can add rooms on each side. If you just put up a flimsy shack it'll satisfy the government, but it'll be money wasted because it won't be sturdy enough to build onto later." He seemed deep in thought for a minute. "If you've not got enough money for anything but a tar-paper shack, I can loan you some. Not having a family to raise, I've got a bit set by. Hate to see you have to break the ice on your stew every time you take a bite this winter."

Will looked uncomfortable, and when he spoke, he sounded the same. "Much obliged, Uncle, but I need to do this on my own. Pa gave us a start ... said it was about the same he'd have spent sending me back East to read law. We should be able to manage on that. We're luckier than most folks starting out homesteading."

Uncle Hiram nodded. "It's the best way to turn a boy into a man. But if you get bad off, remember I'm family."

I got the feeling that was important to the old rancher, and I knew I'd remember him always in my prayers.

Will drew a rough rectangle on the paper and wrote the dimensions on the lines. Uncle Hiram's stubby forefinger indicated where the doors should be. "Sometimes folks just put in one door, to save time and money, but that's a bad idea," he said. "You need a front and back door, in case of fire. And in the summer, you can open them both and get a good breeze going."

Will marked in doors on both sides. Then he added windows. "What about the chimney?"

"You ought to have the bed in one end, and the cookstove in the other. Probably the east end, so it won't be in the lee of the hill, and the chimney will draw better."

I relaxed my fingers where they'd been crossed under my apron. I'd been seeing those pitiful little homestead shacks with their tin stovepipes leaning crookedly in the wind. At least we'd have a brick chimney, like regular folks.

While the men turned the measurements into how many joists and rafters to buy, and how many feet of boards for the outside and the floors, I filled the enamel wash basin with the water that had been heating on the stove, and washed dishes and cleaned the kitchen. My mind was trying to picture how we'd manage in a fourteen by sixteen feet house for a couple of years. Finally, I could see the cookstove in one end, the bed in the other, and a table and chairs in the middle.

I hung up the dishtowel and sat back down at the table. "Will you be able to build some cupboards in the kitchen end? And a table and chairs? And maybe a settee? I could make pillows to go on it, to look nice."

Will nodded. Uncle Hiram said, "Why don't you wait for your frills till we've got the house boxed in, to see how much lumber we've got left over? Then you can buy whatever else is needed. I've got some scrap lumber out in the barn, too."

I didn't really consider cupboards for the food and a table and chairs to eat on to be frills, but I swallowed a little flare of resentment and obediently nodded my head. I had a lot to learn.

Will slid his list under the sugar bowl. "We'll go in first thing tomorrow and get the wood and bricks, and ask about a cookstove. If we have to order one, we better do it right away. I'd like to not have Pa send one if we can get it ourselves."

Out in our bed in the wagon, I had a hard time getting to sleep. My mind was filled with hopes and pictures, and worries, too. "You asleep, Will?" I whispered.

"No. I keep going over that list in my head, wondering what I'm forgetting."

"Will we have enough money?"

"I think so. We'll have to be mighty careful, though."

"I was just thinking ... if first thing after you get the supplies, you could plow up a garden spot, I'd get it planted while you're working on the house. I could get the seeds in Choteau tomorrow. It's kind of late, but still time for a lot of vegetables. I won't bother with the ones that take too long to grow."

Will yawned. "That sounds like a good plan." He was quiet for such a long time I thought he'd gone to sleep. Then he spoke again, his voice serious. "We've got us a big job, B'Anne. I hope we're up to it."

"I don't think we've got much choice." The wind whipped the canvas, and a coyote howled from far away. I scooted a little closer to Will. "I think God will help us to make a home for our baby. It's what I pray for every night."

Will murmured, "Me, too. But my prayers probably don't go much higher than the wagon top. I've not done much of it since I was a little boy."

"Maybe we could start having evening prayers together, like my family did, back home." I waited for a reply, and it was a long time coming.

"If that's what you want, B'Anne, I'll try it. But I don't think I'd feel comfortable right now. I'd feel like maybe I was putting on an act."

"That's all right. We'll wait till you feel like it. It'll come. In the meantime, I'll pray for both of us." I found Will's hand under the covers and took it. "Don't worry yourself into a tizzy, Will. It's not like we're completely alone. We've got your uncle."

Will pulled my head onto his shoulder and I felt his chuckle. "I think he's enjoying all the planning. Leastways, he sure seems to be." He pulled the patchwork quilt closer around our shoulders. "We better get to sleep. Tomorrow's another busy day."

Then one thing led to another, and we didn't get to sleep right away. But in Will's arms I didn't worry about coyotes howling, or whether we'd have a warm house by winter. I figured he'd take care of me.

Chapter 11

Next morning we ate a quick breakfast and headed for Choteau. Uncle Hiram said maybe we could get everything in one trip if we took two wagons. Ours wasn't unloaded yet, so Will hitched our horses to Uncle Hiram's hay wagon, and Uncle Hiram took his farm cart.

While Will and his uncle headed for the mill to get the lumber and the brickyard to get the chimney materials, I went to the general store for seeds. I asked the storekeeper what I could count on growing this late in the season, and he called his wife from their living quarters behind the store. "Bessie's the gardener in the family," he explained.

Just like back home, I thought. *Men grow crops, women grow gardens.* The storekeeper's wife helped me pick out seeds for lettuce, radishes, spinach and kale greens, onions, peas and green beans. "Do you have room for potatoes?" she asked.

"Room is what we've got plenty of." We added a bushel of seed potatoes to my stack behind the counter.

"It's a little late for corn, but if it were me, I'd plant it anyhow. Seed's cheap, and maybe we'll have a late frost. And if it doesn't have time to ripen good, you can feed it, stalks and all, to a cow."

"I'll take some corn seed. We'll have a cow by autumn." I sounded a lot more positive than I felt. Who knew what we'd have by autumn?

"Now, beets and carrots and turnips are good around here because you can leave them in the ground even after first frost. Just get them out before a real hard freeze," Mrs. Haysom advised. "Plant lots of cabbage, too. It does fine up here, and it keeps good in a root cellar. Say, I've got some tomato plants I started in little pots. They've come along right good. Come out back with me and I'll let you have some."

"Oh, I'll buy them. I can't let you give them to me for nothing."

"Pshaw! Call it a get-acquainted gift. Besides, I always put in a lot more than we can use."

"That's just like my ma. Every year she says she's going to plant less the next year, but she never does."

"I bet you miss your ma. I knew Hiram Carter's nephew and his wife were coming out, but I didn't expect you to be so young."

"I miss Ma some, but I don't think I'm going to have time to be very lonesome. I'll be too busy getting us ready for winter."

"You don't have many neighbors out your way. There's one family, the Yeagermans, about a half-mile west of Hiram's place. I imagine they'll be over to help get your cabin up."

She placed the tomato plants in a basket and we started back inside. Stopping by the back door, she said, "Say, do you like pie-plant? Let me give you some cuttings. It needs divided this year, anyhow."

I helped her dig up the rhubarb and placed it in the basket with the tomato plants. "Once you get the plants safely in the ground and can tell they're doing well, go ahead and cut these stalks off for a pie. Next year they'll grow even better."

Will and Uncle Hiram hadn't returned from their buying yet, so Mrs. Haysom, or Bessie, as she insisted I call her, took me into their living quarters and we had tea and muffins. "Mrs. Brill, down the street, made these. She's one fine cook, and pretty often she brings in baked goods to sell in the store. Her husband died last year, got kicked in the head by a horse down at the livery stable, where he worked. She's doing her best to hold things together. Two little ones to care for, too."

"Oh, no," I murmured sympathetically while I remembered thinking I could take care of a baby and support us, all by myself. I made sure to add two loaves of Mrs. Brill's bread and one of her applesauce cakes to the seeds and few supplies I'd picked out. I paid with the money Will had given me that morning, and just as I finished Uncle Hiram and Will came in.

"Do you have a cookstove in stock, or do I need to order one?" Will asked Mr. Haysom.

"We'll need to order one from Fort Benton, but it can be here in a couple weeks," the storekeeper answered, and took down his order book to look up the price.

When Will heard the cost, his jaw tightened. I could tell it was more than he'd hoped. "Well, we have to have it anyhow."

Bessie Haysom put her hand on her husband's arm. "Wait a minute," she said. "That big fancy stove the Dickinsons ordered, the one with the hot water reservoir, should be here next week. Maybe they'd sell them their old one."

Mr. Haysom gave his wife an annoyed look. I got the feeling he didn't want to lose the profit he'd make by selling a brand new stove. "John Dickinson told me they were going to put it outside, put a roof over it and use it for summer canning. He won't want to sell it."

Bessie ignored her husband's frown. "Best check with them first, anyhow. You could save money now and get a fancy cookstove later. I'll tell you how to get to their ranch."

Uncle Hiram was hiding a grin by smoothing his mustache. "I know where they live. Thank you for your help."

As we went out to the wagons, Mrs. Haysom called after us, "Now, young lady, if you get lonesome you just drive in and have tea with me."

The hay wagon Will was driving had long boards jutting over the passenger side of the bench, so I had to ride with Uncle Hiram. I didn't look forward to the trip home, trying to make friendly conversation with a stranger who maybe didn't even like me.

I'd begun to learn that Uncle Hiram wasn't much for idle conversation, so I was surprised when he said, "Bessie Haysom is a mighty fine woman. She'll be able to help you with things you need to learn."

I swallowed hard to hold back a sassy answer. I wanted to tell him that my own ma had already taught me everything I need to know. Instead, I just said, "It'll be nice to have a woman to visit with when I go to Choteau for supplies." For the rest of the drive to the Dickinson's ranch, the only sound was the rattling of nails in their keg and the squeaking of wagon wheels.

Out at their place, Mr. Dickinson invited us in to see the stove. "Would you take ten dollars for it?" Will asked.

"How about twenty?" Evidently Mr. Dickinson figured they needed the money more than his wife needed a cool kitchen in the summer.

He and Will struck a deal at fourteen dollars. We could pick up the stove as soon as their new one came in.

Back in the wagon, Uncle Hiram and I listened to the nails rattle and the wheels squeak for a mile or so. *I wonder if his voice gets rusty from not using it,* I thought. When he spoke, I worried for a moment that maybe I'd said the thought out loud.

"Lonesome for your ma yet?"

"Just a little bit once in a while." I didn't want to sound defensive, but that's how it came out. "It'll go away, once I'm too busy to think."

"Wouldn't be human if you didn't get homesick." He gave a quick glance in my direction.

Probably checking to see if he'd made me cry. Maybe this was a good time for me to talk to Uncle Hiram, without worrying about what Will would think.

"Uncle Hiram, I'm not a spoiled little city girl. I'm not afraid to work, or do without 'frills and furbelows.' I intend to make Will a good wife."

Uncle Hiram nodded and turned to me with the first real smile I'd seen from him.

"I'm beginning to see that. I think you've got enough grit in you to make it."

"Thank you." I felt better than I had since we arrived. "Now, tell me what it's like here in the autumn and the winter. I remember you said you had to chop the ice on your water bucket every morning, but just how thick was that ice?"

He actually chuckled. "Thick enough for a hatchet, but not an axe."

The rest of the way home he told me what to expect here in Montana Territory, both good and bad. Yes, the winters are fierce, but wild game is plentiful. Not many neighbors, but the ones we have are good ones. We're far enough north that it stays light longer in the summer than in Iowa, which is a good thing when there's so much work to do. When our wagon pulled in alongside Will's, I was laughing at Uncle Hiram's story about shooting a deer and having to carry it home in pieces.

Will came over to help me down from the wagon, his face looking puzzled but happy. "See? I told you he'd like you."

And he'd been right. I'd found a new friend in Uncle Hiram.

I hurried inside and heated up a couple of tins of tomatoes, sliced cheese and one of the loaves of bread from town, and we ate a quick meal before going over to our place to put down stakes to mark the foundation for our house. Our place! Our house! The words gave me goose bumps, but in a good way.

For days, all three of us worked from sunup to sundown, then we ate and fell into bed. Before we started on the cabin, Uncle Hiram drove his Clydesdales and mower over, and Will used them on the prairie grass from the creek up to the house site. After it dried and was raked up, he plowed and harrowed a big garden space between the house site and the creek, where if I had to carry water to the garden, it wouldn't be so far. The garden patch was turned over to me while the two men got started on the house. That evening Will and I cut the potatoes up, each piece having an eye. At least that was work we could do sitting down after supper.

The next day I planted so many hills of potatoes that by noon my back felt like I might never stand up straight again. I'd brought a basket of food that morning, so we washed our hands in the creek and sat under the cottonwood trees to eat. Not wanting Uncle Hiram to think we were taking advantage of him, I made sure we used supplies from our wagon to cook most of the meals.

It was pleasant there, with the wind rustling the cottonwood leaves and the creek burbling nearby. It had been hot while I worked in the garden, but here in the shade it was comfortable. The matted grass made my tired body feel better.

Will gave me a sharp look when he took the cheese and onion sandwich I handed him. "B'Anne, you need to take some time off and rest. You're overdoing it."

I saw Uncle Hiram give me a quick glance from under his shaggy eyebrows. Was it approval? He seemed to like women who were good workers, so maybe it was.

"I'm healthy as a horse. By the time we've finished eating, I'll be ready to go again." But I did lie in the grass and rest awhile before I started with the seeds. I'd already set out the tomatoes and pie-plants along the edge of the garden closest to where the house would be, the pie-plants on a little hill that would drain well from both sides.

That afternoon the Yeagermans, the neighbors we hadn't met, showed up. Mr. Yeagerman and his two sons, one grown and one a gangly youth, pulled shovels off their wagon and began digging the foundation trench Uncle Hiram and Will had started. Mrs. Yeagerman and her three daughters, Phoebe, Bertha and Josephine, carried a jug of milk down to the creek and set it securely among rocks in the cold water. Then they joined me in the garden. "Ours is all planted," Mrs. Yeagerman explained. "You're getting a late start, so we'd better pitch in. Many hands make light work."

I had to blink my eyes hard to stop the tears that threatened. That was one of Ma's favorite sayings. I hadn't been homesick for days, but my tiredness must have made me weepy. God knew just what I needed to hear from these kind, new friends. If only I felt worthy of His goodness. "Oh, you're right," I agreed, "and do I ever appreciate your help. We might have something to fill a root cellar with, after all."

The women came the next morning, too, and we were able to get the whole garden planted, even a big plot of corn. Mrs. Yeagerman kept up a flow of questions about Iowa, my family, Will's family, and Will and me. I told myself she was probably just lonesome for woman talk, but inside I was thinking she might be a tad bit gossipy. Since there was nobody much to gossip to, I put it out of my mind.

As their wagon pulled away in the afternoon, Mrs. Yeagerman called out, "Now you let me know if we can do anything to help you."

I waved and thanked her again. Suddenly the country didn't seem so big and scary, since we had neighbors ... even if they were half a mile away.

Now that the garden was safely in and there were enough men to work on the house, I kept busy at Uncle Hiram's place, cooking a good breakfast every morning and driving a hot dinner over in his wagon every noon. When they got home at dark, I fixed them a light supper.

They got a rest, too, after a week, when we had two days of rain. "Sure a good thing we got that foundation dug and the rocks bedded," Uncle Hiram said. "It'd be pure misery to be digging now."

"But think how good it is for the garden." They agreed with me. It wasn't the driving rain that would wash out newly planted seeds, but a soft, gentle, insistent rain.

On the first afternoon that the weather kept us indoors, the three of us hurried out to the barn through the rain to see if any of the odds and ends stored there could be used in the new place. There didn't seem to be much but scrap wood until Will noticed something in the far corner covered with old horse blankets.

He pulled the blankets off. "Don't you need these things in the house, Uncle Hiram?" A lovely oak rocking chair stood there, and leaning against the wall behind it was an oak bed frame, the headboard carved with flowers and curlicues.

Uncle Hiram walked over to join us, and even in the dim light of the barn, I could see the pain on his face. He stood staring at the furniture for a moment. "No, I'm not able to use them. But I'd like to see them in your house." Then he turned and walked out of the barn.

Will and I stared at each other. There was something strange here. Uncle Hiram slept in a bunk on the wall, and we all sat on plain old kitchen chairs with caned bottoms. Why didn't he have these nice things in his house?

We had already turned to leave the barn when I noticed something smaller behind the bed frame. Will helped me lift the frame aside to see better. It was a cradle. "Why would your uncle have a cradle?" I whispered.

"I get the feeling we shouldn't ask questions. If he wants to explain, he will." I knew he was right, but my heart hurt for the pain on Uncle Hiram's face.

Back in the house, Will and Uncle Hiram sat down with froes and the blocks of cedar Will had bought at the mill, and shaped shingles. I watched them for a little while, amazed at how the simple L-shaped tool could split wood so thinly and evenly. Then I got busy.

Will had hauled the sewing machine off our wagon, so I started on curtains from the red and white checked gingham. It was an odd feeling, for the house to be so quiet, with the only sound the rain on the roof and against the windows, the crackling of the fire, and the off-and-on clatter of the sewing machine as I treadled away on the long seams. The kerosene lamps lit in the middle of the day were unusual, too.

On the second day of rain, I finished the curtains and got out the bolt of white outing flannel for diapers. Uncle Hiram stopped at my side after refilling his coffee cup, picked up one of the hemmed diapers. "Dishtowels?"

I shook my head. I could feel the heat of my blush on my cheeks. "Diapers." I figured Uncle Hiram knew why we were sent away in disgrace, but the baby had never been mentioned.

He rested his hand on my shoulder. "That's good, B'Anne," he said. "That rocking chair needs to rock a baby." Then he got back to his stack of shingles.

A little later, when I reached the end of a hem and stopped treadling, Uncle Hiram cleared his throat. "You're probably wondering about those things you found in the barn." His voice was flat, like he was preparing to tell us something he wasn't sure we'd take to.

Will snuck a quick glance at his uncle. "Only if you want to tell us."

Uncle Hiram gave a deep sigh. "Well, I wasn't always alone. I had me a fine woman. We slept in that bed you saw, and I got that rocking chair when she was in the family way." He smoothed his mustache in a self-conscious gesture before he went on. "I made that cradle, got it finished just in time. But the baby never drew a breath. And Mary died the next day."

"Oh, Uncle Hiram." I got up and went to stand behind his chair, and put my hands on his shoulders. "I'm so sorry." I felt his shoulders relax. Had he been bracing himself for our disapproval? He put one callused hand on mine for a moment.

"It was a long time ago, down in southern Montana Territory in the 1860s. I was there to get rich in the gold rush." He gave a rueful chuckle. "Never got rich, but I managed to make a little money. When I decided to come up here and homestead, I just couldn't leave those things behind."

Now why on earth would Will's ma think he was a black sheep for getting married and having a child? That's the most natural thing in the world.

When Uncle Hiram began talking again, I wondered once again if I'd spoken my thoughts out loud.

"Mary was Shoshone. Her man had been a trader, and he gave her an English name, but when he got killed in a fight they hadn't had any children. She'd been alone for awhile, wasn't sure she wanted to marry me. Her man hadn't been good to her. But I convinced her."

Ah, now I understood. Will's prim and proper ma wouldn't have been pleased to have an Indian sister-in-law, much less a little papoose for a niece or nephew.

"I wasn't worth much for a long while after Mary and the baby died. Did a lot of drinking. Didn't feel like life was worth living."

Will spoke then. "Was that when Pa came out here to visit you?"

"Yes, he did. Spent some time with me, got me away from the mining and up here. Somehow he got me back in the land of the living. He might be my little brother, but he stepped in like a man. He's a good one, your pa."

Before I went back to the sewing machine, I said, "Thank you for telling us, Uncle Hiram. Is it going to make you sad to see those things in our cabin?"

"Oh, no! I think it's going to make me happy to see a baby being rocked in that chair, and sleeping in that cradle. Do you suppose I could be a substitute granddad?"

"I should say so!" Will exclaimed. "In fact, you might be the only grandpa he ever knows. Or she."

"Every baby needs to be dandled on a granddad's knee," I added. "I'll bet you'll be real good at dandling."

Uncle Hiram nodded, smiling. "Never done it before, but I can learn."

I didn't know how it had happened, but Uncle Hiram seemed to have weighed us up, measured us off, and found us suitable for the job. He was going to be part of our family. One more thing to thank the Lord for when and if He listened to me again.

Chapter 12

W hen the rain stopped, the men were back working on the
cabin. With the help of Mr. Yeagerman and his sons, the
rough shell structure had gone up quickly. The place got
wet, but June turned hot after the rains, and it didn't take long to dry
out.

I still had sewing to do, but it would be months before the diapers
were needed, so each morning I packed a basket dinner and rode over
with Will and Uncle Hiram to help in any way I could. We brought
along the chunks of cedar wood, and I sat on the rock that would
someday be our door stoop and learned how to make shingles with the
froe. My first few were pretty uneven, but I soon caught onto the right
amount of pressure to put on the froe to get each shingle thin at one
end and thicker at the other, so they'd lap over each other and make a
weather-tight roof.

I'd never pictured myself as a carpenter, but it was enjoyable to
work in the shade of the cottonwood. The fragrance of cedar mixed
with sun on prairie grass to make a smell I liked to sniff up in big
gulps. The trilling of meadowlarks and wind through the tall grass
was punctuated by hammering and sawing. Best of all, I admired
my growing stack of shingles and told myself smugly that Victoria
certainly wouldn't have been able to make shingles for her own house.

One noon as we rested under the cottonwood tree with our cold bacon sandwiches, Will said, "I think we can move in, B'Anne. We don't have the windows in or the roof shingled, but we don't have to worry about getting cold or wet. Feels like summer's here for good."

Uncle Hiram looked a little doubtful. "I'd get those floorboards down first if I were you. You can do the inside walls while you're living in it, but it's mighty hard to put down floorboards once you've moved in."

"We've got the rough floor in," Will said. "Couldn't we wait till later for the flooring?"

"Come winter, the wind will whistle in through the cracks in that sub-floor. You'll be a lot warmer with another layer on there. You don't want our B'Anne, there, to take a cold."

Our B'Anne. My, how good that sounded.

It took a day to get the wide floorboards nailed down over the rough floor with a layer of tar paper between. Then Mr. Yeagerman came over to help with the chimney. He'd had experience with his own masonry work.

Uncle Hiram had offered us a little potbellied stove that was stored in his barn, to put in the end of the room where the bed would be, so Will had bought enough bricks for two chimneys. Now Mr. Yeagerman said, "You know, small as this place is, I think you could get by with just the cookstove. It'll put out plenty of heat, and it'll be burning all the time anyhow, for cooking."

I remembered how hot the kitchen got at home, and it was bigger than our cabin. "I think one stove would be fine," I agreed. "Besides, then Will could return the extra bricks and flashing we won't need, and get some money back."

The chimney had to dry for a few days before it could be used, but they weren't wasted days. Will and I drove in to pick up the Dickinsons' cookstove. Then we went into the general store to get supplies we were running low on.

Mrs. Haysom was arranging a new shipment of tinned goods on the shelves. She hurried over to welcome me. "My stars, girl, you're brown as a berry."

"That's what gardening does. I hate a sunbonnet. Like to feel the breeze on my head." I suddenly wondered what Will thought of his wife being brown as a berry instead of ladylike white, like a lily. Well, too late to worry about it now. "Those tomatoes are thriving. That nice rain was just what they needed. The pie-plant is growing good, too. And all the seeds are coming up fine. I can't thank you enough for all your help."

She took my list and handed it to her husband. "Come have a cup of tea," she insisted.

I went with her gladly. There was something about her I liked. Maybe because she reminded me of Ma. I appreciated the help our neighbor Mrs. Yeagerman gave, but I didn't think we'd ever be good friends. There was a kind of persnickety air about her. I hadn't been in her house, but I figured it'd probably have fancy doilies on the tables and the backs of the chairs, and beeswax on the furniture an inch thick. But Mrs. Haysom, now … I felt comfortable with her. I had the feeling she probably wouldn't even be judgmental if she knew I had to get married. Well, maybe a little judgmental, that was to be expected, but I'll bet she'd get over it quicker than some.

She brewed tea and set out a little plate of Mrs. Brill's cookies. "These are *some* good," she said. "Polly Brill calls them 'hermits,' don't know why."

Bessie Haysom was right. The cookies were delicious, with candied fruit inside, like the fruitcake Ma always made at Christmas. Bessie made sure I took a couple so Will could eat them on the way home.

I was eager to be in our own place, but we couldn't use the stove because the chimney wasn't quite dried and seasoned yet, so we stayed at Uncle Hiram's for a few more days. I wouldn't have minded cooking on a campfire, as we'd done on the trail, but there was too much danger now of starting a grass fire.

Finally, it was moving day, and we brought over the three pieces from Uncle Hiram's barn and unloaded our possessions from our wagon. Will had finished the inside wall in the kitchen end, so he could put up some shelves for dishes and supplies. After everything heavy had been brought in and put in place, he and Uncle Hiram worked outside on sawhorses, making the doors and window-frames. Now that the shelves were up, I could start arranging things inside. I was so excited I could hardly wait, almost like a little girl on Christmas morning.

Will carried in the straw tick from the wagon, and I used the linens from my hope chest to make up the beautiful oak bed in one end of the room. The brightest quilt Ma had given me went on top. The cradle would go at the foot of the bed when the baby was born, but for now we stored it in the little loft space Will had made over that end of the room. I folded the quilt I loved, the one with pieces of garments I remembered, and used it to cover the trunk, so it looked like a piece of furniture, not just a trunk. It would make an extra seat if we ever had company, too. After my hope chest was emptied of everything except bed linens, I folded another bright quilt to fit the top of it so we could use it as a chair. I arranged our food supplies on one of the shelves Will had put up. On the other shelf, I put the gifts that were pretty to look at ... the pickle dish, the teapot, and Grandma's sugar bowl. I hurried out the back door, where the prairie grass hadn't been cut yet, and picked a big handful of wild bachelor buttons. Their color matched the blue vase Annabelle had given me, and I set it on the shelf. I put a crochet-edged scarf on my sewing machine cabinet and put the fancy rose lamp Will's sister gave us on it. Our new family Bible went there, too.

Drawing in a deep breath of the fresh scent of new wood, I stood back to gaze at the room. My, it looked nice. When the rest of the inside walls were finished, I could hang the picture of Jesus watching over the two children and the calendar from Will's father's store. When he had time to make us a table, the big kerosene lamp with the painted roses would sit in the middle of it for convenience. When he had more time ... poor Will, so much to do ... he'd put up a shelf in the living end of the room, and we could put our clock there.

I pictured how it would look in wintertime, with the inner walls finished and pictures hung; the windows in place and the curtains looking bright and cheerful, and fires crackling in the cookstove. This would be a home where a baby would be safe and happy, I vowed. God would be with us in this house. We'd done wrong, but we were doing our best to make it right with God, I felt. Busy as I was, I still took time to bow my head and whisper a thank-you to God for this sturdy home.

But right now there were two hungry men ready for dinner. I built a fire in the cookstove for the first time. Using a wood packing box turned on end for a worktable, I prepared a meal of fried ham and potatoes and opened a crock of Ma's piccalilli relish. We ate out under the cottonwood tree, where a gentle breeze from the creek made us a lot more comfortable than we'd have been in the kitchen. That would have been uncomfortable even without the heat since there were no table or chairs in the kitchen. Sitting outside on the ground felt more like a picnic.

When twilight came, Uncle Hiram went home. Will and I sat on the hope chest and shared a tin of peaches for supper, and then went to bed under the bright quilt in the beautiful bed Uncle Hiram had shared with his Indian wife. Will pulled me close for the first time in our own home, and it *felt* like home.

In the days that followed, the weather turned scorching hot, but with the windows and doors being just holes in the walls, the cabin was bearable, at least after I let the cookstove fire go out. We soon decided we'd rather have cold suppers than fire up the stove and have a hot room to sleep in. The flies weren't bad yet, although I knew they would be as soon as we got some animals on the place. In the evenings, though, the mosquitoes found us. As soon as the doors and windows were finished and in place, Will drove into Choteau for a roll of screen wire.

I remembered Ma saying what a blessing it was to have screens on the windows when they had been so hard to get during the War Between the States, and for a long time afterward. Once he covered the windows with screen and hammered two screen doors together, it felt like we were living in a real house, not just a temporary place. The cupboards and furniture could be made when winter came, and nothing much could be done outside.

We had to get a cow and some chickens soon because we needed the milk and eggs. A pig would be good, too, so we could butcher when the cold weather came and have meat for the winter. But before we got animals, we had to have a place to shelter them. If we were going to buy calves to sell as yearlings next summer, they had to be bought soon. And we'd have to somehow get enough hay to feed them through the winter.

We knew we had to dig a well, but suddenly there were just too many things to do at the same time. The well would have to wait. The creek water was clean, and not too far away. Will carried two buckets up to the house in the morning and the evening, and we managed.

I'd been pleased when pregnancy gave me a plump bosom instead of the scrawny one I'd always had, but now I was getting plump in more places than my bosom. Not plump, really, just bumpy. My belly was really noticeable, and Will didn't like it when I started to pick up a water bucket. I knew I was strong as an ox, but he was uncomfortable about it.

There was a huge amount of work ahead of us, but the thought didn't bother me. I was happy and contented to be in a house of our own. But Will became very quiet and out of reach. Maybe it was just a letting down after we were finally in our own home, or maybe it was the back-breaking load of work he knew was ahead of him, or fear that we'd run out of money soon. I hoped those were the reasons, but I was afraid he was regretting the burden he had taken on when he married me.

I tried finding more ways to help him, but he resented it. One afternoon I ran out of water because I'd used some on the marigolds and the tubs of moss roses by the front stoop. I took the two buckets down to the creek, filled them and was starting back up to the house when Will rode in from town, where he'd gone to get a new axe-head. He looped the reins around a cottonwood trunk, ran and grabbed the buckets from me.

"I can take care of my jobs!" he snapped. "You knew I'd be back soon!"

I followed him back up to the house. I wanted to cry from his unfairness, but inside I was blazing with anger for the same reason. "And I can do for myself when you're gone." I knew I should be meek and sweet, but three days of silence and then his little outburst cancelled out my meekness and sweetness.

He spun around, water sloshing from the buckets. "You make it sound like I'm gone all the time. I wasn't going for a horseback ride … I needed that axe-head."

"I didn't say you were shirking, Will. How could I think a thing like that?"

He didn't reply, just stomped up to the house, left the buckets in the kitchen, and slammed the screen door on his way out to the woodpile. I cried for awhile, trying to figure out what I'd done wrong and how to make it better.

In the early evening I fixed a pot of the macaroni, tinned tomatoes and bacon that I knew Will liked and pushed it to the back of the stove to keep warm while I let the fire go out. Then I took the bar of scented soap, not the sturdy lye soap, and my nightgown and wrapper, down to the creek. In the deepest part where the bottom was sandy, I washed my hair and took a bath. When the sweat was gone, and the sadness was a little better, I dried with the clothes I'd been wearing, put on my nightgown and wrapper and trudged back to the house.

Will was sitting on the bed reading a newspaper he'd picked up from Uncle Hiram on the way back from town. He looked up and raised his eyebrows when he saw what I was wearing, and my damp hair wrapped in my apron. "You took a bath in the creek? Should have told me; I'd have joined you."

I stared at him. Ma had warned me that with our rocky start, I'd have to try extra hard to make my husband happy, but there was a limit to how much I had to put up with. My plan had been to present Will with his favorite supper, then a willing, rose-smelling, sweet-tempered wife, but the plan disappeared in a puff of smoke.

"After the way you've treated me the last few days, do you really think I'd come looking for you and say 'Will, come take a bath in the creek with me'?" I could feel my resentment and worry turning into a little fire that was getting hotter by the minute. I didn't care one bit what Ma had said about being meek and sweet. "Besides, my body's starting to be ugly, which is probably the reason you're avoiding me. Even in the creek when it's almost dark, you'd see it." I knew how close the tears were, and I didn't want him to see them. "Your supper's on the stove. I'm not hungry, and I'm going to bed."

"B'Anne ..."

"I'm sure it's still hot enough. Just drop your dishes in that pot of water on the back of the stove when you're finished, and I'll take care of them in the morning."

Can a person be sick from sadness? I doubted it, but suddenly I was so tired that I felt ill. I didn't care about anything. Dropping my wrapper on the floor by the bed, I went around to the side opposite Will, crawled in, pulled the sheet over me, and turned my face to the wall.

I felt him move on the bed and his hand touch my shoulder. "B'Anne ..." he began again.

"It's all right. *I'm* all right. Just go eat your supper."

"No, it's not all right, B'Anne." A long silence, then, "I know I've not been easy to get along with the last few days. I guess it just kind of all hit me ... how much we've got ahead of us, and how little to do it with. And with you getting so big, there's no forgetting that soon there'll be a baby to worry about, and a baby's something you can't make a mistake on. It's just ... I get scared, I guess. A man's not supposed to get scared."

I rolled over to face him. "Oh, Will, I get scared, too. A lot." I thought I'd cried myself out this afternoon, but here the tears came again. "Maybe it's too much. Maybe we handled our mistake the wrong way. It's not too late. I'm sure you could let somebody else take over the claim, sell the house and improvements to them. Like I said before, right after we got married, I can go to my aunt Isabel in Des Moines. We can each make our fresh start in a different way."

Will's face was shocked. "No, B'Anne. That's not what I want. I just want everything to slow down, let us catch up, that's all."

"There's one thing that's not going to slow down, Will." I took his hand and laid it on my stomach, where the baby was moving as if it could sense how upset I was. "We just have to do the best we can to be ready for it." I looked straight into his eyes. "I can do it by myself if I have to. Are you up to it?"

I couldn't tell if it was anger or determination I saw in his eyes. "Yes, I'm up to it."

My anger was replaced by sadness. "Oh, Will, sometimes you just have to turn your worries over to God. You'd feel at peace, and hopeful. That's the only way I can manage."

His hand still on my stomach, Will patted gently. "I'm glad it helps you, B'Anne. I'll try harder. I don't *not* believe; I just don't have a whole lot of faith like you do."

There was no further apology, nothing about the way he'd acted with the water buckets. But when he dished up his supper he brought me a bowl, too, and he held me for a few moments before he went to sleep.

"Good night, B'Anne," he murmured sleepily. "Thank you for the Dutch uncle talk." Then he drifted quickly off. But I stayed awake for a long time, wondering and worrying. Then I followed my own advice and turned it over to God.

The next few days were a little awkward, with Will trying hard to be cheerful and me putting a good front on my uncertainty, but the feeling wore off, and we got back to normal. Maybe not quite normal … there was a guardedness that hadn't been there before, but we managed.

We worked on through the hot summer. Will built a chicken coop and bought eight laying hens, some young pullets and a rooster in Choteau. Now we had eggs, and we could sacrifice a pullet now and then for meat. Next spring the pullets would be hens, and our little flock would grow. After spending an hour adding columns of figures, he determined we could afford to buy a weaner pig. It could live on grain and our scraps, especially when the garden came on good. We'd butcher it in late fall and have pork for the winter.

Will put together a simple lean-to shelter, with a sturdy pig-sty alongside it, and I was able to help him by marking measurements and fetching boards. I even learned to use a saw. The shed didn't have a roof yet, but at least there was a place to tether and feed an animal. We bought the weaner pig and a cow from the Yeagermans. The cow was due to calve in a couple of months, and then we'd have milk.

Shortly after we got the pig and cow, I decided there was one thing I could do to help Will that didn't require any skill. In the early morning cool, I went out to the cow-shed, where he had hung our few farming tools, and got down the scythe.

Will came up from the creek with a bucket of water in each hand. Seeing me, he put down the buckets and said, "What in tarnation do you think you're doing?"

"I'm going to cut the prairie grass out back of the house, where it was too hilly for the mower. It won't make a lot of hay, but every little bit to feed the calves this winter will help."

"B'Anne, that's not woman's work. It might not even be safe, for a woman in the family way. What would your ma say if you lost the baby from working out in the field like a man?"

I hadn't thought about that. I took a few experimental swings of the scythe. I didn't see how it could hurt the baby, like horseback riding or taking a bad fall. "I could give it a try. If it starts to feel bad, I'll stop."

Will got a stubborn set to his chin. "I can do the man's work around here. You go back in the house and cook, or sew, or something like that."

I didn't want to make him mad again, but it only seemed sensible to help him with his load. Wasn't that what husbands and wives were supposed to do? "The work in the house is done till time to get dinner. You've got enough to do out here to keep two men busy till autumn comes. I've fed the chickens, and there's nothing else I can do to help you. I'm going to do this for a couple of hours, just to give it a try." I knew I should be asking for permission, not telling him what I was going to do, but Will had never got away with bossing me around in all the years I'd known him, and I didn't want him starting now. I snuck a peek at him under my eyelashes. He didn't look happy. My mouth surprised me when it said sweetly, "Please, Will. I'll be careful."

He looked at me a long time. "Well, let me sharpen that scythe first, so you don't work any harder than you have to. And let me show you how, so you don't cut your leg off."

He took the water into the house, sharpened the scythe on the whetstone Uncle Hiram had given him, and then demonstrated. "You don't have to swing hard. In fact, if you swing too hard, you might cut yourself. Just a gentle swing from the shoulders, and follow through kind of slow."

He handed me the scythe, took off his hat and ran his hands through his hair in an angry kind of way, and stomped off to where he was sawing boards to roof the cow-shed.

I did it the way he showed me, and pretty soon I got into a rhythm … sweep the scythe, step forward, sweep the scythe, step forward. You had to keep the rhythm because if you made the step forward too quick, you'd slice into your leg. By the time the sun was high overhead, I felt like I couldn't lift that scythe one more time. I headed for the house to fix us something to eat, making sure I stood up nice and straight and walked briskly when I neared Will, so he wouldn't know that every muscle in my body was aching, and my legs trembled so badly I could hardly stand up.

We sat down under the cottonwood to eat biscuit and bacon sandwiches and drink cold water from the creek. I must've made some small noise, or maybe I flinched when I leaned forward to pick up another biscuit, because Will said, "Learned your lesson yet?"

I wanted to say something smart and sassy, but I tamped down my temper. Much as I didn't want to admit it, he was right. "I've learned I maybe did it too long for starting right out. I won't cut hay so long tomorrow, but I'll get stronger. And even if I just do it a little bit at a time, it'll be a job I can do to help."

Will heaved a long, loud, sigh. "Oh, B'Anne, you're just as hardheaded as you always were." He reached over and smoothed back the hair that had come loose from my braids. In the hot summer, braids were the coolest way to wear hair. "If you're so determined to help, can't we find something else for you to do? Besides, before long you're going to be as brown as Uncle Hiram's Mary probably was."

That hurt my feelings. It was one thing if he wanted me to stop because he thought the work was too hard for me; it was another thing entirely if he just wanted me to have fair skin. "Well, it's a little late for me to worry about having lily-white skin like Victoria," I snapped, "so if you can't have beauty, you might as well have a good worker."

"Beatrice Anne Hopew...Carter! That's not what I meant." He scooted over and pulled me into his arms, sweaty and sticky as we were. "Is that what you're doing? Working like a dog so I won't feel like I got a bad bargain? That's the silliest thing I ever heard of."

Having his arms around me was hot, but I didn't mind much.

"I thought we were kind of having a good time," he said. "We're working hard, sure, but we're doing it together. Doesn't it feel good, at the end of the day, to look around and see how much we've got done?"

I didn't lift my head from his chest, but I gave a little nod. I could feel his breath ruffle my hair.

"When we're doing it for us, it's not as hard as if we were working for somebody else." His arms tightened a bit. "B'Anne, I'm not wishing someone else was here instead of you. When I dreamed about getting a place in Montana, you were always the one beside me."

"All right," I murmured. "But if that cow was just giving milk, I could put buttermilk on my skin. That would help."

Will gave a whoop of laughter. "Oh, that'd help, all right," he chuckled. "This Montana sun would heat up the buttermilk and fry you like an egg."

We got to our feet to get back to work, and I was ashamed of a little groan that slipped out when I straightened my back.

"So you're through cutting hay?" Will asked.

"For today. I'm going to keep doing it, but not so long at a time." Out of the corner of my eye I saw him shake his head. "Could you help me carry some water up from the creek? I want to water the garden. It's looking pretty thirsty."

That's how I spent the afternoon, giving each plant two cups of water. By the time I finished, my back felt like it was clamped in a big iron vise, but at least the garden could go for another few days without rain.

Chapter 13

Mr. Yeagerman and his boys came over one morning in early August. Without hesitation, they hopped down from their wagon and pulled out axes, shovels, and mallets. Jim, the older one, wasn't really a boy. He was a young man. I knew from conversation with his mother that the younger son, Arthur, was only fourteen, but he was a husky lad. Whatever they were here to do, it would be helpful.

"Saw Hiram in Choteau yesterday. Said you're going to start some calves to sell next fall," Mr. Yeagerman said. "The boys and I'll help you get enough fence in to hold them. First year we were here, I cut fence posts all winter, then set them out in the spring. It takes a heap of posts and wire to fence so many acres."

Will had good manners; that was one of the things I liked about him. "Ben, how am I ever going to be able to help you enough to pay you back? I don't know how we would have managed without you and your boys."

Ben Yeagerman just laughed. "Jim, here, is sparking a girl in town, and come next summer, they'll probably be getting married and needing a place of their own. You'll be paying us back in sweat, for sure."

I didn't go out to cut my usual swaths of prairie grass because I knew it would embarrass Will for others to see his wife doing field work. I'd fix them all a nice noon dinner, instead. I didn't know what it'd be, though. We'd been needing a trip to Choteau for supplies, but kept putting it off to work on all the things that needed to be done. I decided I'd put the food outside on planks over sawhorses, so they wouldn't see that in the house, Will and I were still using scrap wood over boxes for a table.

I'd baked just yesterday, so there was fresh bread, at least. I looked through the things on our food shelf. Maybe I should go out and decide if any of the pullets looked ready to meet their Maker, but just one chicken wouldn't be enough unless I stewed it, and that took so long they'd be starving by dinnertime. They'd think I didn't know how to manage my kitchen. I could pry the lid off that small keg of salted beef, but it had to soak overnight to soften and leach out the salt. Same with the dried fish.

There was still a little bit of meat left on the bone of the ham I'd been slicing off for days, so I cut off every last tiny speck and chopped it up. There was part of a hard cured sausage, so it got chopped. I boiled and mashed potatoes, and made gravy out of flour and tinned milk with the meat added. A couple of big tins of tomatoes stewed with homemade bread cubes, the way Will liked, topped with a bit of cheese at the last minute, would help fill stomachs. Ah, it was all coming together. The chokecherries Uncle Hiram had brought over yesterday went into a cobbler, and when it was in the oven I hurried out to the garden for leaf lettuce, so I could make Ma's good wilted lettuce salad.

While I cooked, the sound of axes and laughter drifted in the open windows. Two of the men were cutting small saplings down by the creek, turning each one into several fence posts. The rest were digging holes along the line Will and Mr. Yeagerman had marked for the fence.

The kitchen felt like an oven by the time the food was ready. I grabbed a tablecloth and a stack of those thick white dishes Will's pa had given us from his store and hurried out to the sawhorse table with them.

I was pleased to see Uncle Hiram's wagon pull up. He could have some of that chokecherry cobbler. I'd planned to take him some, anyhow. Now I was saved the drive. Shortly behind Uncle Hiram came the Yeagermans' small pony cart, carrying the women of the family.

Oh, my, I hoped there was enough food. I greeted everybody, then hurried to the kitchen, where I opened a jar of store-bought dried beef, chopped it up and added it to the gravy with more flour and tinned milk. Then I dumped in another tin of tomatoes to the stewed tomatoes and hoped for the best.

Mrs. Yeagerman came in. "I knew your cow wouldn't be giving you any milk yet, so I brought some, and some butter and cream," she said, setting the containers on my improvised work table. "Oh, you poor thing, how can you manage?"

I saw my kitchen area through her eyes. Yes, I'd been right, she was a bit judgmental. "Thank you for the milk. I've been missing it. And the cobbler will taste much better with cream." Seeing that she was still looking sharp-eyed around the room, I said defensively, "It's just for now. As soon as things ease up a bit, Will's going to build me some cupboards, and a work counter, and some furniture."

"Oh, I know how hard it is to start. It's been quite a few years, but I remember."

I saw her sneaking a look at my waist, which had thickened some since she saw me last. Thickened a lot, in fact. I was getting big so fast I wondered if I should cut down on my eating, but I was hungry all the time. As her eyes took in my apron tied up high over my belly, I tried to remember how old I'd been when I finally realized that when Ma or one of her friends said so-and-so was tying her apron high, it meant she was in the family way.

Now Mrs. Yeagerman's gaze traveled up to where my bosoms puffed out the top of the loose dress my cousin had loaned me. *Yes, Mrs. Yeagerman, I do look exactly like a pillow tied in the middle.*

"Are you in the family way?" A smile came with the question, but it didn't really look like a friendly smile to me.

She doesn't know how long we've been married, I reminded myself, willing down a blush. "Due in late November."

"If it's a bad winter, you might want to take a room in Choteau when it's close to your time. Might be hard for the doctor to make it out before the baby does."

I hadn't thought of that. "I hope it's a mild winter, then, because I want Will to be close by, and he wouldn't be able to leave the animals for too long."

"Well, keep us in mind. One of the boys could come over and tend the animals."

Maybe I could put up with a little bit of her being judgmental, I thought. At least she was helpful.

Her three girls carried the food to the sawhorse table outside, and we spread quilts on the ground to sit on. The workers left their fencing to join us. Will had started to pick up his spoon when I quickly asked Ben Yeagerman to say the blessing on our picnic. I saw a little flush on Will's cheekbones, embarrassed that he hadn't thought of saying grace.

There was enough food to satisfy everybody. Will savored the stewed tomatoes like he always did, and Uncle Hiram had two helpings of chokecherry cobbler with cream. Afterward, we all rested awhile, then we women carried everything back to the kitchen and cleaned up while the men returned to the fencing job.

I heard Uncle Hiram tell Will that he was going back to his place, where he had a lot of wire in coils in his barn for a project he wasn't ready to start yet. Will could use the wire and there'd be plenty of time to replace it. Thanks to Uncle Hiram's generosity and the Yeagermans' help, by twilight that evening there would be a nice fenced-in pasture for our cow, and the calves we were going to buy.

While Mrs. Yeagerman … Adelia, she insisted I must call her … and her daughters helped in the kitchen, the girls admired the red and white checked curtains I'd finally gotten hung, and the pretties on the kitchen shelf. They thought making a seat out of my hope chest, and covering the big trunk with a quilt, were the cleverest ideas ever. I hoped they weren't just feeling sorry for me and pretending, but it didn't feel that way. They seemed like nice girls. When their mother whispered, like it was a big secret, that I was going to have a baby in November, they were very excited. The oldest, Phoebe, was seventeen, same as me. She'd be having a kitchen of her own to clean up before too long. Bertha, who hated her name and wanted to be called Bertie, was just a year younger than Phoebe. The youngest girl, Josephine, was only seven.

The women went back home in midafternoon, and when the men left at twilight the house seemed quiet and empty, in a good way. I wasn't used to having company. Will and I sat out on the little stoop in front of the door and had bread and milk for supper, thanks to Adelia Yeagerman's gift. We had to use it up quick, in this heat. We'd put the milk, butter and cream that was left after dinner in jars in shaded water at the edge of the creek, but still, they wouldn't keep long.

"That was some good dinner you cooked, B'Anne," Will said, slapping at a mosquito. "I don't know how you did it, low as we were on supplies."

"I was a little worried when the last two wagons showed up," I admitted. "We can't put off the trip to Choteau much longer. I want to send a letter to Ma, too. And maybe there'll be some mail to pick up at the post office."

The frogs down at the creek were giving us a concert, and enough of a fresh little breeze had sprung up that the mosquitoes weren't too bad. It wasn't quite dark; we could still see the nighthawks swoop and soar above the cottonwoods and willows. A feeling of peace filled me. *Thank you, God, for all the blessings You've given us. Thank You for this life.*

Will set down his bowl and put his arm around my shoulder. "It's going to be a good life, B'Anne."

I rested my head on his shoulder. "That's just what I was thinking. A good life."

Inside, I lit the kerosene lamp and got out the letter I'd been writing to Ma and the rest of the family, so I could mail it tomorrow. I'd sent one shortly after arriving at Uncle Hiram's, and had been adding every few days to this second letter. When it finally reached them, it'd look like a diary, I thought ruefully. Each time I added to the letter, I told Ma what we'd accomplished since the last writing. Now I told her about the neighbors who had come to help put in the fence, about how pleasant it had been to have Adelia Yeagerman and her daughters for woman company. I described the meal I'd cooked, and how pleasant it was in the evening listening to the frogs and watching the nighthawks.

Then I put the cork in the inkwell and joined Will under the bright quilt.

Next morning, Will dropped me at the general store and went looking for fence wire to repay Uncle Hiram and information about buying calves. As usual, Bessie Haysom handed her husband my list and took me back for tea and cookies.

As soon as the curtain that separated the store from the living quarters dropped into place, she looked pointedly at my waist and raised her eyebrows.

"Late November," I told her, and she gave me a warm hug.

"With our young'uns gone we've got extra room. If it's a bad winter, I want you to come in and stay with us just before the baby's born, so I won't have to worry about a doctor not getting to you in time."

"Oh, I couldn't …"

"Oh, yes you can. I insist."

When we were settled with the teapot between us, Bessie said, "This is your first, isn't it? I'll bet you miss your ma."

"I do. When I have time to think about it, I'm a little bit scared."

"Wouldn't be natural if you weren't. But you'll do fine. You're young and healthy, and you don't look like a weak little clinging violet."

I wasn't sure I liked that description, made me feel sort of like a brood mare, but I nodded agreement. Her words were true.

"Besides," she continued, "there's chloroform now. The doctor just puts a cloth on your face and you take a few sniffs and when you wake up you've got a baby."

"That doesn't sound very safe. I'd rather have some hurting and know what's going on."

"We'll just see if you're still saying that when you're almost there." Then, looking like she was afraid she'd scared me, she said, "Of course, you don't have to have it if you don't want it. Just good to know it's there." She held the cookie plate out to me, then spooned some sugar into her tea and stirred vigorously. "Did your ma know you were carrying before you left Iowa?"

"Yes, but we didn't have a chance to talk much about it. Wish we had."

"Well, let's see," Bessie said, "in the store we've got some good ointment to rub on your belly when it starts to get big. Helps with the itching you get when the skin stretches." She looked at my waist hard. "Looks like you could start using it right soon. You're awful big for late November. Any twins in your family?"

Oh, my, I just thought I had been eating too much. I'd already let out the seams in my two oldest calico work dresses and still couldn't button them in front. Today I was wearing one of the loose shirtwaists Lorinda had loaned me over my gray skirt with the waist button undone. Suddenly I remembered Ma talking about her twin brothers. I'd never met them because they stayed back East when the rest of the family came out to Iowa.

Bessie continued, "Later on, you need to be sure and have some bismuth on hand for the heartburn. Tastes like dirt, but works like a miracle. Ginger helps, too. Brew a pot of strong ginger tea in the morning and have a cupful a few minutes before you eat, all day long. Never could understand how something spicy and burny could help heartburn, but it does. Do you have baby clothes?"

"Just diapers, but I imagine Ma and my aunts will be sending some things. And I've got the cloth to sew some, when I have time."

Bessie nodded in understanding. "Yes, it's always hard to find time for anything when you're on a homestead, or any farm, for that matter. But it slows down after autumn."

We talked on and on, about her grown family and how she missed them. "Two daughters in Kansas and a son and daughter in Oregon. Eight grandchildren, and I've only seen two of them. But when the railroad comes through, we're going to visit them. George promised, and I'm going to see he sticks to it."

We had another cup of tea and talked about back home in Iowa. I told her about the nice party my aunts and cousins had given me, and she wanted to know about my wedding.

"We got married in a hurry," I said briefly, looking her straight in the eye.

"Not the first and not the last. Our Dora got married in a hurry. She's got three now, and happy as a hen in a corncrib."

I relaxed. That was the reaction I'd hoped for.

"Just the same, I'd not share that with your neighbor, Mrs. Yeagerman. She rules her girls with such a tight hand; it'll be a miracle if they're not all old maids. She'd probably be some shocked."

"I sort of got the feeling she might think badly of me."

"She thinks badly of most folks," Bessie said with a chuckle. "But she's a good soul, for all that. She's generous to a fault."

Will arrived as we finished our third cup. We picked up the muslin bags and paper-wrapped parcels from the store counter and headed home.

"I mailed the letters," Will said. He'd written one to his family, too. He handed me two envelopes, one from Ma and one from his pa. I opened mine and read it to him. Pa had added a paragraph, reminding us to keep the Sabbath holy (which gave me a little jolt of guilt; we hadn't been, partly because I didn't feel worthy calling on the good Lord), and wishing God's blessings on us. He added a p.s. at the end, after he signed it: "B'Anne, I hope you're not being too sassy with Will." Will and I had a good laugh reading that.

Then I read the one from his pa. Like the letter from my family, his was full of honest questions and good advice, both written with love. I wished Will's mother shared the feeling. Although the letter brought my family close for a minute, I wasn't homesick and hadn't been for quite awhile. I was too busy, and too happy, to be lonesome.

We stopped at Uncle Hiram's to drop off the fence wire, and some of Polly Brill's cookies I'd bought for him at the store. He bit into one right there by the wagon, didn't even wait to get inside the house. "That woman is some baker," he said, brushing crumbs out of his mustache. "I think I'll ask her if she'd be able to cook for the threshers next week."

"I'm going to do the cooking, Uncle Hiram. I've been planning on it. I could cook for threshers until I was too old to do it anymore, and it still wouldn't repay you for all you've done for us." I knew what a big job cooking for a threshing crew was; I'd been helping Ma with it since I was big enough to peel potatoes and scrub carrots. The hired crew of men who traveled the countryside with their big horse-drawn threshing machine during grain harvest needed lots of food. They worked hard and ate hard.

"That's a mighty heap of work, B'Anne. Adelia Yeagerman did it for me for the last couple of years, wouldn't let me pay wages, which made me feel uncomfortable as a preacher in a bawdy … in a saloon." I could tell he'd meant to say something worse, and saw Will was grinning.

"It was a heavy job even for her, an old hand at the cookstove. And she had her two oldest girls to help her. I appreciate the offer, but it's just too much."

"No, it's not. I'm used to cooking big meals. I always helped Ma and my aunts at threshing time."

"We'll see."

I could tell by the stubborn set to his chin that "we'll see" meant "no." I glanced over at Will. He was looking from me to Uncle Hiram and back again, like he was trying to guess which one would win. "She can be awful stubborn when she gets her head set," he told his uncle.

I figured I needed to bargain. "How about we hire the Yeagerman sisters to help with the noon dinner, but I do the morning and evening food myself? I'm sure Adelia would let you pay the two girls. She probably just didn't feel neighborly taking money for herself."

Uncle Hiram was still shaking his head, but Will knew how much I wanted to repay him. "B'Anne really wants to do it, Uncle. With someone helping at noon, I think she can manage it."

Uncle Hiram came around reluctantly. "All right. You decide what you're going to cook, then check to see what supplies I need to lay in. They'll be here three or four days. Four of the men will be with the thresher, and sleep out in the barn, so they'll need all their meals. The rest will be neighbors, and only here for noon dinner."

I'd been full of brave talk, and now I needed to be sure I could do all I'd promised. When we got home I put away our supplies, and then sat down to plan, so Uncle Hiram could buy what was needed. Harvest helpers were entitled to a mid-morning heavy snack, a bountiful feast for noon dinner, and an afternoon refreshment of something sweet along with a cool drink. The men that came with the machine, the real threshing crew, also expected a big breakfast and a hearty supper.

When I finished my plans, I drove the wagon over to Uncle Hiram's and checked his pantry against my list. Tomorrow wasn't too soon to start getting ready, I told myself. I'd go into the store next morning.

Back home, after cooking our dinner and washing up, I tidied the room and gathered dirty clothes together. It was scandalous to do laundry this late in the day, but if I put the washtub and the scrub board outside in the shade by the side of the house, it wouldn't be as hot as inside, and I could easily get two tubs done and dried on the fence before time to get supper. The bright Montana sun was good for at least one thing besides growing prairie grass ... it dried laundry in a hurry.

When I picked up the shirt Will had worn to town that morning, I felt something crinkle in the pocket and pulled out a letter. That's strange; the two letters we'd read in the wagon were there on the shelf by the clock. I pulled it out and saw an envelope with the fancy, hard-to-read handwriting of his mother. He'd evidently decided not to share that letter with me.

Before my better self had a chance to take over, I slipped the letter from the envelope and read it. I wasn't surprised to find myself called ill-bred and conniving. I was hurt, but not shocked, to learn that according to his mother, Will had thrown his life away on a country bumpkin carrying a child that probably wasn't even his. But the lines at the end of the letter chilled me:

"You asked if Victoria's aunt and uncle knew how she had taken the news of your perfidy. I talked to her aunt Cornelia at Ladies' Guild recently. She said Victoria was heartbroken that such a thing could have happened; that she couldn't believe you would swear deep devotion to her and then get another girl in the family way. In her letter to them, she asked if it were possible that you had been hoodwinked by an innocent-seeming floozy. They received another letter a short time ago, in which Victoria told them she is marrying one of Boston's financial leaders. He is considerably older than she is but worships the ground she walks on, and is already spoiling her outrageously.

"William, I am deeply disappointed. You could have made a wonderful marriage. You know how wealthy Victoria's parents are. You could have stepped into her father's business and become very comfortable yourself. You never listen to my advice, but I am going to give you some now, and I hope you pay heed: If Victoria is marrying an old man that means she will probably be free again, and maybe soon. And rich. When Beatrice's child is born, you must be very sure it is yours. If it does not have the look of a Carter, abandon your mistake as soon as possible. If you cannot be sure, leave the strumpet and her child with Hiram. It would do his black soul good to spend the rest of his life with a floozy and her offspring. You could obtain a divorce, and I am sure Beatrice would be perfectly content as long as she is cared for financially."

The letter went on for many more lines, but I didn't read them. Sickened, I carefully put the letter back exactly as I'd found it. Will's shirt could be laundered another day. Or maybe never. I knew Mrs. Carter hated me, but I had no idea Will had written to his mother about Victoria. It was obvious he still cared about her. And that horrible part about abandoning me with Uncle Hiram ... would Will see that as an easy way out? I thought I knew my husband, but now it appeared I didn't.

I knew I had to talk to Will about this letter, but how I dreaded it. If it had only contained the horrible things Mrs. Carter said about me,

I could just assume he'd kept the letter from me because he knew it would hurt my feelings. But why had he asked how Victoria handled the cancelled engagement? If I asked him, and learned he still cared for Victoria, it would mean the end of the life I'd been trying to build.

Maybe I'd be raising a child in Des Moines with Aunt Isabel after all. I had always taken my problems to God. He seemed as real to me as my pa. But maybe neither one of them could help me with this.

Chapter 14

At bedtime that evening, I was still rehearsing in my head what I would say. Will fell asleep quickly, so I put it off till the next morning. I tossed and turned. After a while Will asked sleepily, "Are you sick?""

"No," I snapped, "just thinking."

The next morning I dished up Will's oatmeal and before he could spoon on the sugar I said, "I read the letter in your pocket."

Suddenly the oatmeal needed a lot of his attention. Finally he said, "I didn't tell you about it because I knew it would only upset you."

"The part about being a floozy who trapped you didn't surprise me, but suggesting you should leave me and the baby with your uncle was low, even for your mother. What really hurt me, though, is the part about Victoria."

I watched Will stir his oatmeal in silence for a while, and finally had to say it. "Why did you ask how Victoria took it, Will? You must still have feelings for her."

"No. No, I don't. I just felt guilty, is all. I mean, we were planning to get married, and then I broke it off. Her father could have taken a horse-whip to me, and I'd deserve it."

"So could my pa!" I was too hurt to use the gentle touch Ma had tried to teach me. "I wish he *had* horse-whipped you and then sent me off to live with Aunt Isabel. Then I wouldn't have to worry all the time, and walk on eggshells, wondering if you're mad or sad."

"Oh, B'Anne, I'm sorry. I was just trying to be a gentleman. I shouldn't have asked Ma that question."

I nodded, trying to hold back the tears. "No, you shouldn't have. But you did. And now what happens? Are you going to help Uncle Hiram add on to his house, so the baby and I'll have a room of our own when Victoria's rich old husband dies and you decide to cut your losses?"

"No!" Will's voice was fierce. "We're all staying right here … you, me, and the baby." He got up from the table and tried to put his arms around me, but I twisted away.

He grabbed the skirt of my dress and pulled me back. "You've got to believe me, B'Anne. I don't want Victoria."

I cried then, and let him hold me and kiss me. I wasn't sure I truly believed him, but I tried to. All my dreams were ended if I didn't. Finally I dried my eyes, rinsed my face in the washbowl by the back door, and picked up my list. "I have to go to Choteau to get supplies for Uncle Hiram," I said.

Bessie Haysom was sweeping the boardwalk in front of the store when I pulled up to the hitching post.

"Two days in a row?" she joked. "You must have forgotten a lot of things." Then her gaze sharpened. "You don't look very good. Are you all right?"

"Sure, I feel fine. Just a little tired, I guess." Then I perked up so she wouldn't suspect anything. "No, these supplies are for Uncle Hiram; he said to put it on his bill. I'm cooking for his threshing crew next week." I climbed down and went inside, grateful for the darker coolness.

Bessie followed me in, tsk-tsking as she came. "That's a lot of work. Sure hope you haven't bitten off more than you can chew."

"I'm sure I can do it. I've cooked for threshers back home. And Uncle Hiram's hiring the two older Yeagerman girls for noon dinner."

Bessie helped me, making suggestions and adding a few things I'd forgotten. "Put the oatmeal on the back of the stove before you go to bed at night. By morning, it's cooked, and it'll keep the men quiet while you cook the meat and eggs." I nodded, grateful. "Boil up a big pot of potatoes while you've got the stove hot, cooking dinner, and you'll have 'em ready to hash next morning for breakfast. Won't take 'em as long to fry as raw potatoes." I nodded again.

She reached up and got eight tins of peaches. "If you run out of cake or pie, just open these up and serve them with bread, butter and jam, and the men will be satisfied."

I hadn't been too worried before, but now I was beginning to be. "Um … I was thinking of ordering some things from Polly Brill and picking them up the day before they start. Do you think that'd be awful wasteful?"

"Lordy, no," Bessie exclaimed. "That just makes good sense. Soon as we're through here, I'll take you down to meet her."

Polly Brill turned out to be a woman who was probably not over thirty, but her worry lines made her look older. Raising her children after her husband died had obviously been hard. Guiltily I remembered again how I'd pleaded with Will to let me raise our baby alone. For all I knew, that might still happen. I could have worry lines of my own; maybe even more than Polly had.

Although she must have been tired, Polly was chipper and energetic, and happy to help me. I ordered three applesauce cakes and four dozen hermit cookies to be picked up the day before threshing started, and two lemon sponge cakes and four dozen sugar cookies to be picked up on the third day the men were there. Then I went home to get started, myself.

With the weather so hot, there wasn't a lot I could do ahead, but at least I had everything planned out and the supplies bought, so I wouldn't humiliate myself by forgetting something important. Thank goodness Uncle Hiram had a well at his place. The things I could do ahead that had to be kept cold could be lowered in a bucket down to where the air was cooler. Things like butter and milk could be sealed up and put right into the water.

I don't think I'd ever worked as hard as I did for the next week. In a way that was good, because being busy kept my mind off that letter. When I fell into bed exhausted, I only saw those hateful lines in Mrs. Carter's handwriting for a few minutes before falling asleep.

Will tried to be very helpful, coming in with buckets of water, asking if I needed more wood, reminding me to call him instead of lifting heavy pots by myself. He was trying so hard I almost felt sorry for him. Almost. Then I remembered the hurt of knowing he'd asked about Victoria, and I answered him with a cool voice. When I crawled into bed with my back and legs aching, I stayed well on my side of the bed, with my face to the wall. Even if I hadn't been so tired, I wouldn't have wanted him to touch me.

I still said a prayer before going to sleep … seventeen years of trusting God doesn't disappear … but my spirit was so angry and rebellious that even talking to God didn't seem to make me feel better.

So being busy was a blessing. I sliced up a gallon of cucumbers and onions in vinegar and alum, sealed them in big jars and lowered them in Uncle Hiram's well so they'd be crisp and seasoned when I needed them. I baked Ma's gingersnaps that improved with age, and stored them in the pantry. I mixed up a starter of sourdough for every breakfast's flapjacks. Wild plums had ripened down by the creek, and Will picked me a bucketful for cobbler. On Sunday, I baked twelve pies, four each of dried apple, dried peach, and wild blackberries I'd picked in the cool of the morning. I wrapped the pies in tea towels and hoped the last of them would still be edible for breakfast at the end. Our garden was coming in good, so last thing on Sunday evening I picked a dishpan full of leaf lettuce and radishes for the next day.

The next morning, Will and I drove over to Uncle Hiram's way before daylight, so the threshing crew could eat breakfast and be out in the field by the time the sun came up.

My stomach felt so shaky it was almost like morning sickness again, but it was just nerves. Threshing crews expected good food and lots of it. A ranch got its reputation by those meals. I remembered how back home, the Birkenbachs had a hard time getting a crew because Mrs. Birkenbach stinted on breakfast, sometimes didn't have meat for noon dinner, and once even served bread and milk for supper. But the Johnsons never had to ask twice for a crew, even though the kitchen looked like it hadn't been swept in days, and sometimes Mrs. Johnson had to shoo a couple of chickens out the door before the men trooped in to eat. They didn't care because she stuffed them full of tasty food.

Although at the end of that first day I thought I might melt into a pool of grease from tiredness and the heat, everything seemed to go all right. The men swilled down their oatmeal and coffee, then flapjacks, ham and eggs and more coffee, finished with dried apple pie, patted their bellies and went out to work. About nine-thirty, Will drove the cart in from the far field and took back a huge stack of fresh bread, butter and jam sandwiches, and a big jug of hot coffee. Just a little later, Phoebe and Bertha Yeagerman drove in with the milk and egg supplies Uncle Hiram was buying from them.

Mr. Haysom had delivered meat the previous evening, even though it was the Sabbath. I guess for an order that profitable he didn't mind bending a Commandment a little. I'd had a huge slab of beef roasting in the oven since breakfast time.

The kitchen was hot as Hades, but I guess all three of us women were used to that. The girls tied on their aprons, grabbed paring knives and started on the potatoes and carrots. By the time the men were washing up out by the pump for dinner, roast beef, mashed potatoes and gravy, buttered carrots and succotash were dished up on the table, hot and ready. Bowls of wilted lettuce salad, bread, butter and jam were spread along the length of the table. They ate fast with not much talking, just the sound of chewing, slurping and lip-smacking. They finished it off with slabs of applesauce cake and mugs of hot coffee. Then they stood up, shoved their chairs back under the table, said "thank you, ma'am," and "mighty good eats, ma'am," and went outside. They lay in the shade of the barn for a short nap to digest the meal, then they went back to the field.

Phoebe, Bertha and I were almost too tired to eat, but we managed, then we washed and dried the mountain of dishes.

"Oh, my," Phoebe said, fanning her sweaty face with her apron, "I'm going to marry a city man for sure."

"Not me," Bertha giggled. "I want to marry Solomon Heinz. But I hope he can afford to hire some kitchen help at threshing time."

"Is that the fellow whose coffee cup you refilled without him asking and made sure he got the biggest piece of pie?" I asked. I'd seen a few secret glances flitting back and forth between the two of them, and wondered if Bertie's rosy cheeks were caused by more than the heat of the cookstove.

Bertie's eyes sparkled. "Yes, that was Sol. He's working the threshing crew as much as his pa can spare him, and saving every penny." Looking like the cat that ate the cream, she said innocently, "Sol says he's going to have a place of his own by the time he's twenty."

"Bertie, you better not let Ma hear you talk about Sol Heinz. She'll lock you in the bedroom till you're so old Solomon won't even recognize you. You know she's got big ideas for us girls." Although she was only seventeen, Phoebe sounded just like her mother.

Bertie shook her curls at her sister. "You and Josephine can be her big ideas, then. It's Solomon Heinz for me!"

"I'll come help you at threshing time, Bertie." I liked this sassy, independent girl.

Phoebe gave me a pitying look. "By the time Ma lets her get married, you'll have so many babies you'll never be able to leave the house."

Hmmm. Phoebe was indeed a lot like her mother, I decided.

"That's what you think," Bertie told her sister teasingly. I didn't know whether she meant it wouldn't be a long time till she was married or that I wouldn't be spouting babies like a mama sow did piglets. Maybe I was better off not knowing.

After they left, I rested with my feet up for a few minutes, then packed up the afternoon snack of hermit cookies and sweet cold tea. Lots of both. After that I cooked a big pot of macaroni with tinned tomatoes for supper, baked enough cornbread to feed an army (or six hungry threshers) and sliced a platter of cold leftover beef and cheese to go with it.

Will sneaked in to dry dishes when I washed them after supper. I could tell he didn't want the other men to see. I also knew he was still trying to make up for the horrible letter.

"You don't have to do this, Will. I can manage."

"I know you can, but you're worn to a frazzle. I'm helping."

I checked on the sourdough starter in the pantry, put the oatmeal on the back of the stove, and let Will help me … almost haul me … up to my seat in the wagon. As we drove home through the twilight, the lantern on the front of our wagon cast a bouncing shadow a little way ahead of us. The air had cooled, and a fresh breeze lifted the hair that had straggled from my bun and lay sticky on my neck. Night birds made their sleepy sounds, and frogs thrummed out their song down by the creek. In spite of my intentions to keep Will at arm's length, I fell asleep on his shoulder long before we reached home.

Next day I did it all over again, and the day after that. The only difference was fried steaks for noon dinner the second day, and chicken and dumplings the third day. Same huge breakfasts. Different suppers, but always hearty enough for hard-working men. Wild plum cobbler with cream, instead of applesauce cake. On the third day, slabs of dense chocolate cake with thick fudge frosting. The cobbler and cake I made myself, as well as the breakfast pies, and Will seemed proud as a peacock. I heard one of the men tell him, "You got yourself a good one, Carter. Looks like an angel, and cooks like one, too."

Hah! I thought bitterly. As if he cares.

The work was constant and exhausting, but I knew it wouldn't last long. Getting to know the girls better was a treat that helped make up for the tiredness. Seventeen-year-old Phoebe I could take or leave, but Bertha, or Bertie, sixteen, was a different story. We talked and laughed through our work. Phoebe looked on, sometimes with a scornful little smile, but we didn't pay attention.

Uncle Hiram had left me money to pay them on the last day. Phoebe took hers daintily and slipped it into her apron pocket. "Mrs. Simmons, in Choteau, is going to make a bonnet to match my new winter coat. She's a marvel. You should go there, B'Anne."

Bertie slipped her money in her apron pocket, too, but she didn't say what she would spend it on. Not right then, at least. She waited until her sister had gone out to the privy, then whispered excitedly, "Sol and I are saving money to get married. If Pa and Ma say no, we'll just elope."

"Oh, Bertie, be really, really sure before you take such a big step." I hated to sound like somebody's old ma, but she was such an innocent young thing.

"You're not very old, but you and Will seem happy."

I hesitated a long time. "Yes, but … we'd have been better to wait till we were older." Then I made the plunge. "We didn't have a choice. I was in the family way. I'll always know he didn't marry me by choice, but because he had to. Don't tell your mother, or Phoebe. Please, please, don't tell."

Bertie's eyes were round. "I won't tell a soul. I promise. But … but that's so romantic."

"No, it's not romantic. It's scary, and embarrassing, and lets down everybody who trusted you. We're doing all right, I guess, but it was really hard at first, and sometimes it still is. Will had to give up a lot. I'll never know if he really loves me or he's just doing what he's supposed to do." I was embarrassed to have to dab at my eyes with my apron. "Don't let it happen to you, Bertie. You and Solomon may love each other, but take it slower, please. Believe me, it makes you feel … well … worthless sometimes."

We heard Phoebe's steps on the back porch, and Bertha leaned forward to kiss my cheek quickly. "I will, B'Anne. And I won't tell anybody." She waved over her shoulder as the girls rode away.

Chapter 15

Life got back to normal after the threshing was finished. Will helped his uncle for a few more days, hauling the grain to Choteau, where wagonloads would be taken to Fort Benton and go by Missouri River steamboat to railroad for Eastern markets. After that was done, he helped gather in the straw that was left in the fields. It didn't have much nourishment in it, but Uncle Hiram said that in a bad winter, we might have to use it to help feed the stock we hoped to have.

I welcomed the quiet of my own home again, and for the first couple of days I mostly rested. I fed our cow and chickens, so Will wouldn't have those chores added to his full day's work at Uncle Hiram's. It wasn't like before, though, when I worked hard because I felt sorry that his load was so heavy. Now I did it because it was a duty. Other than cooking and cleaning the kitchen that was the only work I did. Even though I'd surely been busy enough to burn up the food I ate, my belly was still growing faster than I thought it should. My legs and back hurt from being on my feet so much, but I tried not to let Will or Uncle Hiram know. In their absence I rested, and by the end of a few days I was feeling much better.

We had a nice rain not long after Uncle Hiram's wheat was harvested. It was good for our garden. I was especially grateful because it meant I wouldn't have to water the plants by hand again. I'd done it several times, but the rain should see the garden through to harvest.

It was too wet to work outside, so Will began making a table and benches. Finally, I'd have something to work at besides the up-ended packing crate, and we wouldn't have to sit on the bed holding our plates to eat dinner.

I got out the bolt of white outing flannel again and made more diapers. It would be a luxury if I had enough that I wouldn't have to wash them every day in the cold winter. When the diapers were finished, I cut out and stitched tiny nightgowns. I had learned to sew a fine hand-seam from Granny when I was just a little girl, and as soon as my legs were long enough to reach the treadle on Ma's sewing machine, she taught me how to use it, marveling all the while on what a wonderful invention it was. I remembered the nightgown pattern Ma had cut out of newspaper when all the aunts and cousins helped cousin Lorinda get ready for her baby, and I had finally gotten it right myself.

For awhile, we worked on our separate projects, but it's hard to ignore someone when the rain closes you together in a fourteen-by-sixteen-foot cabin. One wet afternoon, Will finally said, "B'Anne, you're going to have to forgive me sometime. I don't want us to be one of those couples that have to ask their children to 'tell Pa to pass me the salt,' like the Frobishers, back home." He pulled me into his arms, me stiff as a board. "I'm sorry. Can't we get past this?"

I cried awhile, and he wiped the tears away. He sat down in the oak rocker and held me on his lap, even though I was way too big to fit comfortably. Then he carried me to the bed without groaning, although I knew it took a lot of self-control. Under the bright patchwork quilt, he tried to show me he meant what he said, being very careful of my belly.

Over the next few days and weeks we gradually got back to almost the way we'd been before I read that letter. I was able to enjoy our home with him again, but with a little edge of doubt in the back of my mind.

We were both trying, but I think it was harder for me than for Will. Will, I was sure, just wanted to smooth things over for his own peace of mind. But I knew that the bitterness in my heart saddened God. I prayed for help in forgiving Will, but I agonized over whether I wanted to forgive him to please God, or just to ensure the future of my baby. Sometimes I even wondered if I still loved Will. Maybe we'd just settled into an arrangement. Maybe we were a housekeeper and a ranch hand living in the same house. We were polite to each other, but it was the kind of politeness you'd give to a guest in your house: "Would you like more coffee, Will?" "Yes, B'Anne, but let me get it. You've been on your feet all day."

Maybe we just needed a time away from each other, I thought, but there was no way for that to happen. And I had the sinking feeling that if we were apart very long, Will would quickly get used to my absence. If only we had a day or two free of back-breaking work, a time to be together and learn to enjoy each other's company again. Rich people went on little trips, I knew. Why, even my best friend Minna and her husband once left the baby with her folks and went to Des Moines just for the fun of it ... saw a play, stayed in a hotel, ate in a restaurant. Thinking about the things she'd described while I scrubbed clothes on the washboard or picked another basket of prickly cucumbers in the blistering heat didn't improve my frame of mind. We were stuck here, for better or for worse, and this sure felt like worse.

When this feeling dragged me down into what felt like a swamp, I tried to pray it away: *Dear God, please help me to be a whole person again. Please help me forgive Will, and be satisfied with the things I do have, not hunger for the things I don't have.*

One morning, Uncle Hiram drove over. He accepted a cup of coffee and a biscuit, then got down to the purpose of his visit.

"It's time for the huckleberries. You ought to get some. They taste mighty good in the winter, on pancakes or in preserves."

Will said, "We don't have huckleberries back in Iowa. What are they like?"

"They're like a blueberry, only smaller and sharper tasting. Little bit sourer, too, but my, oh my, are they good! Haysom usually gets baskets of them from the Indians and sells them at the general store. Polly Brill makes them into preserves, and he sells them for her."

I thought of the time Will spent with that little journal he kept. It was supposed to be a farm record when we had something to sell or trade. Right now, there was only one column: "Expenses."

"Maybe we can try them next year. Right now, all we can afford is what we grow and preserve ourselves."

"Oh, I don't mean buying them from the store. Haysom makes a killing on what he buys from the Indians." He took another biscuit. "I know the best place to pick them. It's a good three or four hours up in the foothills from here, but if you stay long enough to pick a bunch, it's worth the trip."

Will looked thoughtful. "That sounds like a good idea. Since we don't have the calves yet, we could be gone for a couple of days."

Uncle Hiram nodded. "When I first came up here, several families would go up together. I went once. It was a good time … picking all day, cooking a good meal in the evening, sitting around the campfire, sleeping under the stars. You ought to see if any of the Yeagermans want to go up with you."

"You're coming, of course." It wasn't a question; I just figured for sure he'd come along.

He chuckled. "Not me. I cooked over a campfire and slept on the hard ground enough to last a lifetime when I was mining. I can give you good directions on how to find the best place, and I'll come over and feed your critters while you're gone."

Will went over to the Yeagerman place that afternoon. Sure enough, their oldest boy, Jim, and my friend Bertie wanted to come along. I was glad Phoebe didn't.

We packed the wagon with enough food to last a few days and empty containers to bring the berries home in. Will carried out the straw tick from our bed and heaved it into the back of the wagon, along with quilts and pillows.

"You don't need to be sleeping on the ground, B'Anne," he explained when I raised my eyebrows. "You're uncomfortable enough in the bed."

I thought I'd kept my tossing and turning to a minimum, and Will was usually so tired he fell asleep right away. But I guess he knew. "I'm sorry if I bother you. It's just that I'm used to sleeping on my stomach, and I can't do that now. And the baby seems to choose nighttime as the best time to somersault around."

Will grinned. "He's a rough little rascal. I'll bet he'll be helping me herd calves before he's five."

I pictured a tow-headed little boy with Will's blue eyes and cleft chin. Then I pictured the pig-tailed little girl I sometimes daydreamed about. "Or maybe she'll be helping me scrub clothes on the washboard," I retorted.

Jim Yeagerman drove up with Bertie, and we headed out, Uncle Hiram's penciled map in Will's pocket.

We hadn't been under way too long when I saw another wagon following us. The Yeagerman wagon stopped and waited, so we did too. When the wagon drew up, I was surprised to see Sol Heinz driving it, with a pretty girl beside him.

Oh, no, I thought. How could Sol be so cruel? Didn't he know how Bertie felt about him? Her heart would be broken.

Bertie didn't seem to be heartbroken, though. She hopped out of her brother's wagon, and the other girl left Sol's, and they traded places. Each girl slid across the wagon seat to sit closer to the driver than they should have, chattering and happy.

"Who's that other girl?" I demanded. "Is that the girl Jim's been sparking?" Will nodded sheepishly. "Oh, Will, we're in trouble. Adelia Yeagerman is going to be fit to be tied. They planned this. Did you know about it?"

"Oh, no. I wouldn't be that stupid." Will's voice didn't sound as upset as it should, it seemed to me. "Looks like they're planning to have a good time, though."

"Well, Bertie and that other girl are going to sleep in the wagon with me. I'm not about to be responsible for either one of them having a baby in nine months."

Will's next remark seemed serious, but I could tell he was trying hard not to smile. "They wouldn't even have a blizzard to blame it on."

"I never blamed it on the blizzard. I just blamed it on you!" I shot back, trying to decide whether to have my feelings hurt or laugh.

"That's all right. You can blame me. But I blame it on your hair smelling too nice, and your skin feeling so soft." There was warmth in his eyes when he looked into mine. I knew we were both remembering that night. He leaned over and tucked a strand of hair behind my ear. "And I'm not a bit sorry," he whispered. I remembered my own guilt and sorrow, and my prayers for forgiveness and hoped Will was just joking.

Jim introduced us to Flora, the girl from town he was sparking ... the one his pa had said he'd probably marry next summer. We started out again, three wagons following a rough, rutted trail up toward the foothills.

"I didn't know the road was going to have this much jolting," Will said. "Do you suppose it's bad for the baby? Maybe we should turn around and go back."

"If we turn around and go back it won't be because of the bad road, it'll be because I don't want Bertie's ma to skin me alive." The jolting *was* uncomfortable, but I wasn't about to let Will know it. It was the first time we'd done anything just for the fun of it since … forever. Since long ago, before Victoria came to town and our courtship ended. I sure hadn't had much fun when I was so lonely and sad from losing Will. We hadn't had time for fun since we got married. "I'm sitting on a pillow," I reminded him. "I'll be fine."

After several hours we started to climb, and before long began to see scattered bushes that looked like what Uncle Hiram had described. We kept going, though. According to Uncle Hiram's instructions, the bushes thickened farther up in the hills.

It was dusk by the time we stopped to camp. I felt cumbersome and ugly as Will helped me down from the wagon. I was stiff and slow-moving, and my loose shirtwaist barely covered my gapping skirt front. And here I was with two pretty young girls who were flirting and simpering with their fellows. Had I ever been that young? I sure didn't feel like it.

The two young men began setting up tents. *Might as well get it over with*, I thought. "The girls are sleeping in the wagon with me," I said firmly, "and the axle squeaks pretty loud when somebody gets in or out of it."

Jim Yeagerman's face took on a stubborn expression. "We've got two tents, one for the girls and one for us boys."

Will spoke up. "We're not having your ma come after us with a hatchet, Jim," he said calmly. "I'm sure your folks didn't know there was going to be any sparking going on, just harmless berry-picking."

Jim shrugged, and the matter was dropped.

As we prepared supper, Bertie confided that she and her brother were covering for each other, and their parents were indeed unaware that their sweethearts would be present. "Shoot, I don't think Ma even knows I *have* a sweetheart," she said. "I never talk about Sol at home."

"I'm sure Phoebe took care of that for you."

The other girl, Flora, nodded. "But Jim won't say a word," she assured Bertie. "He wouldn't dare because if it got back to my folks, there'd be a chivaree before you could blink." Blushing, she added, "Jim and I are going to get married, but not like that." She was staring at the ground when she ended with, "Ma and Pa think I'm spending a few days with my cousin at Fox Creek."

I couldn't stay mad at them long. They were too fun-loving. We spread out quilts on the ground and ate supper with our plates in our laps. Thankfully, Will got a box from the wagon for me to sit on. Somehow the bacon and fried potatoes tasted better in the pine-scented air, with smoke wisping up among the trees, than it ever did in the kitchen.

The food smelled so good that Will got his rifle from the wagon and laid it beside him on the ground. "Uncle Hiram said there's plenty of bears around here, stuffing themselves full of huckleberries before holing up for the winter. If one of them comes sniffing around, I want to be ready."

Sol followed his example.

"I didn't bring my rifle," Jim said. "I guess if two shots don't take care of him, we're in trouble."

Jim got his guitar out of the wagon and strummed chords while we decided what we wanted to sing. "I don't play fancy," he explained, "but I can chord along with most songs, as long as I've heard them before." Soon all six of us were singing "O Susanna," "Old Folks at Home," "Swanee River," "Home on the Range," "Love's Old Sweet Song," "Little Brown Jug," and others. I felt a little pang of guilt when we shouted out "Little Brown Jug" boisterously, with the fellows stomping and us girls clapping along in time. Pa couldn't abide drinking songs, so we never sang that one at home, but I'd learned it at play-parties and such.

We sang on and on until the moon was high in the sky. Then I opened a tin of milk and made hot chocolate. It felt good on our tired throats. When we were finished, the boys spread out blanket rolls in the tents. Will and I pretended not to notice the lingering glances and soft voices, but when Bertie and Sol headed into the edge of the woods, Will cautioned, "Better be careful. Could be a bear close by." They wandered back, hand in hand.

The men stood guard facing the campfire, backs to us girls as we found bushes to do our business behind, and we separated for bed. Will helped me lumber up into the wagon. Jim and Sol helped their girls, too. The girls were so spry they didn't really need help, but the feel of hands around their waists might have been what kept them whispering and giggling as the fire died down. I struggled to get comfortable, missing the warmth of Will against my back. He had rolled up in a quilt in Jim's tent.

"This is so much fun," Bertie whispered to me. "I'm so glad you invited us."

"Yes, I'm having a good time, too. I just hope we don't get in trouble with your folks."

"Oh, we won't. Just relax and enjoy yourself." Changing direction suddenly, she asked, "Are you afraid about having the baby?"

"Oh, no, I'm not ... well, yes I am. I miss my ma something dreadful. I don't know what to expect. I wish I'd paid more attention when my cousin Lorinda was carrying, and when she had the baby. The aunts and Ma and Lorinda were always talking about it, but I was too busy to pay them much mind. Never guessed I'd be having a baby all by myself, far from home, nobody around to answer my questions."

I'd thought Flora was asleep, but now she said softly, "Oh, B'Anne, you're so brave. I don't know what I'd do without my folks nearby."

"I have Will. He'll be enough." I hoped I was speaking the truth.

Bertie leaned over and patted my cheek. "You could always come talk to my ma. If you ever get that desperate, that is. I've never asked her a question about anything. She's so proper. She'll probably say the doctor brings the baby in his little black bag."

"Well, we know *that's* not going to happen. But I'll be all right. Bessie Haysom at the store helps me some."

The campfire settled, sending a little shower of sparks drifting up. The wind stirred our blankets, and a desolate howl came from somewhere not too far away.

"It's not a wolf, it's just a coyote," Will called out to us. I pulled my blankets closer and went to sleep.

Next morning, we were up at daylight, teeth chattering in the chill air. A big pot of campfire coffee warmed us up, even if our flapjacks were cold by the time we finished eating. We hung our food supplies in a tree, as Uncle Hiram had directed, and set out with baskets. The berries were small but plentiful, and I soon learned how to strip them down the branches. There'd be a lot of twigs and leaves to sort out afterward, but I could do that in the comfort of our cabin, or out on the stoop.

We picked all day, stopping for lunch and a short rest in the heat of the afternoon. Will helped me into the wagon and stayed there with me. I was so tired that even the deer-flies couldn't keep me awake. I'd rouse up enough to shoo them away, then drop off again. At one point, I noticed how very quiet the campsite was.

"Will, have they gone off together?"

"Not all together ... two by two." Will sounded as sleepy as I felt. "There's not a thing we can do about it, B'Anne. They're old enough to have a little sense."

Evidently I agreed with him. I fell back to sleep.

After the rest, we all picked again till suppertime. Hot and sticky, we washed off in the creek before starting to cook. Sol had caught a string of trout during the rest time, which made me relieved. At least they hadn't been misbehaving *all* the time. The boys cleaned the fish and threaded them on sticks over the fire. Flora fried hushpuppies in the big spider skillet we'd brought, and we washed the meal down with cold water and hot coffee.

After the supper dishes were scrubbed at the creek, we sang like the night before, and played Twenty Questions. But we were all so tired and achy that we welcomed the warm blankets as the mountain air grew cold.

Next day we picked again, but we'd covered the nearby area pretty well, and all the containers we'd brought were full, so we broke camp and headed home in the late morning.

Jouncing along the bumpy trail, Will said, "Well, I had a good time. Did you?"

"I did. It was the most fun I've had in a long time."

"I know. It'll get better, B'Anne. Soon we won't have to work so hard, and we'll be able to enjoy ourselves. Get acquainted with the neighbors around us, and maybe some folks in town. Maybe go to church. I'm sure there's things going on ... pie suppers, and barn-dances, that kind of thing."

"I can just see myself square-dancing, clumping around like a cow. I'd bring the barn down."

"You don't clump around like a cow. Besides, tired and stiff as I am right now, square-dancing is the last thing I'd want to do. But later, after the baby comes, we'll do things to make life better."

Just then, we got to a turn in the trail. Flora and Bertie changed places once again, and Sol headed for Fox Creek to deliver Flora. I shook my head, feeling like an old granny. "No good will come of this, I'm afraid."

It had worked out well for us, though. Neither Sol nor Flora could take berries home, or the secret would be out, so the Yeagerman family got half, and we got half.

After we got home, Will stretched muslin between poles out in front of the cabin. When his pa had given us the bolt of cloth at his store back in Balsamview, I'd pictured someday making sheets and pillowcases. I'd never dreamed I'd be drying huckleberries on it. I sorted and washed berries, and we spread them on the muslin. Then we covered them with a layer of cheesecloth to keep flies off and hoped the hot Montana sun and wind would do the rest. When they were dried, I'd use the cheesecloth to make bags to store them in. That way the air would circulate around the berries, and they wouldn't get moldy. The muslin was from the bolt Will's pa had given us, and I could use it later when I needed it for sewing. Will had got the cheesecloth from the general store, and Bessie Haysom had told him how to do the job. I hated the expense, but the food would be a welcome change in the winter.

We unloaded the wagon and had a simple supper. When I crawled into bed on the straw tick Will had brought in, it felt like heaven. The cabin was hot, but the feel of his body against my back was so secure, I fell asleep while I was worrying about whether the wind would tear the cheesecloth over the huckleberries. But before I fell asleep, I thanked God for the way a little bit of pleasure had eased things between Will and me.

Chapter 16

Now that the wheat harvest was finished, I concentrated on the garden, going out every day in the cool of the morning to weed a little, although the plants were healthy enough to fight off the weeds now. I picked everything that was ready each morning, and we enjoyed all the fresh vegetables. Sometimes green beans or spinach cooked with a little bit of bacon was our whole supper. I picked the last of the peas and dried them before the heat took the crop. I could hardly keep up with the tender summer squash.

Since the house was in a place where Will could quit working on it for awhile, he and Uncle Hiram concentrated on finding us some calves. A hired hand of the rancher who sold them the calves helped them drive home eighteen that were weaned, healthy, and looked big enough to survive the cold of winter. They made our fenced pasture look suddenly very small.

"We'll brand them," Uncle Hiram said. "Then you can let them loose to graze if you run low on hay. During the winter they'll stay around, as long as you put hay out when you can."

I could see Will was worried. I was, too. We'd stored the grass Uncle Hiram had mowed before the house was built, and I'd scythed a couple of hours a day until threshing time, but that was just a drop in the bucket compared to what these fellows would need over the winter.

That night, Will got out the book he kept records in and added columns again and again. "I shouldn't have bought so many, B'Anne. I don't know how we'll feed them."

"We'll figure out something. Just think, if they all make it through the winter, and they go for forty dollars a head like Uncle Hiram says, we'll be off to a good start." I sat down across from him. Uncle Hiram had loaned us two of his caned-bottom chairs to go with the table Will had made during the rainy spell. At least we had a table to worry at, now. "Maybe we can get by without buying any more supplies for ourselves. We can butcher the pig in November, and not have to buy bacon or ham in the winter. We've got a big garden coming on, and I can put a lot of it away."

In my mind, I was filling a pantry and root cellar. I'd pitted and dried many buckets of wild plums in the hot Montana sun, and chokecherries earlier in the summer. The huckleberries we'd just brought down from the hills would be welcome. The wild blackberries along the creek had already provided several baskets dried, and I'd preserved some in Mason jars, although I'd have to be careful with sugar and jars from now on. Next year preserving would be cheaper, when I'd just have to buy new rubber sealers, and could use the jars and lids again.

We should start the cold weather with a winter's supply of potatoes, turnips, pumpkins, carrots, squash, and cabbages in the root cellar Will was going to dig, and we'd have more carrots and turnips in the ground till the first hard freeze.

We'd have dried onions, leather-britches beans and corn hanging from the kitchen rafters. I remembered helping Granny thread green beans on long strings to make what she said the old folks called leather-britches because they were hard as leather to chew. I'd been making the cucumbers into crocks of pickles. I'd use the precious Mason jars for tomatoes and a batch of piccalilli.

If our corn crop was good enough, we'd have some to take to Choteau and have it ground into meal, as well as what I'd dry in the sun and kitchen. We'd make it, but we'd not buy anything for ourselves we didn't absolutely need. We'd probably have to buy hay for the calves.

Will chewed his lip for a moment, his eyes still on the rows of numbers. When he looked up at me, the sad expression on his face made me feel as bad as he evidently did. "I didn't plan on having us go hungry the first winter."

"We won't go hungry, Will. And just look around us, and remember those homestead shacks we saw on the trip here. Why, we've got a comfortable house. We'll be warm all winter, and so will our baby."

Will still looked gloomy. "That reminds me. We've got to get a few wagonloads of coal. Can't very well cut down all the trees on the place the first winter we're here."

"Coal's better anyhow," I reminded him, "burns slow and steady, holds a fire all night on just a shovelful." And coats everything with a dirty layer of soot, I thought, but didn't say. I could always wash off soot.

We went out to admire our calves once again before bedtime. They looked healthy and fine, curled up next to each other in the shed. "We'll probably be using Uncle Hiram's leftover straw sooner than he thought," Will said.

We went to bed, but even the bright patchwork quilt didn't seem to bring Will comfort. I was six months along now and felt big as a barn as I curled up against his back. Suddenly he began to chuckle. "Not even born yet, and he's already kicking his pa for doing something stupid," Will said between gusts of laughter.

The baby was kicking up a storm, that's for sure. "Well, I must have been doing a lot of stupid things lately," I complained, "because I've been getting kicked all day long." Will's chuckles were contagious, and soon I was laughing so hard I was afraid I'd have to run out to the privy.

Finally, we laughed ourselves out and rolled to our other sides, so Will was snuggled to my back. That way, at least only one of us was getting kicked. "We'll make it, Will," I whispered, just before going to sleep.

"We don't have any choice," he murmured against the back of my head, "but we might get awful tired of potatoes."

In early September, Will borrowed Uncle Hiram's Clydesdales and mower and cut the ripe, golden prairie grass for acres around our place. It made the pitiful amount I'd scythed back of the house look like a drop in a rainstorm. By the time he'd finished mowing, the first he'd cut was ready for raking, so the Clydesdales went to work again.

Then the Yeagerman boys showed up with a team and hay wagon to go along with the one we'd borrowed from Uncle Hiram, and hauled it in to make huge stacks behind our shed. Uncle Hiram said he had canvas covers we could use to protect the haystacks from the weather.

My belly was big enough now that there was nothing I could do to help. I wouldn't have tried anyhow, for fear of embarrassing Will. So I cooked good enough meals that the boys would be able to tell their ma that I might be young, but I could cook. Or at least that's what I hoped they'd tell her. Being boys, they probably didn't even notice.

While they were out in the fields, I was busy harvesting the garden, except for what we'd leave in the ground until the first hard frost. Thank heavens the hay work would be finished by the time the potatoes would be dug because I knew that was more work than I could do alone, big and clumsy as I was. I couldn't reach my own shoes, much less a hill of potatoes! But I was able to make kraut and pickles, and even pickled some of the early beets. I knew that if our winter diet were going to be skimpy and plain, things that were spicy and vinegary would be welcome.

One afternoon when I was braiding onion stems together so Will could hang them above the cookstove to dry, I heard hoofbeats and squeaky wagon wheels. I was sitting under the cottonwood tree where it was a little bit cooler than the house, so I hurried inside to put on a clean apron and smooth my hair back. If we were having company, I hoped it was Bertie by herself, not with her ma and persnickety sister.

But it wasn't anyone I knew. It was a rickety wagon that seemed filled with little ones and was pulled by two swaybacked old mules. Half-grown children and grown-ups walked alongside. I watched as it slowly disappeared down the wagon ruts. Looked like we were going to have new neighbors.

I made a big jug of cold ginger beer to have ready when the men came in, hot, thirsty and prickling with hay. While they gulped down the vinegary drink, I told them about the wagon that had passed.

"Must be the folks that were in town yesterday, buying supplies and asking about homestead land," Jim Yeagerman said, shaking his head. "My ma was at the store when they came in. Said they all looked like something the cat drug in ... skinny, clothes practically rags." He took another big gulp of ginger beer. "Mrs. Haysom sent for the

German fellow who runs the mill, to take them out where there was still homestead land for the taking."

"Is there more homestead land down past our place, Uncle Hiram?" I asked.

"Yes," Hiram replied, "but if we're lucky, they'll go on a little farther. I was hoping that section wouldn't get claimed, so Will and I could buy it together when the time was right."

Hah! The time wouldn't be right for so many years I couldn't even see that far. "It would be nice to have neighbors," I said. "I don't speak German, but I'll bet we could understand each other if we tried hard enough. Maybe I should wait a few days to let them get settled, then take them a cake or something."

That night as I unbraided and brushed my hair before bed, I was still thinking about the new people. They had looked so tired and beaten down ... the horses, the people, and the wagon. Like they couldn't go a single mile farther. I looked over my shoulder where Will was already on the edge of sleep. "Will, I want to take the wagon tomorrow and find the new people, take them a big pot of stew or something."

Will clasped his hands behind his head and gazed at me thoughtfully. "I don't know."

"What do you mean, you don't know?" I couldn't believe him. "I've driven a wagon from the time I was twelve."

"Now don't get lathered up. What I mean is that these people are from another country. Maybe to them, a woman in the family way who drives a wagon over the hills to go visiting by herself would be a disgrace." My disappointment must have shown on my face because he added. "The hay's in. I'll take you. I'd like to meet them, too. A few extra pairs of hands not too far away makes a big difference." He gave a huge yawn and patted the bed beside him. "Now come to bed and get some rest. We'll drive over there first thing tomorrow."

Chapter 17

Next morning, Uncle Hiram rode in early and sat down to have a cup of coffee with us as we finished breakfast. He'd been to Choteau the day before and picked up mail for us. I put the letters from Ma, and from my old friend Minna, under the sugar bowl. I'd have the pleasure of looking forward to them all day, and reading them in the quiet evening.

I told Uncle Hiram that we were going to see our new neighbors. He offered to go along.

"I know a little German," he explained. "Maybe it would be helpful."

We gazed at him in amazement. "How do you come to know German, Uncle?" Will asked.

"A little German, a little Italian, quite a bit of Spanish," Hiram replied. "When you're looking for gold and living in mining camps, you meet people from all over." He was grinning, enjoying our astonishment. "I think we should take food. Lots of it. When I talked to George Haysom in the store yesterday, he told how they couldn't get nearly all they needed; just didn't have the money. We wouldn't want to descend on them empty-handed."

"We could take dinner," I said, then, "but maybe that would offend them. What do you think, Uncle Hiram?"

"I think a picnic dinner to share with them would be best, and if I work on it all the way over, I'm pretty sure I can come up with enough German to explain to them that in America, neighbors greet newcomers with gifts of food." Hiram looked thoughtful for a moment. "Were they leading a cow behind the wagon, B'Anne?"

"I don't think so. No, I'm sure not."

"They're going to have a hard winter, without even milk for the young ones."

"I didn't see how many people were in the wagon," I said, "but I know there were children of all sizes, and there were several almost grown walking alongside."

Will drank the rest of his coffee and stood up with a deep sigh. "I think there are three pullets out there whose time has come." He looked at me for agreement, and I nodded. You have to feed hungry people in this world. Fried chicken would be a good start. The Bible told us to do unto others as we would have done unto us. If I was as beaten-down and ragged as that wagon full of folks looked, I'd appreciate a gift of food. If I had a wagon full of hungry children, I'd appreciate it even more.

When we drove out around eleven o'clock that morning, we hauled enough food to make a dent in hunger. Crispy fried chicken filled a dishtowel-lined basket. Another basket held a triple batch of biscuits. Fresh green beans cooked with chunks of bacon were in a large crockery bowl.

Besides the picnic dinner, we were taking a wooden box containing a small sack of ground coffee beans, a jar of huckleberry jam and one of blackberry, and four loaves of bread, all of the weekly baking I'd done the day before. I'd need to bake again tomorrow, but that was all right, I told myself. The immigrant family probably hadn't had fresh bread in weeks. I wished we had milk and butter to share with them, but our cow hadn't calved yet. We did take a basket of fresh eggs, though, and tomatoes and cucumbers from the garden. And while the chicken was frying, I'd baked a cake with dried blackberries in it. We might be poor, but we could share with folks who were probably poorer.

The cool of morning had disappeared by the time we set out, and heat shimmered over the prairie ahead of us, but it seemed comfortable after cooking and baking all morning in that hot kitchen. We followed the tracks of the strangers' wagon wheels across the grassy rolling knolls. After we'd gone about a half-mile, Uncle Hiram breathed a sigh of relief. "Looks like they're settling farther on," he said. "Maybe we'll still have a chance to get that section next to you."

I couldn't see that there was a chance in the world we'd get more land, when we were poor as church mice already. We'd be lucky to hang onto the hundred and sixty acres we'd already filed on. But like a proper wife should, I kept my mouth shut. I took deep breaths of that hot prairie grass smell and kept a sharp look for anything that might be helpful to us. There were no wild nut trees, like the butternut and hickory nut back home, but I saw a big patch of wild roses, all finished blooming. Now they were covered with little round rosehips. I'd come back and pick them when I had time. I couldn't waste the sugar to make jelly, but dried rosehips made good tea when a person was sick, and Ma always made us drink it when winter was coming on … said it kept us from getting so many colds.

Eventually the tracks led through a break in the willows and directly to the creek bank, then disappeared. They could be seen again in the muddy creek bank on the other side. "There's a good gravelly ford a little farther down. We'll cross there," Uncle Hiram said. "If they made it across here without getting bogged down, we should be able to as well, but why chance it?"

At the crest of the slope after crossing the creek, we could see the immigrants' camp in the shade of a cottonwood tree and a willow. A piece of canvas slanted from the wagon to the ground beside it, and stacked under the canvas were boxes and bundles. Smoke wisped up from a small cooking fire where a large pot rested on coals. Drying laundry covered nearby bushes. Two old mules were grazing in the grass, and several children played nearby.

As we drew near, the children stopped their play and ran under the canvas. The woman sitting close by put down the basin in her lap and came to meet us. She was wearing her apron tied high, but I figured that with all those children, it didn't necessarily mean she was in the family way. Poor thing, she probably no longer had a waistline. "Guttentag," said Uncle Hiram, tipping his hat to the woman. "*Vilkommen.*"

The woman's eyes glowed with her smile, and she called instructions to the children, who dashed through the grass to the lightly wooded area beyond. Turning back to the wagon, she began a rapid stream of

German. Uncle Hiram held up his hand with a chuckle. "*Nein. Nein,*" he said. "*Sprechen Sie langsamer, bitte.*"

The woman spoke more slowly, reinforcing her words with gestures, and it was obvious she was inviting us down from the wagon. Once on the ground, Hiram introduced us in labored German, and she responded with the two German words that had served Hiram well: *Guttentag* and *Vilkommen.* A middle-aged man, several teenagers and half-grown children emerged from the wooded area and came quickly through the meadow grass to the camp.

Watching the group approach, I was glad I'd brought large quantities of everything. With the middle-aged man, there were three young men, the youngest appearing to be about fifteen and the oldest perhaps twenty; and two girls, one around sixteen and the other a little older. Two boys who seemed about ten or eleven didn't look strong enough for physical labor, but they were with the workers. Two young girls had been playing in the grass. The mother carried a baby in her arms while another toddler clung to her skirt, thumb in mouth.

The man who was evidently the father introduced himself as Konrad Schmidt and his wife as Magda. Waving his arm around the group, he said proudly, "Mine kinder."

Eleven kinder! I prayed that poor woman wasn't in the family way, but she had a sallow, sunken look that some women have when they're carrying.

Hands were shaken all around, and Uncle Hiram gave his little speech in slow, fumbling German about neighbors in this country welcoming newcomers with food. Mrs. Schmidt brought plates, cups, and spoons from a box under the canvas.

The teenagers who had been helping their father clear brush knew a little English, and soon everyone was gathering around the food spread out on a quilt in the grass. The older girls helped their mother prepare plates for the younger children, but no one touched their food until the father of the group had prayed a simple blessing over the meal. I recognized *danke* and *Gotte,* but little else. The huskiness in the father's voice and the tears welling in the mother's eyes needed no translation.

Everyone, including the children, ate with restrained politeness. Konrad Schmidt gestured to the feast spread on the quilt and asked his oldest son a question. The young man turned to Hiram and Will and translated slowly. "This ... all this ... come from your land?"

Uncle Hiram nodded, then added, with a gesture to the big enamel coffeepot simmering on the cooking fire, "Not the coffee. All the rest ... yes." Mr. Schmidt nodded, impressed, then rattled off a rapid stream in German to his wife. I couldn't understand the words, but the inflection seemed to be "I told you so."

I wanted to urge seconds on everyone, but remembering that what was left would stay with the family, I didn't. The leftovers might feed them tomorrow. Instead, I unwrapped the blackberry cake. After the first bite, Mr. Schmidt had his son relay to Uncle Hiram the same question: Did this come from your land? After considerable mind-searching and substitution of words, Hiram was able to convey to the son that he grew the wheat, our chickens gave the eggs and the berries were wild, but the sugar came from the store.

Mrs. Schmidt said something to the little ones and they ran to play. Two daughters began to gather up the empty plates and take them to the large pot of hot water that sat on the ground by the cook fire. Mrs. Schmidt picked up the bowls and baskets with food still in them and started toward the wagon. "No," I said, rising and following her, "for you," gesturing to illustrate the words. I carried the basket of leftover fried chicken to the area under the canvas and put it on a box there. "For you," I said again.

"*Nein, nein!*" Mrs. Schmidt exclaimed, following with a spate of words I couldn't understand. She beckoned to the oldest daughter, who was feeding the baby a biscuit crumbled in water. The girl slung her little sister on her hip and came to help translate. Through her, I was able to make Mrs. Schmidt understand that the food was to remain, a gift to her family.

The men were by this time involved in a deep three-way English/German/hand gesture discussion about crops and climate. Mrs. Schmidt beckoned, and I followed her as she spread another quilt in the shade and sat down. She put her hand on her chest. "Magda."

I followed her example. "B'Anne."

"Byann," Magda attempted.

"Bee-Ann." Someday I'd explain nicknames, but it was too difficult a concept for now.

"Ah," Magda said triumphantly, "Bee-Ann."

Pointing to the older daughter, who looked to be about the same age as me, I asked "Name?"

"Elsa," the girl replied. She came and sat down with us, handing the baby to her mother.

"May I hold it?" I held out my arms to illustrate my request. Magda said something to Elsa, and the girl hurried to the laundry drying on bushes, coming back with a square of age-yellowed outing flannel. Magda deftly unfastened the baby's wet cloth and replaced it with the dry one before handing the child over. The baby gurgled up at me, chortled and blew a good-sized spit bubble, then began to squirm and fuss.

I returned the baby to her mother, who offered her breast. The baby fell asleep nursing. When Magda had laid the child on the quilt beside her, she leaned over, touched my stomach, and said something to Elsa, who translated. "When?"

"Late November, maybe early December," I replied. Magda chattered away, and Elsa translated. "Mama says your baby will be a Christmas gift." Wondering how a woman with eleven children could consider a baby to be a gift, I smiled and nodded agreement.

Magda patted her own stomach. "Kinder," she said with a smile and turned to Elsa with a questioning look.

"February," Elsa told me. When I gave Magda what I'm afraid was a sympathetic glance, Elsa said firmly, "We will manage."

The men paced off the area where the cabin was to be erected and walked up a line of trees on the hillside to a small area of lush green grass. A little stream of crystal cold water burbled from the ground, ran a few feet, and disappeared into the earth again. The settlers had hollowed out a good-sized basin and lined it completely with rocks for water collection.

When the men returned, we said our goodbyes and got ready to climb in the wagon. I remembered the loaves of bread and the jars of jam, and Will got them for me to give Magda.

"*Danke*," Magda whispered, and then impulsively pulled me to her and kissed me on both cheeks.

"*Vilkommen* to America," I replied.

As we drove away, waving, Will said, "That was better than the welcome they had when they landed in New York. Konrad had his pocket picked. They've had to make the journey this far in stages, stopping to earn money whenever they ran out. It's taken them two years. That's why they got here at such a bad time, too late to plant crops."

Uncle Hiram added, "The long trip cross-country must be how the older children picked up so much English. I'm sure they did rough labor right alongside their father. They were headed for Oregon, where Konrad's brother and his family live, but some horn-swoggler convinced Konrad that taking a boat up the Missouri River would be quicker, and said Konrad and the two older boys could earn the family's passage. When they got off the boat up at Fort Benton to earn more money, they decided ... I think Mrs. Schmidt decided ... that they weren't going on to Oregon."

"They're going to have a hard winter," I said. "No money, no crops, very little supplies. How will they manage?"

"Even though they seem to be good people," Uncle Hiram said, "I don't make rash decisions. I'll hire the older ones to help with work around the place, and by the time autumn comes I'll know the family better. I could loan them money for supplies on next year's crops."

"It's a good thing we came to visit," Will told me. "They were so excited to get started that they hadn't filed on the land yet. They found what they wanted, but they hadn't made the trip back to town to file. Uncle's going in with Konrad tomorrow to take care of it."

We rode on in comfortable silence. Then I said, "I surely learned something today."

"What did you learn?" Will asked.

"I learned how very, very fortunate we are to have Uncle Hiram. Without him, we wouldn't have had any more chance than a snowball in August." I leaned over and gave him a quick kiss on the cheek. "Thank you, Uncle."

"You're very welcome, my dear," the old man replied. "It's good to have a family again."

At our house, Uncle Hiram mounted his horse and headed home. I was eager to read the letters he'd brought that morning but made myself leave them untouched until bedtime. Will took one of the envelopes Uncle Hiram had left and slipped it in his shirt pocket and went outside. He never had to wonder about how to fill his time ... he could just step outside and see the work waiting for him.

I watched the back of Will's head as he disappeared around the calf-shed. I'd been too excited about my own letters to pay the envelope much mind after I saw it wasn't his mother's handwriting. Now I told myself it must be from one of his friends back home, wanting to know what homesteading was like. Maybe they were interested in trying it, too, and we'd end up with neighbors our own age from Iowa.

I could hardly wait for him to share the news with me. But when he came in for supper, he didn't say a word about his letter.

Washing dishes and tidying the kitchen were tasks done silently. My mind was filled with doubts again. I'd finally managed to push down the memory of the awful things Will's mother had said in her letter, and here was something new to worry about.

Chapter 18

In the days that followed, Will didn't mention the letter he'd tucked away. Surely if it were good news about friends coming out to Montana, he'd have shared it with me. I didn't ask him about it. I just wished I'd received a secret letter that same day, so I could keep it from him. But who'd write a big old ugly pregnant woman a letter, except her ma and pa. And Minna. She always sent me funny letters … it was almost as good as talking to her. I wondered what Minna would tell me to do. But she was married to a man who adored her, and soon would have a baby he'd welcome. How could she understand how I felt?

I already knew what Ma would tell me. "Be strong, B'Anne," she'd say. "Every marriage has its rough spots. Yours are just coming sooner than most; that's all. Trust God and pray for Him to help you be sweet and modest and loving and to make Will a good home. Will's a good boy. He'll come around eventually." That's what I was trying to do, but resentment made it a hard job sometimes. I prayed for God to help me bury my doubts, and to make a welcoming home for Will and our baby. It eased my mind, but the worries always came back again.

Busy as I was, the hungry winter facing the new immigrant family was never far from my mind. I made a trip over to their camp one hot morning and took a couple of the oldest children to show them the wild blackberry patch, and the bend of the creek where the wild plums were thickest. With all those hands picking, they'd at least be able to have a lot of dried fruit.

In this mid-September warm spell, I was busy canning and drying everything I could get my hands on. Whenever my back ached, and I felt too tired to move, I remembered the worried look on Will's face when he added up those columns of figures. I'd sit down and put my feet up for a few minutes and then get back to work.

Bertie Yeagerman rode up early one hot morning, bounded into the kitchen and said, "I'm yours for the day. Ma and Phoebe are both mad at me, so I decided to go someplace where I'd be appreciated."

"Oh, Bertie, I can't pay you anything. We're poor as poor can be. Let's just have a nice visit. Then you can go home and apologize for whatever you did."

Bertie looked offended. "I didn't come to earn money. I came to help you and to get out of that house where all they talk about is how to be ladylike and prissy, so we'll make good marriages." She grabbed my extra apron off the hook and tied it behind her. "Besides, what makes you think I'm the one who should apologize?" She looked at what I was doing, then found a paring knife and started slicing cucumbers.

"Well, Bertie, I figured if anybody at your house was kicking over the traces, it wasn't Phoebe or your mother."

Bertie grinned in spite of herself. "You figured right. Maybe by the time I go home this evening, they'll have forgotten I called Phoebe a silly cow."

That extra pair of hands made all the difference. After things calmed down at her house, she still came over for a few hours almost every day. I was big and awkward enough now that harvesting the garden was harder than planting it had been. The heat bothered me more than it ever had, too. Bertie flew down those rows in the hot sun twice as fast as I could, plucking green beans and corn, cabbages, tomatoes, and cucumbers. She helped me thread the young beans to hang from the kitchen ceiling to dry and become leather-britches … tough to chew, but tasty from hanging with braids of onions, and smoke from the cooking fire. We popped the beans that were too mature out of the shells to dry. She spread shelled corn in a single layer to dry out in the sun on cheesecloth, so the air could circulate around the corn. With her chatter, the boring job of chopping cabbage for kraut went faster.

I knew why she wanted my company, and much as I loved Bertie by now, I knew I'd better not get involved. She was head over heels for Solomon, and her mother was sure she could do better.

"Oh, B'Anne," Bertie said one afternoon as we ladled hot stewed tomatoes into clean jars, snapped down lids over the rubber gaskets and put them in the big pot to boil, "why does everything have to be so hard? I don't want a fancy house in town, or a husband who wears a starched collar to work every day, and comes home with soft white hands. I just want Sol. Just a little cabin, like this one," and she waved her arm around the steamy room, "fixed up pretty like this, and Sol to sleep beside every night."

I knew I should try to at least act shocked at such an unladylike remark, but I didn't. "Bertie, you've got to be sensible. It's not all romance. It's not like one of those pretty stories in that ladies' magazine they have at the store. It's a lot more than sleeping with somebody ..." I snuck a peek at her and added, "Nice as that may be. It's hard work, and being friends, and thinking of somebody else ahead of yourself. It's something you've got to live with for the rest of your life."

Bertie had a mutinous look on her face, like she was about to tell me she knew all that already. So I told her more about Will and me. She knew we'd had to get married; I'd confessed that to her when we cooked for the threshers. Now I told her how we'd been sweethearts until Victoria came along. I told her about thinking Will loved me again that night of the blizzard. I described how my brother bloodied Will's nose and hauled him out to the farm to propose to me, and our thrown-together-in-a-hurry wedding. And last, I told her how I still wasn't sure Will really loved me or if he were just making the best of a bad situation.

She dropped her ladle into the kettle of hot stewed tomatoes and threw her arms around me. "Oh, B'Anne, of course he loves you. Why, anybody can see that!"

"Maybe. Maybe not. We're both making the best of it. But Bertha Yeagerman, you'd better not let the same thing happen to you. You and Solomon just hold on for another year, and I'll bet your mother will soften up." I fished the floating ladle out of the kettle. "In fact, by the time a year's up, she'd probably marry you off to Blackbeard the Pirate to get rid of you."

I couldn't help worrying after Bertie went back home. If she and Solomon did something foolish, her mother would blame me, I knew because she'd been spending so much time here. My own mother had been disappointed and heartsick, but forgiving. I didn't think Bertie's ma would take it so well.

My back and legs ached something fierce from being on my feet so long, and there was no sign of Will for supper yet, so I gave the pot of beans a stir and stretched out on the bed for a few minutes. That was one good thing about your house having only one room. You didn't have to walk far to find the bed. I'd just rest a few minutes until he got back from Choteau, where he'd gone to get scours medicine for one of the calves.

I was still sad and worried, but somehow I fell asleep, no matter how hot the room was. When Will walked in, I sat up guiltily. "Supper's ready in just a few minutes. I only have to heat up the cornbread left from dinner."

"Don't hurry," Will said. "Bessie Haysom at the store asked about you." He sat down on the side of the bed and pushed me back down. "Rest a while longer. You look done in."

I felt so mixed-up when he treated me like he really cared for me, but I knew he hid a secret letter.

"Bessie sent you this." He handed me a little muslin sack. "It's a special tea that's supposed to build up your blood when you get close to your time."

I took the bag and sniffed it. It smelled pretty awful. I'd have to doctor it up with spice or something to get it down.

"Bessie said she was surprised she hadn't seen us at church since we came here. You know, with your pa being a minister and all. Do you want to go tomorrow?"

I thought longingly of church back home, surrounded by friends and relatives who loved me. At church, I could make friends with other women. When the baby was born, they'd chuck him under the chin and say how beautiful he was, and give me suggestions about taking care of him. But that feeling that I no longer belonged near to God choked back my words.

Will waited patiently. "Well?"

"I suppose we should," I said slowly, "but I'm big and awkward. Do you want to go, Will?"

"Sure, if you want to. And don't be silly about that 'big and awkward' business. Of course you're big. But you're not awkward. You're carrying our baby, B'Anne."

I hadn't planned to, but I burst into tears. "Oh, Will, how can you act like you care about the baby and me, and carry around a secret letter?"

Will didn't meet my eyes for a long time. Then he lifted his head and said, "I'm not carrying around a secret letter. I burned it."

"It was that bad?"

"It was from Victoria. Congratulations on marriage and fatherhood."

Oh, yes. I certainly believe that! "Did she have any suggestions about where I should live after the baby's born? She doesn't know Uncle Hiram. Probably she thinks I should go back to Ma and Pa."

"No, it wasn't anything like that. She said she was very happily married. Has servants, a carriage of her own, and a new ball gown for every party. I think the letter was just to remind me that she'd done better than marrying an Iowa storekeeper's son."

"But you hid it, and let me worry myself sick for days!" I was angry, but sad inside, too. Will was acting like the letter didn't mean anything, but for all I knew he was just putting on an act. Seemed like he was very good at that … a lot better than I'd ever dreamed he'd be.

"I didn't want to upset you with something that wasn't important. Truly, B'Anne, that's all it was. Just a bragging letter that would have made you unhappy. But I'm sorry I didn't show it to you. Then you would know it's nothing to worry about." He took me in his arms, although it was awkward with my big belly. "You lie down again, and I'll dish up the beans. We don't need to warm the cornbread; the beans will heat it up."

I did what he suggested, watching his back while he filled our bowls. If only he *always* seemed like the straightforward boy I'd grown up with. If only we could have started a new life in Montana Territory without bad memories hanging between us.

We sat at the table and ate our supper while the sky darkened outside. It was September now, and night came earlier.

Will crumbled more cornbread in his bowl and got up to ladle beans on top. When he sat down again, he said, "So are we going to church tomorrow?"

I thought for a moment. This wasn't about letters and Victoria. It was about Will having to marry me because I hadn't done what I'd been taught.

"Yes. I want to go." Maybe the familiar hymns would soothe my worries. In my next letter, I'd be able to tell Pa about the service. He'd like that. If only my heart were truly in it.

Next morning, I put on the prettier of the two loose shirtwaists my cousin had loaned me over my gray serge skirt. I'd sewed ties at the waist of the skirt, so I could leave it unbuttoned over my stomach, and the shirtwaist was long enough to cover the gap. Then I pulled my hair into a ladylike bun and put on my old straw summer bonnet with the silk roses around the brim. I hated hats, but I wanted to look as grownup as possible.

The ride into Choteau was pleasant, even if I was worried about what these new people would think of me. We left early enough that the morning was still crisp, and when the little breezes stirred the long grass, I was glad I'd worn my gray shawl. Down along the creek and in the little hollows between hills, the trees were beginning to change colors. A few flocks of geese honked that lonely sound as they straightened into their vee and made an early start south.

We drove past the Catholic church and tied our horses to a hitching post outside the only other church. Will said Bessie Haysom had told him it started out to be Methodist, but Choteau wasn't big enough for a lot of churches, so now several other religions joined forces and met for services. It was a community church now.

Will helped me down from the wagon, and we went inside, where people chatted with their neighbors. Thank goodness we were a bit early, so everyone wouldn't turn heads at the interruption. But they turned their heads anyhow, and folks came to welcome us. Bessie Haysom beckoned, and I was glad to sit by someone I knew.

"You look so pretty," Bessie said, and touched the pink silk roses on my bonnet. "What a stylish new hat."

"Stylish about three years ago," I replied. "And looking new because I only wore it when Ma made me."

Then a lady sat down at the pump organ and began softly playing the hymns I'd grown up with: "What a Friend We Have in Jesus," "Rock of Ages," and "Blessed Be the Tie that Binds." I remembered sitting with my cousins on Sunday morning, or being planted firmly beside Ma if we'd been giggling, and hearing Pa's deep voice reading verses from the Bible. I blinked and swallowed hard to hold back tears.

Like she knew what was in my heart, Bessie squeezed my hand, and it almost felt like being beside Ma again. Will put his arm along the back of the pew, and I felt its warmth across my shoulders as we shared a hymnal. We might be miles and miles away from Iowa, but suddenly it seemed home.

Chapter 19

As we neared Uncle Hiram's place on the way home from church, we noticed there was no smoke coming from his chimney. "That's not right," Will said. "When we passed on our way to town, it was still pretty early, and I figured maybe he just slept a little longer today. But it's late enough now that he should have a fire going. You know how he is about his coffee. He'd have a pot boiled down to tar by now."

We could hear Rex, Uncle Hiram's old collie, whining when we walked up on the porch. When we pushed open the door and walked in, the smell hit us like a wall of poison.

Uncle Hiram lay on the floor about halfway between his bed and the back door, and it was obvious he'd been trying to make it to the privy. He'd vomited, too, and it was caked on the front of his long underwear. His skin was a waxy white, and for a minute I thought he was dead, but when Will put his finger against his uncle's neck, he nodded in relief. Uncle Hiram was unconscious, but at least he was alive.

I touched his forehead. It was fiercely hot. "Pump some water and get it heating, Will. We've got to get him cleaned up and back into bed where it's warm. Feels like there hasn't been a fire in here for at least a day."

Will started a fire and soon had a large pot of water heating. I filled the teakettle to get a basin of warm water quicker, so I could clean Uncle Hiram. All the time I worked I repeated a little prayer in my mind: *Lord, please help Uncle Hiram. He's such a good man. Please don't take him from us. And please help me know what to do to help him.* I washed his face, neck and hands, and down his chest where the vomit had caked. Will helped me strip off the soiled long underwear. I refilled the basin five times before I had his scrawny hind-end soaped and rinsed.

Uncle Hiram came to during the last part. "Get away! What are you doing? A girl can't see me like this." He moaned, trying to push my hands away.

"Well, this girl isn't looking at you, she's just getting your rear clean." I laid my cheek against his for a moment. "Don't be upset, Uncle Hiram. We've got to get you clean and comfortable. Then we'll get you back to bed."

"Need a drink of water," he muttered thickly, through dry, chapped lips. Will brought him a cup of the fresh water, and he gulped at it thirstily.

"Not too much right away," I said, pulling the cup away. "Let that settle in your stomach for a few minutes. Then you can have more."

I turned to Will. "See if you can find some salve or ointment of some kind. His rear is getting sore. He must have been lying there for quite awhile."

"Bag Balm," Uncle Hiram murmured. "Shelf by the back door."

For Uncle Hiram's comfort, Will smoothed on the salve, instead of me. Meantime, I pawed through the chest at the end of Uncle Hiram's bunk and found a yellowed old nightshirt, worn to soft comfort. We got it on him, and Will carried him to bed. By this time, his teeth were chattering with chills. We covered him warmly and gave him more water.

Once he was settled, Will emptied all the dirty water, and I carried the soiled clothing out to the back porch and put it in a tub to soak.

"B'Anne, you need to drive to town and get the doctor," Will told me.

"No, you go, and I'll stay here and take care of Uncle Hiram."

"I have to be the one to stay here. If he falls out of bed, or has a fit and has to be held down, you're not strong enough."

I knew he was right. People with high fevers sometimes thrashed around and had what folks called fits, although they for sure weren't just hissy-fits. They were the kind of fits where their arms and legs jerked and their eyes rolled back in their heads.

So I rode back into town and returned with the doctor, after waiting for him to finish delivering a baby. That surprised me, a doctor delivering a baby. Back home a midwife took care of the job. He explained on the way to Uncle Hiram's place.

"She's a lady from back East. Built like a Percheron mare, but thought she was too dainty to have a country midwife deliver her child." He looked me over carefully. "How about you? When are you due?"

"End of November, thereabouts."

You look pretty big to go another two months. Might be a good idea to stop by my office next time you're in town."

"I'll do that. Bessie Haysom is going to introduce me to the midwife, too. Right now I'm just worried about Uncle Hiram."

Back at Uncle Hiram's place, his chills had eased, and he was sweating, so Will had peeled off all the bedding except a blanket. Uncle had kept down the water and had some more. Seemed like he needed that more than anything.

We explained the condition we'd found him in. The doctor examined him, then shook his head. "Well, he doesn't have typhoid or smallpox or cholera." He gave us a serious look. "You two can be thankful for that, especially with a baby on the way. "I think he must just have the summer complaint, even if summer is over. I've got some drops here that'll make him feel better; make him sleep a lot." He turned to speak to Uncle Hiram now. "You've got to stay in bed till you're a lot better, old friend." He turned to me again. "Light food … tea, milk toast, broth, custard. Plenty of water. He can't be here by himself, of course."

"We could wrap him up good in quilts and take him to our house," Will suggested.

The doctor looked thoughtful. "I hate to see him moved right now. In a few days, maybe."

"I'll stay with him now," I said quickly. "He's some better, so I shouldn't have to lift him or anything like that."

"I can be here a lot, too," Will added. "I can keep our chores and garden up, and still spend plenty of time here to help you."

The doctor sized us up with a long look, then turned to Uncle Hiram. "You're a lucky man, Hiram. These young folks saved your life, and now they're going to take care of you."

"Don't I know it," Uncle Hiram said weakly.

"We're family," I protested. "That's what families do."

The medicine was evidently relieving some of Uncle Hiram's pain because his eyes were drifting closed as he murmured, "We're family right enough. You're like the son and daughter I never had."

The doctor left. Will made sure I had plenty of firewood and water, checked on Uncle Hiram's horses, and then went home to see to our animals. When he returned just before dark, he brought with him a freshly dressed chicken and a basket with a few eggs in it.

"Figured Uncle could eat some chicken broth by tomorrow," he said softly because the sick man was still sleeping. "Eggs always sit well on an uneasy stomach, too."

We piled blankets and quilts on the floor and slept there. At least Will slept. I was so busy trying to get comfortable that I only slept a few minutes at a time and was grateful when the windows began to show daylight. Will got up several times during the night to check on his uncle, and once to give him medicine and again to help him use the pot. It was awkward tipping the thunder mug on its side for Uncle Hiram to use. I was glad Will was going to spend part of the day with us, too, because now that Uncle Hiram was more aware, he'd probably just force his bladder to wait until Will could help him.

Next day, I cooked a nourishing chicken broth, and Will brought over fresh peas, carrots and onion from our garden to go in it. I rolled out a sheet of noodles and hung them to dry from the cookstove's warming rack. I knew they wouldn't be as tender as Ma's ... I hadn't learned how to have a good hand with noodles yet ... but if Uncle could get a few down, they'd be good for him. As it turned out, he only drank the broth, but Will enjoyed the rest.

Over the next few days Uncle Hiram slowly improved. He continued with chicken broth and water, and by the fourth day he was able to eat soup, custard and a soft-boiled egg.

The oldest Schmidt boy stopped by that afternoon. He'd stopped at our house first, to ask some questions about supplies. Of course, we weren't there, so he was glad to see us at Uncle Hiram's.

He was concerned when he learned how sick Uncle Hiram had been. "Elsa can come and take care of him," he exclaimed. "We want to help."

Will explained that we were going to take Hiram to our house soon, and the Schmidt boy quickly offered to come see to Hiram's stock each evening.

On the fifth day, we bundled Uncle Hiram up in quilts and drove him to our house. I knew my garden would be going wild, and at our place I could begin to catch up and still take care of a sick person. Will helped me gather in cucumbers, zucchini and cabbages. We had to discard some that were too large and tough, but the pig enjoyed them, and we knew that every scrap he ate would benefit us in the winter, after we turned him into ham and bacon. The cabbage we put down in brine would make excellent sauerkraut to go with spareribs.

I was happy when Elsa and a younger sister and brother showed up next day. "I will help you in the house," she explained, "so you can rest. My brother and sister will take care of the garden."

And they did. Elsa did a huge laundry, and then went to Hiram's house and did the same, including the clothing that had been soaking on the back porch since he first became ill. She baked bread, cleaned house and insisted that I put my feet up and enjoy a cup of tea prepared by someone else. The two youngsters had the garden looking trim as Mrs. Snively's prize flower beds, back home.

When they were all finished, I insisted they take most of the bread Elsa had baked. "Tomorrow I come back and make more," she promised. "And some German noodles."

As they started off over the fields toward their own place, I poured some tea for Uncle Hiram. "I never realized just how wonderful it could be to have neighbors," I told him.

He took hold of my hand as I set down his cup. "And I never realized just how wonderful it could be to have family," he said, his voice husky.

We wrapped a quilt around Uncle Hiram when Will took him home on a late September morning. It wasn't wintery cold yet, just a little brisk, but a lively breeze blew over the browned prairie. I sent a pot of soup home with him, and Will stayed there for a few hours, building a fire and getting the little cabin warm. The boys had done a good job of taking care of Uncle Hiram's animals, and one of the girls had evidently been there the day before because everything had been dusted. I was sure the boys weren't responsible for the sprigs of Queen Anne's lace arranged in a drinking glass on the kitchen table that Will described when he got back.

That night when I knelt awkwardly by our bed for my evening prayers, Will joined me. Putting his hand on my shoulder, he explained haltingly, "I've got a thank-you to say, too. I've gotten to love Uncle Hiram like my own pa. I'm sure grateful God saw fit to let him be with us a while longer."

Chapter 20

By the beginning of October, I was big as a barn. My feet were swollen, and I had such a hard time reaching them that Will had to help me put on my shoes each morning. I was glad the heavy work of the summer was finished because I doubted I'd have been able to do it now.

Our cow had a healthy heifer calf, and we were grateful for the addition of milk, cream, and butter to our diet. We were trying to buy as little as possible from town, and it helped. Most farm wives do the milking, so I thanked my lucky stars that Will didn't mind that extra chore. I'd never have been able to squat on that little stool, much less get to my feet afterward. Just straining the milk and scalding the straining cloth and bucket was effort enough.

Whenever we had more milk than the two of us could use, Will took it over to the Schmidts. Mr. Schmidt and his older children had hollowed out a dugout in the hillside to make a primitive dwelling that would keep out the cold, even though it would be a crowded place to spend the winter. I couldn't imagine existing in a dugout, but people often did on the prairie. They planned to build a cabin in the spring.

I was able to make one visit there before I was too far along to safely make the wagon ride over the rough, trackless ground. Poor Magda had one baby teething on her lap, and one just beginning to kick in her belly, but she was managing. The whole family was doing the best they could with what they had available.

Uncle Hiram wanted to help them as much as possible, grateful for their willingness to do whatever they could when he was sick. He gave them a piece of stovepipe and the potbellied stove that we hadn't needed, so the family could cook and have a fire to gather around. They used the canvas from their wagon, and a piece Uncle Hiram loaned them, to cover the roof and walls of the dugout, and spread evergreen boughs and dried prairie grass on the floor, covered with old quilts. Two of the German families in town had given them some quilts and blankets, and Uncle Hiram had provided several sturdy horse blankets. They used packing boxes from their wagon to sit on and for a table, and were managing as well as anyone could under those circumstances.

Two of the girls had found work in Choteau as household helpers for little more than their keep, but at least it was two less mouths to feed. Uncle Hiram hired the older sons, Sev and Josef for odd jobs as often as he could. Our potato crop had given us more than we'd need over the winter, so after we'd crammed as much as would fit in the root cellar Will dug, he took the rest to the Schmidts. It would be a hard winter for them, but then, it might be a hard winter for all of us.

I got busy on Ma's sewing machine, turning that bolt of outing flannel into little gowns and belly-bands. Often Bertie Yeagerman rode over to help me. For such a flibberty-gibbet girl, she had a fine hand with the needle and embroidered flowers or lambs or chicks on the gowns. "They'll get peed on first thing," she said with a laugh, "but they're pretty. A new baby deserves pretty."

I used every opportunity I saw to remind her about not marrying in a hurry. When I dropped my thimble, and she had to get it for me because I couldn't reach the floor, I said, "See, this is what happens when you're carrying. Don't let it happen to you for a long time yet."

She laid the thimble in my waiting hand. "You can't scare me, B'Anne. You only get that big if you're carrying a baby moose."

The girl was irrepressible.

Will stayed busy weather-proofing the cowshed against the coming Montana winter, extending the fences and hauling in downed wood from the little creek valley after every wind storm. He drove into Choteau and brought back wagonloads of coal, and extended the roof by the back door to store it out of the weather. Then he got out that little ledger where he kept track of what we spent and what we had left, and chewed his knuckle while he added and subtracted again.

When the cold was bitter at the end of October, he worked on the inside jobs that had been put off for so long ... a work counter in the kitchen end, a wash-stand by the back door, and more shelves for storage. He even spent long hours on his hands and knees sanding rough spots in the floor, so the baby wouldn't get splinters crawling on it.

One frosty morning in early November, Uncle Hiram came over. When he finished his cup of tea, he said, with a twinkle in his eyes, "I've got a surprise out in the wagon," and went out to fetch it. We heard a clanging noise from outside and hurried to the door. Lo and behold, he was struggling to lug a big iron bell.

"I was in Choteau yesterday when a peddler came through. He had this on his wagon. He got it from one of those old mining towns down south that are getting dried up and empty. They closed the school down, and the man who'd donated the bell took it back and traded it to him for blankets and beans and kerosene." Uncle Hiram smoothed his mustache, looking a little bashful. "I figured it'd be handy to hang by your back door, so you can ring Will in from the fields if you need him."

I reached across my belly and threw my arms around his shoulders. "Oh, thank you, Uncle Hiram! What a wonderful idea!"

He grinned. "I'll probably be able to hear it over to my place. And maybe the Schmidts will, too." Then he pulled a string-tied bundle from his mackinaw pocket. "These are for you, too. I saw the other day how you left your shoes unbuttoned."

It was a pair of soft Indian moccasins. I sat down, and Will pulled off my uncomfortable shoes. I slipped my feet into the buttery softness of the new moccasins. There was even room to wiggle my toes. "A-a-ah, that feels like heaven," I sighed.

They were the only shoes I wore from then on. Except on Sundays, of course, when I forced my feet into my button-up shoes for church. Now that I'd returned to God's house, it felt like home. I still carried a heavy load of guilt for my sin, and doubts about Will, but I was no longer going to let those feelings keep me away from where I belonged.

On a cold, windy afternoon, I was surprised to hear the wheels of several wagons pull up outside the house. I whipped on a clean apron and smoothed my hair down with my palms. Who on earth could it be?

I opened the door to Bessie Haysom, Adelia Yeagerman, and eight other ladies from church. Their arms were full of plates, pots and packages.

"Surprise!" Bessie called out and bustled over to the table to empty her armload. "We're here to welcome the baby." Glancing at my belly, barely covered by the apron, she added, "Looks like not a minute too soon."

I was glad that earlier Will had made a bench to go behind the table, and I pulled it out for seating. There were places for everybody, with the bench, the bed, the trunk, my hope chest and our three chairs. I made sure Adelia Yeagerman got a proper chair, not wanting her to tell everybody in Choteau that we didn't have enough furniture for civilized people to sit on.

The ladies spread out their treats ... little biscuit and ham sandwiches from Mrs. Grenville, who still had her Virginia accent. "Mammy used to make these for us," she confided, "back before the War Between the States, of course." There were teacakes and fresh bread with strawberry preserves. Mrs. Brill had brought some of her special cookies, and Adelia Yeagerman brought chess tarts. Bessie arranged a plate of soda crackers, sharp cheese, orange marmalade, pickles and sugared dates from their store, made tea, and we enjoyed the special food.

After we ate, they piled their gifts on the table in front of me, and I opened them. One of the ladies had made a sweet little quilt. There were hand-knit sweaters, caps, booties and shawls. One had sewed a thick wool bunting, saying as she watched me untie the string and spread back the white tissue paper, "That'll keep the little tyke warm when he's old enough to bring out to church." Another had made four small outing flannel blankets, just the right size to swaddle a newborn baby.

They insisted that I bring out the box I'd received from Ma and my cousins the week before. They'd sewed and embroidered pretty little gowns and sacques, knitted booties, sweaters, hats and shawls.

My cousin Lorinda, who had loaned me the loose shirtwaists I'd worn for the last few months, enclosed garments her baby had outgrown, some a little worn and stained, but all clean and useable. Ma had even crocheted a jacket for me to wear in bed, dainty and pink. Looking at it now, awkward and ugly as I knew I was, I couldn't imagine putting it on.

Afterward, we had more tea and they shared their childbirth stories with me until I began to wonder why God hadn't figured out a better way to populate the earth. Bessie snuck a glance at me and said, "We're scaring the poor child to death," and they went on to advice about how to care for a baby. I learned about colic and teething and how long it takes the dried-up bellybutton to fall off, and about browning flour and using it to treat sore bottoms. I learned about croup and heat rash, which it didn't seem my child would have to worry about, being a winter baby.

When the sky began to darken, they gathered up their coats and empty dishes. I thanked them from the bottom of my heart, and they hurried out to the wagons. They left any uneaten goodies behind, which meant Will would have a nice supper after spending the cold afternoon out in the cowshed.

I called him in, and he admired the little garments spread out on the bed while he munched biscuits and ham and warmed up with the tea I'd poured for him.

"Do they really come that small?" he marveled, touching a pair of tiny booties with his work-roughened finger.

"I guess they must." I hoped my voice didn't sound as uncertain as I felt. The thought of caring for anything that tiny frightened me a bit. I wished heartily that Ma lived just down the road, instead of clear back in Iowa. For the first time, I wasn't afraid of *having* a baby. I was afraid of what came afterward. I had a new subject for heartfelt prayer … the health and well-being of the child in my belly.

Chapter 21

By the second week of November, the mornings were frosty. Ducks and geese landed regularly on the creek, evidently a stopover for the latecomers' way south, and we had them for dinner often enough to get tired of them. Anything to stretch our supplies was welcome.

One blustery morning Will said, "Well, I think it's time to dig the rest of the turnips, carrots and rutabagas. Feels like we're in for a really hard freeze." I helped him as much as I could, which wasn't a great deal. I couldn't dig or bend enough. Mostly, I just shook as much dirt as I could off the vegetables before Will carried them to the root cellar he'd dug into the hillside not far from the cabin, and laid them on the straw inside.

Sure enough, when we woke the next morning the windows were etched with ice. After breakfast, Will slurped down the rest of his coffee and put on his sheepskin jacket. "Got to go round up tools, buckets and stuff," he said grimly. "It's pig-butchering time tomorrow or the next day, soon as I have everything ready. Hope Uncle Hiram knows more about it than I do."

Turns out Uncle Hiram did. And so did Konrad Schmidt ... a whole lot. Magda Schmidt was a lifesaver, too. We'd butchered pigs every winter back home, but I'd never been involved. Will had helped at our butchering once, but that was all.

The men built a sturdy hoist on a calf shed rafter. "Back home we'd hang the carcass over a tree branch," Uncle Hiram joked, "but not too many tree branches around here." They built a fire outside and hung a huge pot of water over it to boil, and we were ready to go.

I turned aside and covered my ears during the killing part. I moved my hands from my ears to my mouth during the next part, when Magda Schmidt caught the fresh blood in buckets. "Blut sausage," she said sturdily. "I teach you." It took me a second to realize that with her accent, 'blood' became 'blut.' *I might let you teach me,* I thought, *but that blood sausage is going home with you.*

When the hanging pig was gutted and all the organ parts put to soak in salt water, the carcass was taken down and placed in the boiling water long enough to soften the bristles, then was hung up on the hoist once more. The smell was bad enough that I doubted I'd ever be able to eat pork again. Now we women stepped in. With sharply honed knives, we scraped the hair off the skin while the men built a small, simple smokehouse, just large enough to hold hams and bacon with space for smoke to circulate around them.

They cut the meat into hams, loins, and shoulders. Will brought our table outside and fastened securely to it the meat grinder his dad had insisted on putting in our wagon at the last minute. Elsa and I took turns grinding all the scraps too little to be used any other way while Magda mixed salt, pepper and sage I'd dried from our garden. With our hands, we kneaded the seasoning mixture thoroughly into the meat, and we stuffed it into the intestines Magda had cleaned and soaked in salt water. This job continued off and on during the day. As scraps became available, one of the older girls would grab the handle of the grinder.

Magda scrubbed one of the large pots used previously, moved it to the back porch, and mixed the brine in it. Fortunately, she'd told Uncle Hiram what to buy for it because I'd never have had enough salt. I winced to see precious sugar stirred in, but I knew it'd give the hams and bacon a wonderful flavor.

"We put the meat in," she said authoritatively, with Elsa translating a few words, "two-three days, maybe, we start the smoking."

We washed our hands, rested awhile, and I brought out the big pot of beans that had been simmering all morning, and the triple batch of cornbread I'd made before we started working. I was glad to see Magda eat heartily. She was far too thin for a woman six months along, and no wonder. She was nursing nine-month-old baby Greta and nourishing the baby she carried, too.

Afterward, Magda stood up purposefully. "Now," she said, "the lard." That job also took all day, as the fat scraps were melted in a kettle over the open fire.

By the time the brief sun went down, the job was finished. Well, mostly finished. There was still another kettle of fat scraps to melt into lard, but that could be done tomorrow. The brining kettle was full of meat waiting to be put in the tiny smokehouse the men had built by the cowshed. Another brining kettle was full of a sickening coil of sausage, which would also be smoked. Lard was congealing in little tin buckets, ready to be covered and stored on the cold back porch. One loin was hanging to freeze on the back porch, where we'd cut from it until it was gone. Another loin was in the Schmidt's cart, after much protest on their part. They also had the jugs of blood, brain, heart and kidneys, which Magda assured me disapprovingly were "fine food."

They drove home. I heated a pan of water and tried to scrub the pig smell out of my skin and hair, and changed clothes. Then I cooked a fine supper for Will and Uncle Hiram. It was boiled potatoes and fried liver and onions ... the liver we'd split with the Schmidt family. As for me, I ate a piece of bread and butter, drank a cup of tea, and went to bed.

Chapter 22

On the morning of November 18, Will and I had an argument about whether I should accept Bessie Haysom's invitation to stay at their house until the baby was born.

"Who knows when the first bad storm will come?" Will said. "With that wind and gray cloud, a blizzard could be on its way, and we wouldn't know about it in time to get the doctor out here before it hit."

We'd discussed midwife and doctor earlier and often. A midwife would be cheaper and lived closer. I'd met her and liked her. Besides, none of my relatives back home ever had a doctor deliver a baby. But Will was determined it was going to be the doctor. I had finally agreed on the doctor, but I stuck to my grounds about going to town too soon. Once again, we had discussed it sensibly for a few minutes before the talk heated up. Now Will was so frustrated his neck was turning red.

I jabbed my finger at the page of the *Farmer's Almanac* I'd been reading. "It says right here in black and white that human gestation is two hundred eighty days. Unlike other women, I know *exactly* the day this baby started. I don't have to guess."

"That book is about cows and sheep. They just threw human beings in there to make it more interesting." He gave me a sober look. "B'Anne, I don't even know how to deliver a calf or a lamb. I'm sure not going to start on humans!" He grabbed his mackinaw from the hook by the backdoor and turned for one last shot before he slammed outside. "You just think long and hard about that while I feed the calves."

Of course, I didn't want Will delivering our baby. But I didn't want to go to town too early, either, and spend days or weeks in the way at the Haysom's living quarters behind the store. Besides, my cousin, Ma, and the visiting church ladies had all said the first baby takes a long while to come. I'd know in plenty of time to send Will to town for help. I'd seen Dr. Milton a couple of months earlier, and he'd said I should do fine, although he was a little concerned because the baby was bigger than it should have been at that time.

"It might be a long, hard delivery," he warned. "Send for me as soon as labor starts."

And that meant I'd have plenty of time, I told myself. I grabbed a dust-rag and began my housework by wiping the coal soot off the pretties on the shelf.

I'd just finished cutting up potatoes and onions to make a stew with the rabbit Will got the day before when he stuck his head in the door.

"Two of the calves took off. I've got to go find them." He was gone before I could do more than tell him to be careful.

I set the stew to simmering and sat down with my knitting basket. I had a low backache and didn't want to stand anymore. Must have strained it. It hurt almost as bad as when I cut meadow grass last summer.

Will hadn't returned by noon dinnertime, so I pushed the stew to the back of the stove. My back was hurting something fierce, and I warmed a blanket on the oven door to put in the back of my chair to lean against. Maybe the heat would help. I'd never had such a bad backache. If the pain was in my lower belly, like monthly cramps, instead of my back, I'd be worried.

I had just folded the blanket for a second heating when a grinding cramp had me bent over, grasping my belly. Oh, my. This was ten times worse than the monthly cramps I used to have. And then I knew. That hadn't been just a backache. It was the beginning of labor.

I made it out the backdoor and pulled that bell rope so hard I'm surprised it didn't come off the wall. I clanged it and clanged it until another pain came. Then I changed into my oldest nightgown, took the pretty quilt off the bed and replaced it with newspapers and a sheet. All the time I prayed, "God, please send Will. And please, please let me deliver this baby safely."

When I heard hoofbeats above the howling wind, a wave of relief swept over me. Maybe Will didn't even know how to deliver a calf, but he had to be better than nothing.

But it was Uncle Hiram.

"Will's out rounding up some lost calves," I explained as soon as the cramp eased and let me speak. "You'd better go for the doctor."

Uncle Hiram's voice was as panicked as his face. "I can't leave you by yourself. The baby might come before I get back with the doctor." He ran to the backdoor and clanged the bell, loud and long.

"I hope you know how to deliver a calf," I snapped.

He stared at me and shook his head. "Well, I've caught a calf or two, but you're not having a Guernsey." He put the biggest pot on the stove and began filling it with water. "We'll just have to do the best we can."

The sound of more hoofbeats was welcome. It wasn't Will this time, either, but Magda and Elsa Schmidt on their old horse.

I think Uncle Hiram was even more relieved than I was. "Thank God you're here, Magda. I'm going for the doctor."

Magda felt my stomach with her icy cold hands, then looked between my legs. "*Ja*," she muttered, and then said something to Elsa in German. Elsa pulled a little bag from her mother's ragged coat pocket and made a cup of hot tea from some of its contents. I drank it down and started to feel a little drifty, until the next pain came.

When it eased, I told Elsa, "Oh, I'm so glad you're here. How did you know I needed you?"

Elsa replied, with some searching for words, "We hear bell ringing. We never hear it before, and it sound ... frightened, like someone need help. Mama said, 'That's Bee-Anne!' and nothing change her mind. I thought she foolish, but I come along to help her talk, say why she acting like a crazy woman."

I held out my hand to Magda. "Oh, Magda, *danke*. I was so scared." I wasn't sure how much of the words she understood, but her face softened, and she patted my hand. She had understood the tone of voice and knew she was being thanked.

Magda smiled and patted my belly. "Baby for Christmas, *ja?*"

I nodded. "Yes. For Christmas."

At her mother's direction, Elsa tied a couple of tea-towels to the headboard. "For to pull on when gets worse," she explained.

Oh, no, it gets worse? Then the cramp eased enough that I could talk again. "Elsa, I'm so glad you're here. I thought you were working in town."

Elsa nodded. "Mrs. Heintz sent me home for a few days. Was running out of money to pay me." Then she brightened. "But I go back to do Christmas cleaning and cooking."

The hurting seemed to go on in waves forever, with little breaks in between to get my breath and gather my strength for the next one. The windows darkened, and Elsa lit all the kerosene lamps, but Will still hadn't arrived. Between pains, I glanced at the window and saw that it was snowing hard. I had her put a lamp close to the front window on the table and light a kerosene lantern and hang it outside by the backdoor.

Finally, the cramps didn't have time in between them … it was just one long pain. I knew the doctor wasn't going to make it in time and thanked God for Magda and Elsa. The pain and fear for the baby did one good thing. It took away my worry for Will. I guess you just can't worry about the whole world at once. When it eased for a moment, though, while I caught my breath, I pictured Will wandering in the snow. And the wind howled around the cabin like it was trying to get inside.

Before long, I was hanging onto those tea-towels for dear life. Magda said something sharply to Elsa, and Elsa said, "Is coming! Can see head!" Then came a wrenching pain as the baby's shoulders came through, and a sweet sense of relief, and I knew it was born. I saw Magda grabbing the scissors and string that Elsa had boiled and left by the stove to dry, and knew she was tying and cutting the cord. She cleaned out its mouth with her finger, but there was no protesting cry from the baby. It was limp. It was blue, motionless and scrawny as a newly-hatched chick before it gets its feathers. She puffed into the baby's mouth and gently massaged the tiny chest while Elsa rubbed its feet and hands. "Is very small," she murmured.

"It's two weeks early," I explained, praying that two weeks didn't mean the difference between life and death. Then came a weak, mewling cry that we could hardly hear above the wind, and the three of us released our held breaths.

Just as I was allowing myself to hope, another cramp gripped me. Magda gave the towel-wrapped baby to Elsa, muttering something. I remembered one of the church ladies talking about pain when the afterbirth comes and figured that was what was happening. But Magda looked concerned. Suddenly I recalled another lady talking about bleeding afterward, and how dangerous it could be. I didn't hear the whole story because her friend shushed her, but I knew it didn't have a happy ending.

"Another one!" Elsa gasped. This baby came faster. Magda did the puffing and rubbing she'd done before and was rewarded with another weak cry. Then she massaged my stomach until the afterbirth came while Elsa wrapped both babies snugly in the little blankets that had arrived from Ma earlier and placed one in the crook of each of my arms. "Is cold! Warm them!"

I gathered them close and pulled the quilts up until only the tips of their noses showed. I'd been sweating for hours in labor and delivery, but now the deep chill in the room overwhelmed me. Elsa brought in another bucket of coal from the back porch and heaped it in the stove's firebox. With her at one end and Magda at the other, the two of them wrestled the bed across the room, close to the stove. I looked down at the two little ones in my arms and marveled. So now we had two babies, not one. All the comments about being so big made sense.

In a little pot, Elsa warmed the sweet oil that Bessie Haysom had given me, and gently cleaned the babies' faces and heads, then slipped on little knit hats from Ma's package. "Finish cleaning when gets warmer," she explained. While she made hot, sweet tea for me, I kept a hand on each baby's tiny chest under the quilts. The breathing was so light I could hardly feel it, but at least they were breathing. Their fragile little faces were wrinkled and red, but after seeing the bluish cast of their skin right after birth, red looked beautiful to me. Their eyelids were nearly transparent, and their wee fingers looked like the ones on the wax doll I'd loved as a child. "Boys?" I asked.

"And girl. One each," Elsa smiled as she said it.

I remembered the dreams I'd pictured so many times when I put my hands on my belly and felt the life inside. Sometimes I'd see a son, and sometimes a daughter. Now we had both. There'd be a little boy scattering corn for the chickens, and a little girl helping me shell peas on the porch, I thought. But they were so frail and tiny. And their papa was out somewhere in this freezing, howling wind and snow that even a bucket full of coal was having a hard time beating.

I nestled the babies even closer and turned my face into the pillow so my tears wouldn't fall on them. I thanked God for the two little souls he'd given us. And I prayed as I had never prayed before for Will's safety. In that instant, I realized that I could talk to God like I had all my life. Will and I had done wrong, but God still loved me. I thanked Him for the two little souls he'd given us.

Chapter 23

At Magda's direction, Elsa heated milk, stirred in a spoonful of honey, and had me drink it. "Mama says you need much milk for two babies," she explained.

When the room heated up a bit, Magda and Elsa put dry sheets on the bed. Magda got me all cleaned up and in a fresh nightgown. Elsa remembered the pretty pink bed-jacket that Ma had sent, and brought it to me. With it on, and my hair brushed and in a loose braid, I felt better. The babies had been in a basket on the open oven door while this was going on, and I was glad to get back in bed and have them in my arms again. I hoped I was providing more heat than the oven had.

Elsa translated for her mother. "Mama says when it's a little warmer, you can nurse them."

I looked down at the sleeping babies, more worry filling my mind. "Shouldn't they be hungry? Shouldn't they be crying to be fed?"

Elsa translated my fears to her mother, and her answer back to me. "For a while, they just rest from journey. Not to worry yet."

That was easier said than done. I'd not been around many babies, but these little bundles whose weight I could barely feel on my arms filled me with fear.

A blast of wind shook the cabin, and the blaze of the lamp by the window flickered from the draft. Where was Will? Was he wandering on a snow-blinded horse that was trying to find the way home? Was he lucky

enough to have run into a fence to guide him to an isolated house or at
least a barn? Or was he frozen, not to be found until the snow melted?

"Is the wick up as far as it will go?" I asked Elsa. "Can't that lamp
be any brighter? Here, take this one and put it by the window, too. We
don't need it here anymore."

Elsa moved the lamp while Magda prepared another cup of tea
from the contents of her herb bag. Bringing it to me, Elsa translated
her mother's words. "Mama says drink this, to be calm. If not calm,
milk not come down."

I drank the tea, and must have slept. I didn't think I could, but
my tiredness after labor, the warm milk, and whatever was in the tea
caught up with me. I woke when the babies began to stir. The wind
seemed to have stopped. I couldn't tell if it was day or night because
the windows were plastered with snow.

Magda was sleeping in a chair, bent over to rest her head on the
foot of my bed. Elsa was stretched out by me on the side of the bed
farthest from the stove, which was probably why I felt warmer than I
had earlier. They both woke at my movement. Elsa poured more coal
in the stove, and Magda helped me arrange myself to nurse for the
first time. Each baby nursed briefly, although I couldn't tell if they were
getting any milk. But at least they were strong enough to suckle.

"Good stuff comes, even before milk," Elsa translated for her
mother.

Afterward, I once again pulled the quilts up until only the babies'
noses were showing, and I asked Elsa to open the door and see what
it was like outside. Snow fell inside when she pulled the door open,
and she used the coal shovel to push it back out and knock down the
drift in front of the door. Then she pulled her ragged old coat on and
waded to the window, where she scraped away the snow so we could
see outside. It was just beginning to be gray daylight.

Elsa heated bread and milk with sugar, and Magda urged it on
me. "For babies," she pleaded, using some of her few words of English.
Worry seemed to have locked my throat, but I forced food down,
hoping it would instantly turn into milk for the babies.

"Go ring the bell," I pleaded to Elsa. "Put on my coat ... it's heavier
than yours, and wrap my shawl around your head. Ring it a long time.
Maybe Will can hear it."

Elsa clanged the bell many minutes, then came in, warmed her hands at the stove, and went out on the porch for another session. "I'll do it again later, and again," she said, "to help Will find way." And she did, throughout the morning.

It was more than an hour after the first ringing that we heard footsteps on the porch, boots stamping off the snow. I sat up excitedly, but it was only Elsa's two oldest brothers, exhausted after wading through the drifts. They had heard the bell and feared we were in more trouble. Which, of course, we were.

They wanted to immediately set out looking for Will, but Magda made them eat a bite first. They bundled up in blankets, saddled our remaining horse and the Schmidt's old nag, and started out.

I closed my eyes and prayed again. Was He listening to me? I pleaded and promised and bargained with God, although I knew that last part would have dismayed my pa. But when I told God that if He brought Will back safely, I'd never lose my temper again, never say or think anything bad about anybody else for the rest of my life, and raise these two babies to be God-fearing and holy, it seemed perfectly right. After all, those people in the Old Testament sacrificed lambs or goats every time they turned around. Wasn't that just another way to bargain with God? Yet I knew in my heart He was listening and would answer however He saw fit.

In their chairs by the stove, Magda and Elsa were praying, too. Magda was slipping a string of beads through her fingers as her lips moved silently.

It was midafternoon when we heard noise on the porch again. The two boys had Will. He was wrapped in a blanket, but able to stumble to the side of the bed. The blanket slipped off, and I saw that he was covered with dried blood.

"Oh, Will," I gasped, "what ... what ..."

"It's not mine. It's Gus's blood. I had to kill him to save myself." A tear slid down Will's grimy cheek as he explained to me. When he knew they were lost and couldn't go on, he and Gus had huddled together as long as possible. Then he'd shot the horse, slit open the belly and crawled inside. "I've lost us a horse, and the two calves are dead, too." He dashed his hand across his eyes and blurted, "I wasn't here when you needed me, and I almost left you a widow." He sank to his knees by the bed while the Schmidts awkwardly turned their backs and huddled by the stove.

"Oh, Will." I shifted the babies a little so I could reach his head, at least. "You're here, safe and sound. That's all that matters." I was crying now, too. "We can get another horse, and more calves. And look, Will, we've got two babies, not just one. We've got twins."

He examined the babies in awe. "They're so tiny. Are they all right?"

"They're tiny, of course. They're two weeks early. But they're breathing good, and they've nursed a little bit. Magda thinks they're going to make it."

He stayed on his knees for quite a while, our heads touching over the babies. Finally he said, "Two. Two. No wonder you got so big. How are you going to manage two babies?"

"Well, I guess God gave women two bosoms for a reason. We'll manage." I sounded a lot surer than I felt. But I knew I was right. We'd manage because what else could we do?

"What will we name them?" Will had extended a finger toward the fist of the closest baby, but wasn't quite touching, with his finger so cold and dirty. "Are they boys or girls?"

"One each. I was thinking Hiram Will, for you and Uncle Hiram, and Magda Caroline, for Magda and my ma."

Magda swung around when she heard my words. "*Nein ...*" she began.

"They wouldn't be here without you," I told her firmly. "It's Magda Caroline."

Elsa melted a bucket of snow so Will could wash off the blood and gore, and the three men sat down at the table to bacon and fried potatoes.

When he'd laid his knife across his empty plate, Will asked the Schmidt brothers if they were up to another trip in the snow. "I figure if we get to them before the wolves, we could drag those calves in, save the hides to trade, and hack off meat. They should help us a lot through the winter." Both boys were nodding, and Will added, "B'Anne and I couldn't begin to use that much meat. We'll saw off a haunch, and you take the rest to your family." When he saw shaking of heads, he said simply, "Yes, you will. I'd be dead without you."

So that's what they did. It was dark before they got back.

While they were gone, Uncle Hiram arrived. A quick glance showed him that I was all right, and his first words were "Is Will still out there?"

I explained that Will was safe, that he and the Schmidt boys had gone to bring in the frozen calves. I told him about the horse, too.

"Good lad," Uncle Hiram said approvingly. "Surprised he thought of that, no more experience than he has."

More stomping on the porch, and the doctor came in. In his rush to check on us, Hiram had left him to fend for himself.

"His *wife* wouldn't let him come yesterday." Uncle Hiram sounded scornful, but the doctor was having none of it.

"Use some sense, Hiram. If we'd headed back when you wanted to, with that storm just starting, we'd never have made it. And what good would that have done, one dead stubborn old rancher, and one dead old doctor? Besides, you left the mother in good hands." This was with a nod to Magda and Elsa. He warmed his hands at the stove before approaching the bed, where Uncle Hiram was already staring down.

"Two," Uncle Hiram shook his head in amazement. "Well, I'll be swanned!" Then he went to the other end of the room, turned his back and studied the ceiling while the doctor examined me.

"Good work," the doctor said, with another nod to Magda, then took the babies from my arms and examined them, one by one. "Small, of course. But seem to be healthy. Breathing all right, hearts beating strong. Just keep them warm, don't take them out. They'll need a lot of care and coddling. Feed them whenever they're hungry." He gave me a look of sympathy. "Probably all you'll get done for awhile is nurse them."

Relief flooded through me; for a moment I almost felt giddy with it. Will was alive, and both babies were going to make it. Soon as people cleared out and I had a minute, I was going to give such prayers of thanksgiving that Pa might even feel echoes of them.

Uncle Hiram looked to Elsa. "Elsa, do you think you could stay and help here for awhile? I'll pay you well, of course." He didn't even know yet that a great-nephew was going to be named for him, and he was making such an offer.

"No ..." I began, but he cut me off with a gesture.

"Don't argue with me, girl. My mind's made up."

"But she'll be needed at her job in town before long, and she can't lose that!"

"Not until close to Christmas," Elsa said reasonably. "Then, one of my sisters can help here. Or at my job in town." Magda nodded agreement.

Uncle Hiram's and my eyes met, and I nodded. Not only would I need the help, but here was an acceptable way to see the Schmidt family through the winter. The extra money, as well as the frozen beef, would help.

Will had checked on our animals before he left to look for the calves, and now Elsa went out to milk our long-suffering cow while Magda fixed coffee and a hot meal for the men before the doctor started back to town. As they ate, the two men talked about how lucky it had been that this wasn't a three-day blizzard, like some they'd seen. I shuddered, knowing that even the lingering warmth of the horse's body wouldn't have kept Will alive for three days.

Uncle Hiram wrote out a telegram so the doctor could send it to our families when he got to town. I dictated it from bed, with a little help from Magda on the time of birth and the doctor on the weight. "Probably about four pounds each," he said, then added, after another look at the babies, "yes, that looks right. Weight of a good-sized roasting hen."

When I said, "Their names are Hiram Will and Magda Caroline," Uncle Hiram's head shot up in surprise, and he beamed with pleasure.

"Well, I'll be hornswoggled. I've got a namesake after all."

The doctor left, but Uncle Hiram decided to stay until Will and the Schmidt boys got back, just to be safe. There was no sign of more bad weather brewing, he said, but if they didn't return in a reasonable time, he'd go out and find them.

When darkness began to fall, Elsa placed the lamps on the table by the window again and hung the lantern on the back porch. The babies were having their third feeding of the day, and applying themselves to the job a little better, when we heard the men on the porch. I already had a shawl draped over my bosom for modesty, since Uncle Hiram was there, so I didn't have to cover anything up.

Magda made cornbread to go with the beans she'd had simmering all afternoon, so the cold men had something to eat before the Schmidt boys started home. They had helped Will saw one calf in half to leave with us, and they took the other half and the remaining frozen calf with them. I had Elsa pour a jug full of milk for her family and wrap up three loaves left from the last baking I'd done. It seemed so long ago, but it had only been two days. Magda went home with them, telling Elsa over and over again to ring the bell if we needed her before she returned in a few days. Will loaned them our remaining horse for the trip, since the two boys, their mother, and the calf and a half couldn't have made it on one horse.

Seeing everyone was safe, Uncle Hiram rode home shortly after the Schmidts left. "Tomorrow I'll bring over a horse you can use for a while," he said as he put on his long coat and wound a scarf around his head and hat.

Elsa put oatmeal on to soak for tomorrow's breakfast, and hacked off a slab of beef from where it hung on the back porch, high enough to be safe from hungry animals. She put it in a pot to thaw, muttering approvingly, "Scraped beef. Good rich broth."

Will went out to tend the animals. When he returned, he piled our extra quilts on the floor in front of the stove and rolled up in his blankets there so Elsa could share my bed. I missed having him beside me, but I knew that she'd be more help when the babies woke in the night.

Now was the time for those thank-you prayers. Comparing the fear and uncertainty of last night to the relief and peace of tonight, I gave those prayers with all my heart, right up until I fell into an exhausted sleep, truly content for the first time in a long time.

Chapter 24

I don't know how we would have managed without Elsa for the next few weeks. She got up in the night and changed the babies' wet diapers before I nursed them, taking turns with which baby nursed first, in case my milk wasn't as sufficient as it seemed to be.

Elsa melted snow and heated a foot-tub full of water every morning to wash diapers and gowns. She hung them on the back porch to freeze out some of the moisture, then brought them inside to finish. Will criss-crossed a rope in the end of the room where the bed would be when the cold snap ended, and most of the time it was filled.

Elsa cooked roasts and stews and rich soups from the beef hanging on the back porch, and on some days she simmered beans or split pea or potato soup to make the beef last longer. She baked bread, prepared homemade noodles and German dumplings, and plumped up dried fruit and seasoned the compote with spices.

When my nipples grew sore, Elsa heated the soothing ointment Magda had left for me to use, and then made sure it was washed and rinsed off before each nursing. I was still bleeding, of course, and she soaked my lady rags and emptied my chamber pot. In short, she made life not just bearable, but more pleasant.

After the first two or three days, the babies became more restless and were not sleeping well. Will, Elsa, and I were all worried sick. Were they not getting enough nourishment from my milk? Were they cold? Were they sickening with something? Although another storm was hanging low over the foothills, Will was ready to go fetch the doctor until Elsa suggested one more thing to try.

"Put them in the same basket," she said. "Two of my little sisters were twins. Mama said they'd been together for all those months, they didn't feel good apart."

So we did, and she was right. They were more peaceful as soon as their little bodies were close enough to each other to touch. Or maybe they didn't even have to touch, they could just sense each other's nearness.

Since we talked a lot while Elsa worked, her English improved rapidly, and I learned quite a few words of German. When Magda came over to check on us I surprised her with a halting conversation in her language.

When the winter weather seemed to even off a bit and the sky between us and the Rockies was clear, Bessie Haysom came to call. I was glad we'd been able to move the bed back where it belonged, so there was more room to move around the stove and table. With her usual generosity, Bessie didn't come empty-handed. She brought two dozen more diapers the church women had hastily hemmed up when they learned we'd had twins, some cookies from Polly Brill, and some treats from the store ... orange marmalade, sharp cheese, and soda crackers. She also brought a big pot of her special chicken fricassee, which gave Elsa a day off from cooking.

Bessie leaned over the basket and admired the babies, but she didn't want to hold them. "They're too tiny," she said firmly. "When folks come to visit, they should leave those babies in peace and quiet. You know how it's not good for little kittens to get passed around and mauled to pieces ... well, it's the same with babies, especially early ones."

A few days later, Adelia Yeagerman came bearing a pan of smothered pork chops and two more flannel receiving blankets. "I was in Choteau yesterday and heard about your babies. Mercy sakes, why didn't you send for me?"

I explained that I hadn't been able to send for anyone, but that Magda and Elsa Schmidt heard our bell, fortunately, and arrived in time to deliver the twins. I could tell she wasn't quite mollified. It didn't help when she started to pick up baby Hiram.

"He's sick," Elsa said, as she pulled the basket closer. "All morning he's been spitting up and crying. This is his first sleep in hours."

Adelia reached for the other baby, and Elsa said firmly, "That one, too. Very bad." She could tell Mrs. Yeagerman was offended, so she asked earnestly, "What do you think we should do? Sugar water? Schnapps water? Chamomile syrup?"

Adelia gave us five minutes of her wisdom, gingerly touched their tiny foreheads for fever, and went home, apparently flattered out of her snit.

I managed to contain myself until we heard her sled runners on the ice, and then I burst out laughing. "Oh, you're terrible! They're not sick!"

"You know what Mrs. Haysom said. We'll keep them not sick."

Will came in while we were still laughing. The poor man invented as much outside work as possible, feeling awkward with Elsa there. But I knew that even if he'd been unable to keep busy, he'd have hidden in the barn while Adelia Yeagerman visited. He'd sensed her sharp nosiness and judgmental way a long time ago.

When I told him why we were laughing, he chuckled too. Then he turned serious. "I know what Bessie means. When they're so new and kind of breakable, I'm afraid to touch the babies, myself. And my hands are always cold. And even when I wash up good, I know I'm coming in from the animals, and I'm afraid I'll make the little tykes sick."

But Will spent a lot of time sitting by their basket admiring them, stroking a tiny back with a big, calloused finger. Once I heard him whisper, "You don't know me yet, but I'm your pa. We'll get to know each other when you're a little bit bigger. And when you're bigger still, I'll be the one you come to when you're in trouble."

Aha, I thought. *Take* that, *Victoria!*

One afternoon Elsa was all caught up with the work and sat in the rocking chair, feather-stitching around a baby gown while I nursed the twins. The lamplight glinted on her golden hair and it struck me suddenly what a pretty girl she was. Her high cheekbones and slightly slanted blue eyes made her face just different enough to be eye-catching.

"I'm surprised you didn't bring a husband with you from Germany," I said lightly.

Elsa flushed bright pink. To my surprise, a tear slid down her cheek. "I didn't want to come. I wanted to stay with Bernhard. But Papa said he would leave no family behind. Bernhard is saving money for passage. We'll marry as soon as he gets here." She raised her eyes from her embroidery. "Before long, I hope."

Then, of course, she had to make a pot of tea and tell me all about Bernhard. The way Elsa's eyes glowed and the smiles lit up her face, I knew it would have been wonderful if she and Bernhard could have married in Germany and made the trip together. Her father had been right to insist on the whole family remaining complete, but to Elsa, Bernhard was her future family. Before time to start supper, we'd mentally filled a hope chest with quilts and linens. Once her family made it through the winter, she should be able to start saving some of her earnings to help with Bernhard's passage and outfit a homestead cabin. There was such a sparkle in her eyes and a lightness to her steps that I could hardly wait for Elsa to go out to the privy so I could tell the curious Will what was going on.

"Well, it's fine for you to help Elsa and Bernhard. But if you know what's good for us, you won't do the same for Bertie Yeagerman and her Solomon."

Will wasn't joking, and I knew he was right. So although I was thrilled to see Bertie at our door a few days later, I was alarmed when she pulled Solomon Heinz in behind her.

After a few awkward moments, Elsa hurried to make tea, and Will invited Solomon out to see our animals … the acceptable way to get away from the womenfolk.

Bertie bent over the babies' basket, oohing about how pretty they were, and carefully avoiding my eyes.

"Bertie, your ma must have finally decided to let you see Solomon. That's wonderful." My voice was calmer than I felt.

She looked up then, with a grin and sparkling eyes. "No, she's still planning on her girls making 'good marriages' with fancy city men … bankers or such. I went to Choteau for choir practice, and just happened to meet Solomon on the way. I decided I'd rather see your babies than practice singing." Another impish grin told me she and Solomon hadn't met accidentally.

"What happens when your ma finds out at church tomorrow that you weren't at choir practice?"

"Oh, I'll cross that bridge when I come to it," Bertie said airily.

We women had tea, and when the men came in, we had more tea with bread and butter. They admired the babies; Bertie gave me two little pairs of long stockings she'd knitted for them, and they left.

Will gave me a long, level look over his cup. "That pair is headed for trouble. I hope Mrs. Yeagerman doesn't find out they were here. She'd expect me to rush right over and tell Ben."

"You're not going to, are you?"

He sighed. "No. It's not my affair. Besides, Solomon seems like a level-headed young fellow."

I stifled a smile. Will was only a year older than the level-headed young fellow. "And Bertie's not such a flibbertigibbet as she seems," I said, defending my friend.

I wasn't tempted to smile next morning, though, when Mr. Yeagerman came looking for his missing daughter.

Chapter 25

Ben Yeagerman knocked on our door while Will was out doing morning chores. When Elsa let him in and I saw his stony face, my heart sank.

"Have you seen Bertie?" It was more a bark than a question.

I was in the rocking chair, having just finished nursing the babies. I pulled the shawl around them more snugly to protect them from the draft coming in the door, and he shut it quickly.

"She visited here yesterday afternoon."

"By herself?"

"No. Solomon Heinz was with her."

Ben sighed and sank down on a kitchen chair. "Adelia is fit to be tied." He pulled off a mitten and rubbed a hand across his unshaven chin. "When Bertie didn't get home yesterday afternoon after choir practice, I went into Choteau and learned she'd never showed up at the church. Her horse was tied outside the store, and somebody said they'd seen her get into Solomon's sleigh and drive out of town."

Without a word, Elsa handed Ben a cup of steaming coffee. He took a big slurp, winced at the heat, and set it on the table behind him. "I went out to the Heinzes, but they claimed to know nothing. Except that their son was missing, of course." He gave me a steely stare. "You and Bertie are friends. Did you know they were planning something?"

"No, I didn't. But I knew how she felt about Solomon, and he obviously felt the same about her. Anytime we've talked, I have urged her to wait and give her ma time to get used to the idea. I guess she didn't want to wait any longer."

Will hurried in the back door and saw how upset Ben Yeagerman was. He set down the milk bucket so quickly a little sloshed over the edge. He crossed the room in two big strides to put a hand on my shoulder. "Now hold on there, Ben. Don't you be giving my wife a hard time."

Ben gave another sigh, this one sounding like it came from the sole of his boots. Then he reached back for his coffee. "I suppose they run off to get married. Bertie's only sixteen."

"I'm sure sorry," Will said awkwardly. "I know how worried you must be. But Solomon seems like a good man. He'll take care of Bertie."

"And Bertie's a good worker," I added. "She's not the kind to think the world owes her a living, to sit around in lace and silk."

Ben finished his coffee and put the cup down. "Well, I'll warn you right now. When Adelia shows up, pitching a hissy fit, you'd both better not repeat what you just said. She's already loaded for bear. Don't set her off." Without another word, he stomped out the door.

Elsa busied herself straining the milk while Will hung up his coat and washed his hands. Sitting on the chest across from me, he leaned over and patted my hand. "Now, don't get upset, B'Anne. It'll spoil your milk."

My, he was getting smart. Wonder if he learned that in his blasted *Farmer's Almanac*?

"I'm not getting upset, Will, but honestly, I never encouraged Bertie. I did just the opposite, but her ma will never believe it."

Maggie started to fuss, as if she could feel the tension in my body, and Elsa hung up the straining cloth and hurried to take her. "Shush, shush, little Maggie," she crooned, rocking her in her arms. Magda had become Maggie, and Hiram had changed to Hi when they were only a few days old ... the babies were too small for their big names.

Surprisingly, Will awkwardly took Hi from me, cradling the baby's head with his big hand. "Why don't you go back to bed? Elsa and I will manage."

"I don't need to go back to bed. They're two weeks old, for heaven's sake." I'd begun to feel a little restless for the last couple of days, thinking about the things I needed to be doing. Still, I knew that without Elsa, I'd be not restless but exhausted.

All the rest of the day we listened for sleigh bells or hoofbeats, but the only company we had was Uncle Hiram, who came by every couple of days to see how we were doing (and to have some of Elsa's noodles or German dumplings, I was pretty sure).

On one visit, he handed me a couple of letters. "I picked up the mail yesterday in Choteau and stopped at the store. Bessie Haysom told me about your friend, Bertie. I'm supposed to tell you to watch your step." Taking the coffee Elsa handed him, he continued, "You didn't get yourself involved, did you?"

"No! I tried to talk her out of it several times. I wonder what Adelia's saying."

Uncle Hiram was frank. "Bessie said Adelia is telling folks you were a bad influence on her daughter and encouraged her to elope. She's hinting that you're no better, that you probably came to Montana in disgrace."

I was stunned. "But how ∴. how ..."

"Probably just guessing because you and Will are so young. She doesn't have anything to base it on, but Bessie says she's always been a troublemaker."

He didn't stay long. Standing over the twins' basket he said admiringly, "They're getting bigger every day. Plumping out and getting right handsome, too. Won't be long before I can dandle 'em on my knee." Then he went out to talk with Will, came back with him for a piece of *kuchen* and another cup of coffee, and went home.

I looked at the two letters he'd handed me, and gave one to Will. His mother's dainty, elegant handwriting gave me a sour feeling in my stomach, even without knowing what the letter was about.

The other letter was from my pa and ma, said how excited they were about the babies, couldn't wait for the railroad to come through so they could visit. If it didn't happen soon, they promised, they'd take the steamboat up the Missouri River to Fort Benton and rent a wagon on to Choteau.

In a happy glow from my mail, I looked across at Will's hard expression as he read his ma's letter. Uh-oh, not good news. He folded it and rammed it in his shirt pocket. "Don't even ask," he said. "I've got to cool off and read it again later."

He was just pulling on his sheepskin coat when we heard sleigh runners on the ice, followed by loud banging on the door.

As her husband had warned, Adelia Yeagerman was loaded for bear.

Chapter 26

"Well, I hope you're happy," Adelia sputtered before she even closed the door behind herself. "My daughter is now a ruined woman, and she'll be lucky to be living in a hovel like this one." She glanced scornfully at the makeshift furniture, gingham curtains and glass pretties Bertie had so admired on the shelves.

My feelings were hurt, but more than that, I was mad. After working so hard, Will didn't deserve to hear somebody call our cabin a hovel. Maybe it wasn't as fancy as Adelia's house, or the two-storied houses in town, the ones with gingerbread trim and verandas with railings, but it wasn't a hovel, like the homestead claim tarpaper shacks we'd seen on our way to Choteau. In fact, I was so mad that I forgot to be polite to my elders, like Ma had always taught me.

"This is not a hovel, it's a perfectly comfortable home!" I shot back. "But I'm sure you didn't come here just to criticize our house!"

Will came over and put his hand on my shoulder ... trying to calm me down, I figured. Unlike her usual fade-into-the-background behavior, Elsa stepped to my other side and put her arm around my waist protectively.

Adelia raised her chin and sniffed dismissively. "How fitting. You brought a German peasant out of the cave where they're living to help you. Maybe my daughter and her clod of a new husband could dig a cave to live in if they can't afford to build a hut."

Will stepped forward. By now the tips of his ears were as red as his neck, so I knew he was *really* angry. "Mrs. Yeagerman, I think you'd better leave."

Oh, my. I'd heard him speak in that tight, controlled voice only once before, back when we were sweethearts and Jack Jenson tried to outbid him on my decorated box at the box supper. He hadn't even sounded that mad when my brother Tad hauled him in, bloody-nosed, to propose to me. Mrs. Yeagerman had better watch her step.

Obviously Mrs. Yeagerman didn't know or didn't care how angry she made Will because she went right on. "Oh, I'll leave," she ranted, "because I'm going straight into Choteau and let everyone know about the den you have here. A young woman living with you, and not even a separate bedroom. You all sleep in the same room. The very idea! I can see the kind of example the two of you set for my innocent young daughter!"

I saw her scornful glare at the army cot Uncle Hiram had brought over so Will wouldn't have to sleep on the floor. We should have folded it up and put it on the porch this morning, expecting a visit from Mrs. Yeagerman, but I hadn't thought to do it.

Will took Mrs. Yeagerman's arm and marched her to the door. "Mrs. Yeagerman, the situation here is as innocent as can be. Elsa is my wife's friend, and I don't know what we'd have done without her. I would never violate my wife's trust, or Elsa's name, in any way. And my wife was nothing but a good friend to your daughter. She advised her to bide her time and not do anything foolish, not to marry so young. If Bertha chose not to listen to her, that's not B'Anne's fault." He jerked open the door and pushed Mrs. Yeagerman firmly out on the stoop.

"You should know, Mrs. Yeagerman, that I've read some law. If you damage the name of any of the three of us, I'll see Attorney Brown in Choteau, and before you know it, a good part of your ranch will be mine. I wouldn't want to do it because I value your husband's trust, but your viper tongue has to be stopped."

Elsa and I stared at him as he slammed the door behind her. "When did you read any law?" I sputtered.

"Well, never. But I read in a book about somebody being sued for blackening somebody's name. Some English novel, I think it was."

No matter how upset I was, I had to laugh as I peeked out the window at Mrs. Yeagerman whipping up her horse to get away from our place. "I guess we'll know in a few days if she believes you. The first time I'm brave enough to go to church, I'll be able to tell if the folks who used to be my friends still are."

Elsa's face had a stricken expression. "I must go home. If my being here is doing damage, I must leave."

"Oh, Elsa, don't go," I cried. "I still need you, and you might not be able to get your town job back. Think how much your family needs what Uncle Hiram pays you."

"You're just about ready to manage on your own. And I'll come over for a few hours every day to help you. Surely the *alte landsau* can't find fault with that."

I didn't know the meaning of the German word, and I had a feeling maybe it was better that I didn't.

Will spoke up now. "Elsa, I can sleep in the cowshed. I'll take a buffalo robe and burrow in the hay, and be warm and snug. It's probably what I should have done from the beginning, but I was afraid I might be needed during the night."

Elsa's face wore a stubborn expression I'd never seen on her before, and she was not about to be swayed. "I'll leave this afternoon, in time to get home before dark," she insisted.

She set the sponge for bread and made a pot of beef stew with tiny dumplings for our supper. She laundered everything that needed it and hung it on the line to freeze partially dry. She rocked fussy Hi and Maggie and crooned lullabies in German to them one last time, and when they fell asleep she eased them into their basket, took her bundle of clothes and prepared to leave.

We made her take what was left of the last baking, and all of the morning's milk, as well as the clabber on the stove that was dripping through cloth for soft cheese. It wasn't like store cheese, but mixed with a little sour cream and salt and pepper, it tasted good. I made her wear my heavy coat, and Will drove her home. He'd improvised runners for our wagon, and she'd never have been able to carry everything if we'd loaned her our horse. I tried not to, but I cried when she left. It was like saying goodbye to a sister.

Elsa cried, too. "But I'll see you tomorrow," she promised, wiping her cheeks with the coat sleeve as they drove away.

Will was wearing a hard face when he returned. As soon as he hung his coat and muffler on the hook, he poured a cup of coffee left over from noon dinner, sat down at the table, and pulled his mother's letter from his pocket. "Well," he said, "it seems like this is a day for bad things, so you might as well read Ma's letter." And he handed it to me.

A banker's check for twenty dollars fell out on the table when I unfolded the letter. I thought she couldn't be too unhappy if she was sending a gift for the babies. But it wasn't. The letter instructed Will that as soon as the twins were well enough to go out, and when they were old enough to lose that new baby look that made them all look alike, he was to use the money to take them to Choteau and have their tintype taken, and send it to her. She was sure they were not going to show a trace of Carter blood. There had been no twins in Will's father's family, or in hers either. Also, he was to look for a birthmark just below the right shoulder blade. Both Will and his father had such a mark, and if the babies didn't, they probably weren't his.

I leaped up from the table, determined to show Will the tiny mark on Hi's shoulder, but he grabbed my arm and sat me back down.

"Pay no attention. We know they're my babies ... *our* babies." He got the paper, pen, and inkpot from the kitchen shelf and sat back down. "It's time to put a stop to this, for once and for all."

He scratched away for minutes, so hard I was afraid he'd split the pen nib. When he finished the letter, he read it to me. He told his mother that until she could speak to and of his wife with respect, he wanted no further contact with her. He told her the babies were the best invention since gunpowder, and it was a shame she was never going to have the privilege of holding them. He told her I was a virgin that night at Ole's cabin, and I could just picture his ma turning red at that bold statement. She'd probably never heard or said the word *virgin* in her whole life. He ended by saying, "I hope to hear from Pa because I respect him. I want to be a man just like him, and I hope little Hiram is, too."

Folding the paper angrily, he said, "That ought to boil her beans. She never got tired of letting Pa know he was just a small-town storekeeper, and she could have done much better."

I tried to feel sad that Will had broken contact with his family because of me, but I couldn't. All I could feel was relief that he'd finally stood up for me.

"Are you going to tear that check up, or send it back to her?"

"Neither. She's buying a gift for the babies ... a wagonload of coal to keep them warm, and groceries to help their mother make milk."

I'd have preferred to see the hateful check sent back to Mrs. Carter, but I knew we'd need more coal and supplies before the winter was over, so I swallowed my pride. The twins howled with colic for hours after their next feeding, so it must have upset me more than I thought.

Elsa arrived soon after breakfast next morning and lit into the work like a house afire. When Will came in for noon dinner, she dished up the beans and cornbread, then folded her hands in her lap and cleared her throat.

"I thought and thought, and this is what I decided. Sunday I will come over and stay with the babies while you and Will go to church."

"Oh, it's too soon ..." I began.

"I'm not much of a churchgoer in the best of times, which this isn't," Will said flatly.

"But this is right," Elsa insisted. "You can tell right away if Mrs. Yeagerman has ruined you. Then they'll ask who's with the babies, and you'll tell them. And by their faces, you'll know if they think I'm a ... a bad woman."

I tried to think up a better protest. "But it hasn't even been three weeks yet. I don't think you're supposed to go out from childbed that soon."

Will leaned across the table and put his hand on mine. "She's right, B'Anne. We've got to strike while the iron's hot. You've got until day after tomorrow to figure out what to wear. We're going to church."

Chapter 27

Next day, I went out on the back porch several times and looked toward the Rocky Mountains in the distance, hoping to see a big storm looming there. I didn't want another blizzard, but I'd sure welcome a snowstorm bad enough to keep us from going to church in Choteau on Sunday. But each time there were just the usual clouds wisping around the tops of the peaks, none of the heavy blackness I wanted to see.

I missed having Elsa there, but we were managing. The babies had cried up a storm while we ate supper, so we took turns eating and holding them. When they woke up hungry in the night, Will brought them to me, and I changed their diapers under the covers where it was warm, then fed them. He carried them back and tucked them in their basket. It was wonderful, being able to cuddle against his warm back when the wind howled down the chimney. I'd missed sharing a bed with him since the babies were born.

In the morning I strained the milk, washed the buckets and straining cloth, and fixed breakfast in bits and starts between trips to the twins' basket. I finished cooking with Maggie in one arm, and the bacon got a little black, but I managed. I was sure glad to see Elsa come in the door, though.

She lit into the work like a whirlwind, same as always. After noon dinner, I fed the babies and put them down, and then she said firmly, "Now we find what to wear to church tomorrow."

We went to the corner by the bed, where Will had put hooks in the wall and I'd made a curtain out of some of the red and white checked gingham left on the bolt after making the window curtains. Of course, I could have worn anything there that fit ... nobody had seen me in any of the winter clothes because I was too big to wear them by the time the weather got cold. But Elsa seemed determined that I look as good as possible. Personally, I thought maybe I'd make a better impression if I wore sackcloth and ashes, but I didn't protest.

She took down my Sunday gray serge skirt and the striped shirtwaist, the outfit I'd changed into after I took off the pretty borrowed wedding dress, all that long time ago back in Iowa. She scrutinized it, then shook her head.

Next came my other nice dress, a brown alpaca with Ma's hand-tatted white lace collar and cuffs. She looked it over carefully, hesitated, then hung it back up.

"Aha!" she said and pulled down my very best winter dress. It was a deep red merino wool, trimmed with black grosgrain ribbon. Ma had wanted to put in a bustle, which was still being worn in our little village although modern people like Will's prissy older sister said it was out of style back East. I didn't protest the bustle because it was out of style, but because it seemed like a waste of time and material to sew a little horsehair-stuffed pillow to the back of your skirt and then add poufs of fabric to make it look graceful. As a compromise, Ma left off the bustle but had three layers of flounces where it would have gone, and they were trimmed with black grosgrain ribbon, too. It was my favorite dress, even if it did make me feel like I was sitting on a pillow, with all those flounces.

"There's no way I can get into that dress," I said flatly. "It fit like my skin last winter, so I know it won't fit now."

"You have ...?" Elsa floundered for the word in English, and finally substituted a gesture of smoothing down from her bosom past her waist.

"Stays, you mean. Yes, I have one, but I never wear it."

But Elsa was determined. I dug the hated stays out of the chest and undressed. I slipped into the torture garment, grabbed the bedpost and took a deep breath while she pulled the laces so tight I was afraid I'd faint. Then she slipped the dress over my head. Although I was right about it being too small, it made me a little happy. The waist fit, but there was no way the back buttons could be fastened because of my bosom. I'd always been ashamed of my little apple breasts. Looked like carrying enough milk to feed two hungry babies had a good effect.

"Well, Elsa," I said, "if my bosom doesn't get back to normal after awhile, you're going to have a cranberry red dress with black ribbon trim."

Elsa shook her head. "You'll get smaller. Just look how the waist fits, and so soon after the babies."

"The brown alpaca is the best choice, really," I said. "I don't want to look like someone from *Godey's Lady's Book*. I just want to look like a respectable grown-up wife and mother who's nothing like what Mrs. Yeagerman has been saying."

Next morning, Elsa arrived early to help me get dressed. The brown alpaca was a little tight across the bust, but not too bad. It had always been a bit loose before. Elsa brushed my hair up in a stylish roll and fastened it firmly in place with my tortoise-shell combs. She carefully brushed off the warm black coat we'd been sharing for the last few days, and I slipped it on.

"You need a bonnet. A lady should always wear a head covering," she said.

"I hate bonnets. And it would spoil the pretty way you did my hair. I'll wear my best shawl over my head. It'll be warmer, anyhow." Actually, it would be a lot more comfortable in that awful snowstorm I was still hoping for.

Will wore his wedding suit. I was shocked to see the sleeves were a little short again, even after they'd been altered for our wedding. Was he still growing? Immediately I felt too young and lost the bravery I'd been trying to build for going to church. But he looked very handsome with his suit brushed and his hair slicked down. I waited on the stoop while he brought the wagon around and looked toward the Rockies one last hopeful time. No approaching storm. Will wrapped the buffalo robe around me, and we headed for Choteau, the runners singing on the ice.

As we neared Uncle Hiram's place, we were alarmed to see him frantically waving his arms from the front stoop. I'm ashamed to say that my first thought was to hope there was an emergency big enough to keep us from going to church.

But it wasn't. Uncle Hiram ran out to meet us. "I saw you coming from way yonder," he said. "I intended to be out at the lane, but I forgot my hat and had to go inside to get it."

As he grabbed the side of the wagon and clambered in, his buffalo coat fell open in the front, and I could see he was wearing a suit. The black wool had a greenish tinge from age, and the tight collar of his shirt must have been irritating from the way he ran his finger around the inside of it as soon as he sat down. My stars, was he dressed up. His boots were polished to a fare-thee-well, and he was wearing an ancient beaver-skin hat, like men wore forty years ago, held down by a muffler wrapped around his head. His chin and cheeks were shaved so clean he looked skinned. He was carrying a fancy walking stick topped with a knob of polished petrified wood.

Uncle Hiram gave us a big smile. "Mind if I tag along to church with you? Close your mouth, girl. If it was summer you'd be catching flies."

"We'd … we'd love to have you," I stammered, "but I didn't know you were a churchgoer."

"I figure once every twenty or thirty years won't hurt me." He patted my shoulder. "Besides, three people can fight off an angry crowd better than two people."

Bless his heart, he was coming along to support me. I had to swallow a big lump in my throat. "Well, I'm glad you're on my side. But you're going to need that fancy walking stick to beat off all the widow ladies. You look handsome as a riverboat gambler."

"How'd you know we were going to church?" Will asked.

"Franz Schmidt told me when he helped me muck out the stables yesterday. Said it was his sister Elsa's idea, and a pretty good one, I think."

The folks clustered inside the front door of the church fell silent as soon as we joined them, but they weren't staring at me. Uncle Hiram had everybody's full attention. Nobody turned their back on me or scurried to a pew. I saw a few measuring looks, but not the disdain that would've been there if Adelia Yeagerman had fulfilled her threat. Probably just from the stir she caused that first morning when they came to town looking for their daughter.

Bessie Haysom was the first to speak. "You're a sight for sore eyes, all of you. But I'm glad you didn't try to bring the babies out in this cold."

"Elsa's with them. I'd trust her with my life." I watched carefully to catch any disapproving looks, but there weren't any. I breathed a sigh of relief, sure now that Will's threat had silenced Adelia.

Then I saw her. Adelia and her oldest daughter, Phoebe, had a small cluster of three women around them in the opposite corner of the church. The women all stared at me curiously, and a couple of them raised their handkerchiefs to their lips to hide what they were whispering. Adelia, though, pointedly did *not* look at us at first. She stared fiercely over our heads like maybe the Devil was hovering there. Then she lowered her gaze to look me right in the eye with a stare so cold it dripped icicles. Turning to Mrs. Clatchett, known to be the town gossip, she leaned close enough to whisper in her ear and tilted her head in my direction for emphasis. Will had *partially* silenced her, I guessed. She must not have spread rumors about Elsa spending nights at our house, or people would probably be shunning us. But she wasn't completely quieted.

With her head held high, she walked slowly toward me, followed by her little clutch of hens. When she got within speaking distance, she just stared at me for a few moments. Then, "Well, Mrs. Carter," she said, her voice frosty, "where are your babies? Don't tell me you were foolish enough to go off and leave them with that German girl?"

Will and Uncle Hiram had been talking to a nearby man, but now they moved toward our little group. Their expressions boded ill for Mrs. Yeagerman.

I swallowed hard before angry, undignified words could pop out. "Yes, Elsa is watching them. She's very experienced and trustworthy, too. Since my mother's not around to advise me, I've really appreciated the knowledge Elsa has from helping her mother with babies."

"Yes, I have indeed heard that the mother has a litter. To be expected from such riff-raff, of course."

I couldn't believe my ears. Most of the women here had more children than they planned for. What else was a woman to do unless, as rascally old Hattie Elwell back home said, she slept with her feet in a five-gallon bucket? After that comment, Ma had quickly sent me on a pretend errand whenever Hattie opened her mouth.

Now I just looked at Adelia and smiled. Ma always said you got more flies with honey than with vinegar. I never could figure out why you'd want more flies, but I decided to give her advice a try. Borrowing my ma's kindly expression and soft voice, I said, "Most mothers love all the little angels God sends them. I know Magda Schmidt does." Several of the other ladies nodded in agreement ... all, I noticed, women whose children were grown, leaving them more time and energy to appreciate them.

I decided I should see this thing through, strike while the iron was hot. "How is Bertha, Mrs. Yeagerman?" I asked, and heard several gasps of shock.

Adelia stiffened, and a deep flush appeared high on her cheeks, making her look like a dance hall girl who was careless with her face paint.

"I have not spoken to her since her shameful behavior, nor do I intend to. Perhaps next time she pays you a visit, you can relay my disappointment to her."

"I'm not expecting her, but I'll be happy to see her if she drops in." Even though it pained me to do it, I laid a hand on Adelia's arm. I felt her freeze and figured it was taking all her willpower not to shake my hand off, or slap me, which of course would be a very undignified thing to do. I continued, "Bertha's a wonderful girl. She has a sweet spirit and thanks to her family, a firm foundation. I'm sure she and Solomon will be very happy together."

Adelia whirled around and stalked away, her boot heels loud in the shocked silence. Her little flock followed her, looking confused.

Mrs. Grenville leaned forward to pat my shoulder. "Don't you fret, B'Anne," she said in her soft Virginia drawl, "she'll soon find something else to gossip about and forget you."

Polly Brill whispered, "My poor husband, Jonas, wasn't a drinking man. He only had a tot of whiskey when his lumbago was paining him real bad. But in her gossip, she had him drunk at the time. Shameless old biddy."

Aged Granny Whitney laid her hand on my arm. "Now, don't you rush off after service. My son in Helena sent me a crock of marmalade and it sets off my heartburn something fierce. I remember at your surprise baby party you really enjoyed the marmalade and crackers Bessie brought. I'll hurry home and get it afterward. I'm right next door, you know. There's only two spoonfuls gone."

Mrs. Taylor chimed in. "While she's getting the marmalade, I want to write down the details about your dress. I've got a piece of alpaca I've been saving, and I think my Susan would look real good in that style."

The pump organ gave a loud wheeze, and then the first chords of "Sweet Hour of Prayer" filled the church. One of my favorite hymns. In my memory, I heard Pa's strong baritone and Ma's sweet alto, and a feeling of peace washed over me. I thanked the Lord that Adelia Yeagerman hadn't taken this place and these people from us.

"Come sit with us," Bessie said as she pulled me down the aisle toward where her husband was already seated. Then she gave Uncle Hiram a saucy look and added, "Or maybe you've picked out a lady to sit by, all spit and polish as you are."

He gave an uncomfortable "Hmph!" and followed us.

After church, folks gathered around to congratulate us on having healthy babies, asked about their names and how they were faring. I got lots of advice on milk fever, sore breasts and rashy bottoms ... flour browned in the skillet, cooled and sprinkled on little red rears seemed to be the common solution, although one lady swore by cornstarch. Before long Will was talking farming with several men by the front door, and Uncle Hiram was edging in that direction, backing away from Widow Kirkman, who was smiling and chuckling and talking a mile a minute. Mrs. Taylor copied the details of my dress while Granny hobbled home for the marmalade, and finally we left the warmth of the church and its people.

Headed home in the wagon, we pulled buffalo robes around us against the sharp wind that had come up. Looked like we might get that storm, after all, now that I didn't need it. "Come have dinner with us, Uncle," I said. "I'll bet Elsa's got something good on the stove."

"I was afraid I was going to have to invite myself. Just let me out at my place so I can get these wretched clothes off, and I'll ride over. That way I'll have a way home later."

At home, I hung my coat on the hook and changed into the skirt and shirtwaist I'd worn while I was pregnant because it was the easiest garment to nurse in. By the time my hands had warmed up enough to handle the babies, milk had dampened the front of my chemise ... after all, it had been almost four hours since the last feeding.

Elsa helped me get them settled comfortably, then hurried to the stove. Will had shot two ducks the day before, and a wonderful smell of roast duck and sage perfumed the air. By the time Uncle Hiram arrived our meal was ready, and the twins' meal was finished.

As he scooped a helping of mashed potatoes onto his plate, Uncle Hiram breathed a sigh of satisfaction. Then he announced, "We ought to have a meal like this at Christmas, and have all your family here too, Elsa. It'd be like family Christmases I remember when I was a boy, with planks set up on sawhorses to make room enough to feed everybody. And even then, the young 'uns didn't eat until after the grown-ups. There's more room at my place, but it'd be better not to take Hi and Maggie out in the cold." He glanced at Elsa. "Maybe you folks could share some German ways with us, some songs and the like. How does your family keep Christmas?"

Elsa's expression became bleak. "Back home ..." She swallowed hard and tried again, a quiver in her voice. "Back home we decorated the house with greens. We all went to church on Christmas Eve, and when we got home, we ate the special supper Mama had made ... sauerbraten and red cabbage, and for dessert, a wonderful torte. Then we went to bed, and when we woke up, Father Christmas had left toys and treats in our stockings." A tear sparkled on her eyelashes. "It will be different this year, but I'm sure Mama will do something for the littler ones."

Uncle Hiram nodded. "Maybe Father Christmas will find a way." I had a pretty strong suspicion that he was going to give Father Christmas a little help. Then he said, "What about it, Elsa? Do you think your folks will go for the idea?"

She nodded enthusiastically. "I'm sure they will. It's only a few days. I'll help B'Anne get ready, so it won't be too much work for her." She stopped suddenly and said a little awkwardly, "If you like the idea, B'Anne. We shouldn't plan without even asking you first."

"Well, of course I like the idea. I was thinking the first Christmas away from home might be kind of sad, especially since we won't have the church Christmas service to look forward to because of the babies being so small. But it won't be sad at all. We'll have a whole new family."

I took a spoonful of creamed dried corn and passed the bowl, my mind busy on other things. After the ugliness of the last few days, it was wonderful to have something pleasant to think about.

Chapter 28

After Uncle Hiram and Elsa left for home, I sat in the rocker and nursed the babies. The wind howled outside, but the coal in the stove kept our little cabin nice and warm. I missed the crackle of a wood fire. However, the occasional soft clunk of coals settling was comforting, too.

Abandoning the exciting Christmas plans that had been racing through my brain all afternoon, I took a few moments to just admire my babies. Their seemingly-constant suckling that made me feel at times like a Jersey milk-cow had changed them from scrawny little stick figures to babies on their way to round cuddliness. Maggie's brown hair had grown enough to stick up in untidy tufts around her delicate little face, and when she opened her big eyes, they seemed wise and knowing. Hi was a bit smaller than his sister, but he had a rosebud mouth and a tiny dimple in one cheek. Although he appeared to be bald, fine blond hair showed when you looked closely.

How I wished Ma and Pa could see their first grandchildren. The railroad couldn't come to Choteau soon enough to suit me. They'd sent a parcel that arrived when the babies were three weeks old. Ma and the aunts had whipped together more diapers and long outing flannel gowns, some with drawstrings in the hems to pull them tight and keep little legs and feet warm. And they must have knitted up a storm because there were four pairs of knitted wool leggings with feet

... two to wear, and two in the wash. There were two crocheted shawls, too. The babies had warm clothing, and when the weather was warm enough to put them in the cradle, they'd have beautiful bedding. Right now, though, they were safer in their basket on the table or bed, where it was warmer. The air on the floor nipped the ankles, even with the good flooring Will and Uncle Hiram had put down.

When both babies fell asleep with full tummies, I put them down and got out paper and pencil. Uncle Hiram had said to make a list of everything I needed for what he was calling the Christmas feast. It made me feel bad to have him paying for everything, but we surely couldn't afford to feed fifteen people ourselves unless it was just beans and cornbread. And maybe stewed beef, from what was left hanging on the back porch.

After we'd been in Montana Territory for awhile, I'd asked Will why Uncle Hiram seemed to have more money than the other homesteaders we'd met.

"Well, he's always lived simple," Will replied. "He hasn't built a big house. He doesn't spend money on clothes or such. He doesn't have a family to provide for." Then, looking thoughtful, Will finished, "Remember, Uncle Hiram told us about my pa coming out here from Iowa and taking him away from the mines when things were so bad, when his wife and baby died. Uncle Hiram told me later that Pa stayed with him till he got off the liquor and got his land claimed, convinced him to put his gold from the mines into improvements on the homestead, where it wouldn't get wasted. So he didn't have to start off on a shoestring, like most homesteaders. When he has a good year, the money doesn't have to go for paying off debts. And the Territory's had some mighty good wheat years. Uncle Hiram credits Pa for being comfortable now."

Still, writing down extravagant things I never would have bought myself made me feel extra guilty, but they were for foods Uncle Hiram had specified. Sounded like he must be making up for the all Christmas dinners he'd missed over the years. In fact, he'd said with a laugh that the only holiday treat he'd had a lot of when he was alone was brandy ... too much brandy.

Now he wanted eggnog and fruitcake and five kinds of pie. Ribbon candy, chocolate drops, oranges and walnuts. If it was available in

Choteau, he wanted celery to go in the stuffing for the three turkeys he was ordering from the Petticord farm outside town. He'd said he'd roast two of them in his oven and bring them over cooked on Christmas Day, since my oven wouldn't hold that many. Oyster stew if any oysters had come down from Fort Benton, where the steamboats sometimes brought them on ice from back East. He'd mentioned something called syllabub, then dropped it when he saw my confused look.

He was going to ride over to the Schmidt place tomorrow and invite them, so it wouldn't just be secondhand coming from Elsa. While he was there, he was going to get a list of what was needed for the sauerbraten Elsa had described. I just hoped the Haysom's store would have everything we needed, and I'd be smart enough to know what to substitute if they didn't.

I was beginning to get an excited, little girl feeling about Christmas, although it still gave me a pang when I thought about Ma and Pa, Tad and Susie back home. I'd miss hearing Pa read the Christmas story at church, and the big dinner where all Ma's sisters and their families came to our house, bringing the dishes that were their specialties. One year, Aunt Sarah had Will's pa order cauliflower special from Sioux City, and she made a fancy dish from the vegetable we'd never tasted before. Everybody missed her usual scalloped corn so much that she never tried anything new again. Aunt Cora's special talent was pickles, and she always brought dill, sweet, and bread-and-butter pickles, pickled beets and spiced crabapples.

I wondered if the folks would get the box we sent in time. I knew they wouldn't expect us to buy gifts for everybody, hard up as we were, but I'd sent them a giant batch of molasses taffy. Will and I had so much fun pulling and twisting the long ropes of taffy until it was almost white, and hardly sticky. I cut it in pieces and let it dry on the table for several days, so it wouldn't all stick together in one big mess in the box.

One afternoon while the taffy was drying on the table, Will put down the froe and block of cedar he'd been shaping shingles from to use on the barn we'd build next summer, and admired the table-top full of taffy.

"Would there be enough to send a small box of it to my pa? I'd like him to know we're thinking about him at Christmastime."

"Of course. I made a triple batch, so there'd be enough for a gift to Uncle Hiram and the Schmidt family, too. There's plenty for your pa. Should be ready by tomorrow, and you can take the boxes into Choteau to the post office. Be sure to write a nice letter to him to go with it. I don't want him to think we're mad at him."

So we'd sent the boxes off to Balsamview, and now all I had to worry about was the Christmas feast, and a present for Elsa. With her there to help, I'd had time to sew Will and Uncle Hiram each a shirt. I wished I could think of something special for Elsa that wouldn't cost any money. She needed warm clothing, but I couldn't afford that. Luckily, the two German families in Choteau that the older girls worked for off and on had given the Schmidts some hand-me-down clothes. They were drab and faded but, as Elsa said, they covered what had to be covered.

I rummaged through my sewing box without finding any inspiration, and came back and finished my store list.

Uncle Hiram came by next morning to get the list and said he was buying something for the Schmidt children ... something to brighten their holiday, but small enough that the parents wouldn't feel uncomfortable. Pocketknives for the boys, maybe, and hair ribbons for the girls. Something different for the smaller ones, though. Maybe a ball or a little toy.

Elsa arrived before he left and followed him out to his wagon. I watched curiously as she handed him a little slip of paper and some coins from her apron pocket. I'd wondered why she needed the paper she'd asked for yesterday ... now I knew. Probably she was asking Uncle Hiram to buy something she could give her parents.

Will hurried in from the cowshed, brushing sawdust off his clothes, and ran out to join Uncle Hiram, calling over his shoulder, "I've got some things to do in town. You'll be all right with Elsa here." I caught the door before it slammed and woke the babies

Elsa warmed herself by the kitchen range when she came back in. "Two more days! We're going to have to work fast, B'Anne. It's a good thing the babies are sleeping longer now."

"Yes, we can't waste a minute. Let's start on the things that don't need anything on Uncle Hiram's list."

I put dried apples and dried peaches to soak and plump up, chopped the pumpkin Will had brought in from our root cellar the day before and put it on to stew. Elsa started a big batch of bread and then started on the piecrusts. Luckily, we could cook and bake ahead and store the food on the back porch, as long as we kept it up high, out of the reach of animals.

When Uncle Hiram and Will returned hours later, Elsa and I were flour-dusted and exhausted, but pies were baking in the oven, and bread was rising on the warming shelf of the stove. It took the men two trips to carry in all the parcels and boxes, and after the last trip Uncle Hiram pulled some letters and a little package from the pocket of his buffalo coat.

Handing some letters and the package to Elsa, he said, "I picked up your family's mail, too, and there was something for Miss Elsa Schmidt."

After a quick glance at the front of the parcel she whispered, "It's from Bernhard."

"Are you going to open it now, or wait till everyone's here for Christmas?" I asked.

"I think ... I think best now. I would feel bad to open it in front of my sisters because they'll have nothing." Painstakingly, she opened the package, untying the knots to guarantee a long piece of string that could be used again. After carefully smoothing the paper flat, she opened the little box, then, with a gasp of pleasure, she held up the gift for us to see. It was a necklace of coral, with large and small beads alternating to make a pattern.

"That's craftsmanship. Bernhard knows beauty when he sees it. That's why he chose you."

Elsa's face pinkened at Uncle Hiram's praise, and she smiled shyly. Then she read the letter enclosed. "He has bought the ticket! He will get here in March."

Uncle Hiram paused in wrapping the muffler around his neck. "If the weather cooperates we can have a place built by then, with everybody pitching in." He glanced at Will and saw his nod of agreement. "Your family ... and your husband ... can work on shares with me if they want to. Might be better than having to buy expensive equipment right off. We'll be able to break that west section and plant it to wheat. I'd been hoping to do that when Will got his head above water. If we work on shares, it can happen sooner. This country's not as flat and hot as the plains are for wheat, but there's a new variety that takes a shorter growing season." He opened the back door and a wall of cold hit us all. "Brrr. Got to make sure my animals are warm enough. See you tomorrow, probably."

After Elsa and I had put away the supplies, there was a box left over with writing in the corner showing it was from Balsamview, Iowa. I didn't know if our box to the folks got there in time, but theirs to us made it. All the while Elsa and I minced up stringy beef from the frozen haunch on the back porch, and set it to simmering with raisins, apples, spices and citron to make mincemeat, my eyes kept straying to that beautiful box.

When Will came in from the cowshed for a cup of coffee, he was covered in sawdust again. Some project he wasn't telling me about, I figured. Standing by the stove and sipping his coffee, he caught my gaze at the box and said, "Shall I get the hammer and pry it open?"

I hesitated, ashamed at seeming so greedy, then I blurted, "Yes!"

For Will, Ma had made six handkerchiefs with whip-stitched hems and his initial embroidered in one corner, and a plaid flannel muffler with yarn fringe.

She made me a shawl of soft, dusty rose wool, with a pattern of roses crocheted along the bottom above the thick fringe. But it was the other gift that brought a wave of homesickness. Ma had made a lavaliere of dusty rose grosgrain ribbon, with a large ivory button shaped like a rose centered and sewed on the ribbon. I had loved that button all through childhood and begged to have it put on a dress. Ma always replied that the button was too special to use. A great-grandfather many generations back had carved it from a plain button. It had been on her wedding dress, and on her mother's before her, and *her* mother's before *her*. My hurried wedding and borrowed dress meant she didn't get to use the special button for me, but now it was mine. Seeing that gift reminded me of playing with Ma's button jar on rainy autumn days while she sewed. I knew that whenever I wore that beautiful shawl and lavaliere, it would feel like Ma was right beside me.

The babies got soft wool nighties that were stitched shut at the bottom, so they couldn't kick off all their covers during the night. For Hi, Ma had made a checked gingham puppy, lightly stuffed, with floppy ears, and for Maggie, one just like it but red-checked.

Next to come out was a tin that had once contained oyster crackers, but now held something much heavier. Will pried off the lid and drew a deep sniff. "Ah, fudge! Your ma makes the best fudge in Balsamview."

There was still one parcel left in the bottom of the box, and I turned it over to read what was written on the brown paper wrapping. "Elsa, this is for you. It's got your name on it."

"But ... but ... how ..." Elsa shook her head in confusion. "Your mother does not know me."

"In my letters I told her you were staying with us, helping me. What did she send you? Open it, quick!"

It was a set of five dainty lawn handkerchiefs, each with a different flower embroidered in a corner, and the initial "E" in another corner. "Oh, they are so beautiful," Elsa murmured, stroking the silky blossoms. "I have never had anything so nice."

Now that the packages had all been opened, we turned our attention to the small items that had been tucked in among the parcels. There was a muslin sack full of popcorn kernels from Pa's cornfield and jars of wild plum and Concord grape jellies, carefully swathed in what turned out to be diapers. There were four bars of Ma's special homemade soap wrapped in tissue paper, with Elsa's name written on one wrapper. Ma was famous for her homemade soap. Some of the ladies jokingly accused her of buying it at the general store and pretending she had made it. Well, maybe not too jokingly, some of them. Ma strained the melted fat until not an impurity remained, and somehow the lye she leached out of ashes and rainwater was milder than what other people made. Fragrance was the final luxury in Ma's homemade soap. Herbs and flowers from her garden ... lavender, bergamot, nasturtium, lemon verbena ... were dried or distilled in oil, and their essence was added as the soap began to thicken. Elsa stroked and sniffed the bars in wonderment. "Next summer we do this, yes?" she asked me.

"Yes, let's. It probably won't be as good as Ma's, but let's try, anyhow." I smoothed the crumpled newspapers that had filled corners. "We can read these later," I told Will, "and catch up on what's happened back home." I examined small items that fell from the newspaper. Butternuts and hickory nuts from the woodlot behind the house, where Will and I had strolled on Sunday afternoons before Victoria came on the scene. A muslin bag of dried sarsaparilla root with a note that instructed,

"For teething: pound to a paste and rub on gums. Steep into weak tea for colic or bellyache. Or with sugar, a little vinegar and cold water, makes a good drink in summer."

I put all the small gifts on the table. Since they had very little money, Ma and Pa had given their time and labor, and I appreciated my parents more than ever before.

Will took the empty box out to the barn, to save until we needed it for the same purpose, and Elsa and I got back to work. Before she left for home, she made a big batch of noodles and hung them to dry on the side of the warming shelf, and we made two fruitcakes, with all the chopping that required. Will came in and cracked the walnuts for us, so that helped. The fruitcakes wouldn't be as good as if they'd had time to age, but I guessed they'd satisfy Uncle Hiram.

That evening after supper, Will and I read our letters aloud to each other. Ma caught me up on family news: Tad had grown another two inches. Susie was singing in the church choir; really too young, but they needed altos. Cousin Rose, away at college, was bringing a beau home for Christmas, looked like there might be wedding bells next summer. Cousin Lorinda was in the family way again, due in May.

"Well, I'd better get those dresses she loaned me in the mail," I told Will, "and the baby clothes, too, the minute the twins outgrow them."

The letter ended, as they always did, with a brief message in Pa's handwriting, sending us love and admonishing us to attend church regularly. *Good thing he didn't know about the scene with Adelia Yeagerman at church*, I thought.

The letter from Will's pa was brief, but heartening. Will's ma was still mad as a wet hen, he reported, but was taking it out in a campaign to close Balsamview's two saloons. Will's sisters were fine, although one's children were sick with chickenpox. He told us how much he wanted to see his two newest grandchildren, and was thinking about taking the steamboat up next summer. He wished us a healthy and merry Christmas and told us to use the money enclosed on whatever we needed most.

Will placed three ten dollar bills on the table. "Maybe we can save it toward building the barn next summer," I suggested.

"I wish we could, but I don't think we'd better. When Uncle Hiram and I were in town, the men at the general store were talking about the weather, said an old Indian who's lived here forever knows the signs and has never been wrong. He says it's going to be the hardest winter in years. Tomorrow I'm going to borrow Uncle Hiram's big wagon and double-team his horses. They'll be able to pull as much coal as thirty dollars will buy."

"But tomorrow's Christmas Eve. And we could really use that money someplace else."

"I'm sure the coal-yard's open on Christmas Eve. And we can go on short rations, but we've got to stay warm. I've just got a bad feeling, B'Anne."

Chapter 29

On Christmas Eve, there didn't seem to be a dawn. The rooster out in the chicken-coop began his raucous crowing when the night sky was still black, and it was a long time before it lightened to a dull gray. We were up well before daylight, so Will could get an early start to Choteau. He chopped through the ice in the creek and brought up two buckets of water, and filled the coal box on the back porch to heaping before he left. As I waved goodbye from the front stoop, I looked anxiously toward the Rockies. The sky looked a little more threatening than usual, but not the heavy leaden gray that meant a bad storm on the way.

After changing and feeding the babies, I got out my sewing basket again. Before Elsa arrived to help, I had to figure out a gift for her. Finally, in desperation, I hemmed a large square of the red-and-white checked gingham left from curtains, filled it with tea leaves, pulled up the corners and tied it with a ribbon. Elsa loved tea, and I knew they couldn't afford it at home. She could even use the cloth for a head scarf when the tea was all gone.

When Elsa arrived, one of her younger sisters was with her. "This is Birgitta," she explained. "I have some chores to do at Mr. Hiram's place, and Gertrude and Margritte are both working in town today. Birgitta's only eleven, but she's good help."

And she was. She did the usual daily laundry of diapers, gowns and leggings, and then pulled a slip of paper from her apron pocket. "This is how to make *lebkuchen*. Shall I do it?"

I looked at the slip of paper written in German. "Yes, please do." Imagine my surprise when *lebkuchen* turned out to be just gingerbread. And I was almost as surprised when this eleven-year-old girl seemed to know as much about taking care of babies as I did. She changed diapers like an experienced mother.

While the *lebkuchen* baked, we decorated the little tree Will had cut down by the creek the day before. We didn't have anything fancy to put on it, but bows of yarn looked cheery. I sacrificed some of my dried rosehips to string with popcorn for garlands and used the tinfoil I'd been saving from Uncle Hiram's pipe tobacco packages to cut little stars.

When Will got home in mid-afternoon, he warmed his hands at the stove and sniffed appreciatively. "Smells like Christmas." He had stopped at Uncle's and picked up Elsa, and both girls helped shovel the coal from the wagon onto the pile by the porch, and replace the tarp. Then we all sat down and had the beans and side pork that had been simmering all day. Afterward, Will took the girls home, returned Uncle Hiram's wagon and team, and rode home on our horse.

It was dark by the time he arrived, and I'd put a lamp in the window to light his way. He pulled off his gloves and flexed his fingers by the stove. "My hands were so numb I was afraid maybe they'd been frostbit," he said. "It's fierce out there." As soon as he had a cup of coffee and warmed up a bit, he pulled on his heavy coat, took a kerosene lantern and started out to the cowshed.

"Why don't you bring whatever you're working on inside, Will," I said. "It's too cold out in the shed."

"I will in a bit," he replied. Sure enough, he was back in about an hour, carrying a little wagon and a sack of scrap wood blocks. "I can sand these inside," he said. Evidently he'd finished whatever his secret project was.

He sanded away while I nursed the babies, and when they were asleep again I fetched the Bible from its shelf and handed it to him. "Let me do the sanding while you read us the Christmas story."

There was a long hesitation before he took the Bible and handed me the blocks and sandpaper.

"Didn't your father read the Christmas story from the Bible on Christmas Eve?" I asked.

"Umm ... no, I don't remember that ever happening. Ma liked to have a party on Christmas Eve. She always tried to have it be as fancy as it had been back East, when she was a girl. Then when the party was over and people went home, she'd explain how much fancier it had been back in Boston, with hoop skirts so big that women had to tilt them up sideways to get through the door, and Lady Baltimore cake, and syllabub, and eggnog in a big crystal bowl, and dancing till midnight." He chuckled. "Those parties got a little grander every year when she described them."

"Why did your family come to Iowa?" I asked. "Mine came to get free land and try to have a better life, but I think yours were already well off."

Will hesitated, then replied, "I heard Ma tell my sister that she had 'married down' when she married my father. She'd been engaged to somebody important, and he jilted her and ran off with another girl. So she married Pa on the rebound. He didn't have as much money as Ma was used to, but her folks gave them a generous wedding gift. Pa wanted to go West and get free land, and Ma was anxious to get away from the humiliation of being jilted. So they came to Iowa."

"Did your father *know* he was second best?"

"Oh, he knew. And he wasn't a successful farmer, either, so as soon as enough people settled to start a town, he became a storekeeper."

"What do you mean by 'successful?' My pa was able to take care of us with just farming, even with all the time he gave the church."

"Ma couldn't stand being a farmer's wife unless the farm was big enough and making enough money to have hired hands and maids. She had some relatives down South, and that was her idea of the perfect farm ... having slaves to do all the work, and going to balls and banquets all the time."

I hadn't thought I could dislike my mother-in-law more than I already did. "I wonder how she'd like living down South now?" I muttered. "She'd be scrabbling in the dirt like the rest of us poor folks." I sanded the corner of a block much harder than necessary. "We have some folks down South, too, but they didn't live on a plantation. They didn't have much to lose. They were poor before the War, and they're poor after it."

"Well," Will said awkwardly, "I'd better read this Christmas story, I guess." He pulled the kerosene lamp closer and leafed through the tissue pages until I took pity on him. I took the book from him, turned quickly to the chapter of Matthew and handed it back to him, with my finger on the starting verse.

"And it came to pass ..." Will began, and I tried to replace the thoughts in my head with the ancient story. When he had finished, Will closed the Bible and said, "You're right. This is a good thing to do on Christmas Eve. Better than a fancy party."

When Will went out to check on the animals, I got into my warm flannel nightgown, but the sound of a baby snuffling and smacking on fingers told me my tired body wouldn't get to bed for a while yet. Luckily it was Hi, since it was his turn to nurse first. I rocked him in the chair by the kitchen stove while he hungrily suckled. "You're a greedy little boy, yes you are," I whispered, and he momentarily let go of the nipple to give me a milky smile. Will came in just then, and I said excitedly, "He smiled, Will! His first smile!" Startled by my voice, the baby's hungry mouth grasped the nipple, and he sucked urgently.

Will leaned over us. "Well, he sure ought to be smiling. He's warm and dry, and he's hanging onto the prettiest mama in the territory." His cold fingers brushed gently across my cheek toward my neck, and I bent my head to capture them between cheek and shoulder.

After Maggie had her turn at supper, we put their basket on the table near the stove and covered them with extra blankets against the cold that seemed to seep through the walls. Then we were finally able to crawl into bed ourselves. Cuddling against Will's back for warmth, I wondered how long it would be before we could be together again. Not that I wanted to get pregnant so soon, but I missed that closeness, and hoped he did, too. Just another thing I should have asked Ma about, although I'm sure I'd have been too embarrassed to try. Back home, I'd have asked my best friend or older cousin, who'd both had babies. Maybe I could talk to Magda tomorrow, with Elsa interpreting. Just thinking about it, my cheeks burned so hotly I was afraid Will would feel the heat through his long underwear, and think I had a fever. I resolutely closed my eyes and willed myself to fall asleep quickly and take advantage of the time before a hungry baby wakened to be fed.

Uncle Hiram arrived early next morning with two roasted turkeys and a bag of small gifts to go under the tree for the Schmidt children.

He gave Will a new pair of boots, their buttery-soft leather slipping on without effort, a result of the outline I'd traced from his old pair. When he gave me the blue cashmere cape he'd had made by the town seamstress, I was embarrassed by our own puny gifts to him. He seemed to love the shirt I'd sewed for him, though, and the taffy Will and I had pulled.

Will hurried through the frigid cold to the cowshed and returned with his secret project, a beautiful sewing box. "See, it has legs so it will sit right by your rocking chair and you won't even have to reach down to get something." He opened the lid proudly to show the little drawers inside. "And look, when you're not sewing you can use the top for your book or cup of tea." I raised my eyebrows, and he added sheepishly, "Not that you have much time for tea and reading," he admitted.

He admired the shirt I'd sewed for him. "Soon as it's warm enough to take the babies out, we'll go to church, and I'll wear my new shirt."

I put the last turkey in the oven, and when the Schmidts trooped in, our little house was filled with the children's noise, and the fragrance of holiday cooking. Somehow Magda had managed to make sauerbraten with the supplies Uncle Hiram had given her, and its aroma mingled with the turkey in the oven, and the spicy scent left from the *lebkuchen* Birgitta baked yesterday.

The children loved Uncle Hiram's gifts, but when Elsa gave me a napkin-covered basket and they got a whiff of the cinnamon-scented contents, I could tell food was more important to them than anything else right now.

"It's *zimtsterne*," Elsa said proudly. "Back home, this is our Christmas treat. I gave Mr. Hiram money to buy what I needed when he went to town, and this is what I was baking at his house yesterday."

"Indeed she baked. And I just about died of hunger, it smelled so good."

We gave everybody one of the star-shaped cookies to hold them off till dinner was ready. I set mine aside to give to one of the children, and I noticed all the grown-ups and older Schmidt boys and girls did the same, so the hungry little ones each had another cookie.

With the heat from the cookstove and all the people crowded inside our little cabin, the windows were soon so covered with steam that we didn't notice the darkening of the sky outside, or the snow that had started since the men made their trips outside. They'd brought planks to stretch across chairs, chests and the side of the bed to make eating space for everyone. The women and girls finished cooking as quickly as possible, and before long we were ready to enjoy the mixture of German and American food.

Everybody found a place to sit, with the littler ones on laps, and Will asked Mr. Schmidt to bless the meal. While we passed food and filled children's plates, a gust of wind hit the house so hard that the windowpanes shook, and the flames in the kerosene lamps wavered. Then the gust changed to a steady, howling force that moaned around the cabin.

The men ran to the door. I hurried to peek over Will's shoulder. All we could see was a whirling white wall of snow, and the wind that blew in the doorway was so cold it took our breath away.

Uncle Hiram spoke first. "Thank God we're all safe inside. This is going to be a bad one."

Chapter 30

Mr. Schmidt leaped to his feet, speaking urgently in German. Elsa said, "Papa says better we go now before it gets worse." In my mind's eye, I saw the Schmidt family hovering around the little pot-bellied stove in their dugout. I was glad when Uncle Hiram said firmly, "It's already too bad. You take those young'uns out in that storm, they might never make it. Your horse is safe in the calf shed here, and there's no more livestock at home to worry about."

People sank back down on their makeshift chairs and benches. The grown-up Schmidts continued looking toward the windows, plainly uncomfortable. Will noticed them too. "I just hauled home a big load of coal yesterday," he said. "We'll stay nice and warm."

"And look at all this food," I added. "We haven't even cut into that third turkey yet. We'll do fine."

Magda spoke to Elsa, who translated. "Mama says not room for all to sleep."

"We'll put down quilts and buffalo robes on the floor," Will assured her. "Might not be too comfortable, but we'll manage."

A gust of wind shook the walls again, and the stove hissed with a few flakes of snow that had blown down the chimney.

Will leaped to his feet and put his plate on the stove's warming shelf. "I've got to make sure the calves are all shut up in the shed. We can't lose any more of them. We need to fasten a rope from the back door so we can get to them for food and water, too."

Uncle Hiram, Mr. Schmidt and his older sons followed suit, lining their plates up on the warming shelf over the cookstove. Then they all pulled on coats and wrapped mufflers around their ears.

"If we've got enough rope, put one out to the privy, too," I said.

"I will," Will said. "Why don't you women and children go ahead and eat. We might be awhile." Will opened the back door as he spoke, and a flurry of snow and wind blew in.

We had the little ones eat, but Magda Schmidt, her older girls and I waited for the men to return. It seemed they were gone for a long time, and when they finally struggled in, they crowded around the stove to warm their hands before taking off their snowy coats.

"Whoo, dogies," Uncle Hiram gasped. "That's a bad one. Maybe the worst I've ever seen."

"They're all locked up safe in the cowshed now, even the chickens," Will said. "There ought to be enough animal heat in there to keep them. We'll have to go out and break the ice in the water from time to time, but they're all right for now. We shouldn't lose any more calves like we did in the first storm. We got all five horses in, too. With so many hands for the work, we were able to wall in the open side of the shed with straw bales, so they should keep from freezing."

"Unless the wind blows down the straw bales," one of the older Schmidt boys said grimly. "That wind is some fierce and cold."

"We had enough rope to string out to the privy, too," Uncle Hiram added, "but a chamber pot on the back porch would be safer for the little ones."

Magda, the Schmidt girls and I exchanged quiet smiles. The little ones wouldn't be the only ones using the chamber pot.

We grown-ups sat down for our belated Christmas dinner while the littlest children slept and the rest of them played quietly on the floor. When we were finished, Magda spoke briefly to Elsa, who translated to me, "Mama says let's wait and have the pies and things for supper. We might have to stretch what food we've got."

I nodded agreement. She was right. We had enough food on hand for a festive Christmas dinner, but the storm could last for several days, and not counting the twins, there were fifteen people to feed. And I'd have to get out every piece of bedding I owned when night came.

As if reading my mind, Uncle Hiram took his coat off the hook and prepared to go outside again. "I've got a couple of buffalo robes in my wagon to bring in before bedtime," he said.

The men followed the rope to the calf-shed. They moved all three farm wagons alongside it to reinforce the wall of straw bales, and brought anything that might be useful into the cabin. Our own wagon had a buffalo robe and two lap quilts, and the Schmidts had the two quilts that had covered the children on the drive from their place.

Then the Schmidt boys filled the coal box by the stove to heaping, and carried in buckets of snow to melt on the stove, since going down to the creek, chopping through the ice for water, and carrying it back in the wind would be a fierce chore. "We'll have to carry water out to the stock, too," Uncle Hiram reminded the men, so they filled our zinc washtub with snow so that the stovetop was completely covered.

When enough snow was melted and heated, we washed all the dishes and put any leftovers that had to be kept cold on the back porch. The rest of the day passed with the men checking on the animals and carrying in coal and more snow. Magda Schmidt and I nursed babies, and the older girls took care of all the younger children. We heard stories about Christmases in Germany, translated by the older Schmidt sons and daughters. The English-speakers learned a little more German, and the German-speakers learned a little more English. Elsa and Margritte sang two German Christmas carols for us, telling us first that "*Von Himmel Koch*" would be called "From Heaven Above" in English; and that "*Kinderlein Kommet*" meant "Come Ye Little Children." The few German words we knew, plus the beautiful melodies, helped us remember how special this day was, even if we were snowbound.

Will's strong bass and Uncle Hiram's reedy tenor combined in "Jingle Bells" had us all laughing, especially when Uncle Hiram threw in a whinny from the horse here and there.

In the evening, the men followed the rope out to the calf-shed again, broke the ice in the stock's water tub and milked our cow. With so many children to be fed, I was grateful once again for the milk we wouldn't have had a few months ago. The little ones had bread in warm milk while the older ones and the grown-ups had pie for supper.

With the coming of night, cold began to creep in. In the autumn, Will had piled straw around the foundation of the house and reinforced it with an earthen berm, as Uncle Hiram had advised, and we had a sturdy floor, but the cold seemed to seep up through the boards. Will brought the chamber pot off the porch, set it by the back door and hung a sheet over two chairs to screen it from open view.

"Ladies, this is no time for false modesty," he said.

We made beds on the floor wherever there was space, and eventually everyone was down for the night, covered with all the quilts, blankets, buffalo robes, coats and clothing available. Will stoked the fire, and I knew he'd be up several times during the night to add coal. When he prepared to go out to the back porch to refill the coal bucket, I urged him to hang the kerosene lantern on the hook, as we had in the first storm. He looked at me quizzically, and I said, "Just think of how awful it would be to be lost out in this. Maybe when the wind stops for a minute, the lantern could be seen." I refilled our big lamp and put it on the table by the front window.

We took the twins to bed between us, and the Schmidt parents took their baby and toddler under the quilts with them, too. We squinched close together and made room for Elsa beside me, and put four of the smaller Schmidt children at the other end of our bed. "We'll keep each other's feet warm," Will joked.

The variety of snores inside the cabin competed with the noise of the storm raging outside, but eventually sleep came. My last thoughts were to wonder how long this blizzard could possibly last … and how on earth could Magda and I hang diapers to dry around the heads of so many people.

Chapter 31

At first, I thought it was the silence that woke me ... the lack of wind whining around the eaves. Then I heard it again ... muffled thudding and banging on the back porch.

Will had heard it too. Stepping over people on his way to the door, he wrenched it open and helped two snow-plastered people inside. Uncle Hiram scrambled to his feet, and the two of them removed coats and scarves to reveal Solomon Heinz, half-carrying, half-supporting Bertie.

We pulled off their frozen boots and hurried them to the stove. Uncle Hiram wrapped the buffalo coat he'd been sleeping in around them, and people on the floor began handing up blankets and quilts. Elsa carried the pot of warm water off the back of the stove and began bathing numb feet in it while I heated milk to warm them from the inside out. Uncle Hiram pulled a flask of brandy from the buffalo coat pocket and added some to the milk. "It'll warm 'em up quicker," he said. "We never did get around to having our after-dinner brandy, but it'll do more good now, anyhow."

Solomon had revived and was rubbing Bertie's hands vigorously. His teeth were still chattering when he spoke. "When the wind died down a little, I got a glimpse of your lantern. We were trying to get to it when we bumped into your fence, so we were able to follow it. Then the snow started coming down again, and we couldn't see anything.

Lucky the fence led straight to your cowshed. We rested there for awhile until we were strong enough to follow that rope to your cabin."

Suddenly the wind hit the house again, so fierce it seemed to be trying to make up for lost time. Solomon shuddered. "We barely made it. A few minutes later, and we'd have been goners."

Their toes, fingertips and the tips of their noses were white, and could be frostbitten, but otherwise they seemed all right when they warmed up enough to tell their story.

"We went all the way to Ft. Benton to get married," Solomon told us. "We wanted to put some distance between us and Bertie's folks, and I figured I could get a job there." He held the cup to Bertie's lips and watched while she took a long swallow of hot milk before continuing. "But we both knew we'd have to face our folks sometime, and wanted to get it over with. Besides, it was Christmas. We hoped that might help. So we headed back home."

He drained his cup and handed it to Uncle Hiram. "We got to my folks' place on Christmas Eve. "They weren't mad that we'd gotten married ... just the way we did it. They'd known since summer how I felt about Bertie. And they like Bertie ... who wouldn't? They're going to help us get started on a place of our own."

Bertie wasn't shivering any longer. She gave me a wry smile. "I don't imagine we'll be as welcome at my folk's place. I dread it. That's why I wanted to get it over with. So we started out about noon yesterday."

"I sure didn't know a storm would hit us before we were halfway there," Solomon continued. "Our horse struggled as long as he could. We kept stopping to wipe the ice from his nose and eyes, and we got off and walked, hanging onto the reins." He swallowed hard before he went on. "Finally, he just couldn't go any farther. We had to leave him."

"It's all right, Sol. There wasn't anything else we could do." Bertie picked up the story. "We took shelter in a hollow under tree roots for awhile, but Solomon said we'd die there, so we started again. Every so often we rested when I just couldn't go any farther, but Sol always made me get started again."

Solomon looked soberly at the rest of us. With his white-tipped nose, red cheeks, chapped lips and eyes shining too brightly with unshed tears, he would have been a funny sight if the occasion wasn't so serious. "Finding your cabin was a Christmas miracle," he said. "By rights, we should be dead."

Our cabin might have been crowded, but it was full of joy as everyone stirred and greeted the newcomers. Will added coal to the stove. Babies woke and were nursed, children were soothed back to sleep. After Solomon and Bertie were fed, Solomon and Will rolled up in quilts on the floor with the other men. We put Bertie in our bed, but she began shivering again so violently that Elsa joined us. There wasn't room to move, much less turn over, but with a warm body wedged on either side of her, Bertie began to warm up. We all settled into an uneasy sleep, or at least rest, glad to be safe from that raging wind.

By the time a dim gray light filled the room, the wind had eased a bit. The men wrapped up and tended to the cattle while we women cooked a huge pot of oatmeal and fed all the children. When they got back inside, Uncle Hiram said, "It's easing up, but we'd better stay put till we're sure it's over."

Around noon a dim sun appeared and it was obvious that this storm, at least, was finished. Uncle Hiram insisted on driving the Schmidt family home in his sleigh while Elsa stayed behind to help me get the house back to rights. Will loaned Solomon and Bertie our horse, and they headed for the Yeagerman homestead, reluctant but determined.

By that evening the cabin was tidied, and diapers and baby garments hung on the line over the bed. Elsa had taken home the Schmidt diapers, still damp but clean, when she rode their horse home. I sent the two turkey carcasses, and part of the meat from the third turkey, with her, along with vegetables to make a big pot of nourishing soup, and some other leftovers.

Will and I sat down to a supper of leftover turkey and vegetables mixed into a hearty stew, each holding a twin on a knee.

"Well, we survived that one," Will said. "Didn't lose any stock this time, at least, and I think there's enough hay and coal left to last the rest of the winter, with any luck."

"And we're safe," I reminded him, kissing Maggie's fuzzy head. "Even Solomon and Bertie made it through." I took a bite of the stew, which tasted as good as Christmas dinner had. "Maybe when Bertie's ma learns how close they came to losing her, she'll be more forgiving."

"Maybe." Will didn't sound too convinced.

Will took care of the animals and stoked the stove with coal while I nursed the babies and put them down to sleep. We stretched in comfort under our bright patchwork quilt, and he pulled me into his arms. "I'd do that for you, you know," he said. "I'd push you and pull you and carry you to safety, like Solomon did."

"I know you would," I replied sleepily. And I did know. I wasn't the beautiful Victoria, but I was the mother of his babies. I was his partner in every way. When he smoothed back my hair and kissed me so deeply I tingled all over, I realized that if this was all there was, it was plenty.

Chapter 32

Maggie and Hi had croupy colds by New Year. Will rode into Choteau for kerosene and salt licks for the calves, and Bessie Haysom sent home a mixture of goose grease and camphor oil, with instructions to rub it on the babies' chests and lay a warm cloth over it. They were cranky and puny for awhile, but within a couple of weeks they were good as new.

We took the babies to church for the first time when they were well. There was a break in the bitter winter after that Christmas blizzard. It was finally a little warmer, and the babies were big enough that we felt safe taking them out.

Uncle Hiram surprised us. "Guess I'll tag along," he said when he heard of our plans. He'd driven over with our mail and a little wedge of sharp cheddar cheese from Bessie at the general store. "Church twice in thirty years might set a record for me." Sure enough, he wore all his finery again.

When I dressed the babies Sunday morning, I used as many of the gifts as possible that the church ladies had brought out to our cabin at the tea in November. The little knit sweaters, caps and booties were the off-white of undyed wool. Hi's crocheted shawl was a dainty blue, and Maggie's was pink. The lady who had made the wool bunting for that special day followed up with another one after the twins were born, so Hi and Maggie were each tucked into a cozy yellow bunting. We hurried out to the wagon before the babies could get overheated, and placed them in a laundry basket at my feet, with a wrapped hot brick at the foot and a quilt over the top of it to keep out the wind.

"B'Anne, are you sure they can breathe?" Will was trying to joke, I could tell, but his voice sounded a little worried.

"Well, we don't want them to get a chill, do we?" I was probably defensive, but this was the first time they'd been out of our snug cabin. On the ride to town, though, I did keep slipping my finger beneath the quilt flap and under little noses to make sure they were still breathing.

When we took them from their basket and hurried into the church, each carrying a baby, the ladies gathered around to admire them.

"Oh, my, look how they've grown." Bessie Haysom held Hi for a few moments before passing him to Mrs. Jensen, who had sewed the wool buntings.

"Oh, let's take them out of these. It's warm enough in here that they don't need them," she said, and removed Hi from his bunting. She clucked with dissatisfaction. "Oh, my, they're not the same shade of yellow. When I dyed the second one I thought I was using just the same amount of tansy blossom water, but I didn't get enough. Maggie's is a paler yellow." She tsked again. "You have to use fresh tansy blossoms, you know, so I picked them in the summer and steeped the blossoms in water to use later."

The lady holding Maggie began removing her bunting, too. "Well, when Hi's is washed again, the yellow might fade to match, especially if you didn't use as much salt to set the dye. You know, in big cities you can buy dye already made, but they don't have it at our general store."

"There's a lot of things we don't have at our store," Bessie Haysom said defensively. "This is not Great Falls, you know."

"I'm so glad I wasn't the only one who crocheted shawls," another woman said, seeing her creation wrapped around Maggie and wanting to change the subject quickly.

"Me, too," her friend agreed, "and I'm glad we chose different colors by accident."

Bertie and Solomon were already seated, but she hurried over to take a turn in baby-passing while her mother watched sourly from across the church. Evidently that meeting after the Christmas blizzard hadn't gone as well as they'd hoped.

After the opening prayer, the preacher surprised us. "We usually have the blessing of babies in May," he told the congregation, "but since these little ones are here for the first time, we're going to do it early."

He had Will and me come forward, each of us with a baby. He gave a prayer, then put his hand on Hi's little head and said, "Hiram William Carter, I dedicate you to Christ." Then, "Magda Caroline Carter, I dedicate you to Christ."

After the service, we rescued Uncle Hiram from the widow ladies, and he took us to dinner at the hotel dining room, a real treat, even if he did lean across his chicken and dumplings and whisper to me, "These dumplings don't hold a candle to yours, B'Anne. I swan, you have to hold yours down with a knife or they'd float off the plate."

"But these taste twice as good to me because I didn't cook them."

That night, the continuing letter home to Ma and Pa told all the details of the special day. I knew Pa would be happy about the babies' blessing. When I finished writing, Will took the pen and inkpot and added to the letter to his pa, too. We'd written to both families right after the blizzard, of course, and now we were working till the next letters got long enough to be worth the postage.

Bertie came to visit often. She and Sol were living with his parents. "Sometimes I just have to get out of there," she confessed one day as she helped me hang diapers out in the cold wind. "Sol's ma means well, but it seems like she's always looking over my shoulder, telling me what to do. Of course, it's her house so I can't say anything. And there's not much privacy for … well, you know." Even naughty Bertie could blush once in awhile.

"Soon as spring comes, everybody will pitch in and help you build a cabin." The idea seemed to comfort her a little.

"Well, spring can't come too soon." She flapped the last diaper, slipped the wooden peg in place, and picked up the empty basket.

"Could be worse. What if you had to live with *your* ma and pa?" I had to practically shout to be heard over a gust of wind, but Bertie heard it.

"Hah! We'd live in a dugout like the Schmidt's first."

After she left later that afternoon, I began to worry again about the Schmidt family. The winter was hard on us, even with our tar paper-insulated double floors and the hard-working Kitchen Queen range that turned coal into warmth. How on earth did they manage in their dugout?

Will went over next morning with a jug of milk, a crock of butter, and a batch of yeast bread. Making do with a little pot-bellied stove, there was no way Magda could bake. I knew the four loaves would be appreciated.

"They're managing, but just barely," he reported when he got home. "Uncle Hiram has had the older boys doing jobs I know he'd usually do himself ... mucking out horse stalls, spreading manure on the fields. He had them build some cupboards in his kitchen. The money he pays them helps." He carried his coffee cup over to the basket where Hi and Maggie were sleeping, and gazed down on them for a moment. Coming back to the table, he said, "The two littlest ones are sick. The baby is *really* sick."

I had a sudden picture of Hi and Maggie, sick in a cold, dank dugout. "Oh, Will, we have to do something." But what on earth could we do?

Chapter 33

We didn't have money to set the Schmidt family up in a comfortable place in town, but the thought of babies suffering in what amounted to a cave was more than I could bear thinking about.

"You have to bring Magda and the two little ones here, where it's warm. Whichever older girl is still home can manage the others. We can have the doctor come out, and pay him next summer, when we sell the calves."

Will's face was troubled. "What if they've got something catching?"

"How could they? They never see anybody to catch things from."

He was reluctant. Later I learned that the Schmidts were even more reluctant, but Magda wanted to do what was best for her babies.

The first thing we did when they arrived that afternoon was arrange beds ... another basket for year-old Greta, and a quilt-padded box for toddler Heinrich, on a bench close to the stove. Both had fevers, so we gave them lukewarm baths in the dishpan, rubbed their little chests with mild camphor and goose-grease, and put on the clean nightgowns Magda brought with her. When settled in their beds again, Heinrich, the toddler, cried fretfully. Greta, the baby, was beyond crying. She gave a few weak wails from time to time, but that was all.

Will went to Choteau to fetch the doctor. Magda put baby Greta to breast, but the child nursed only listlessly for a few minutes and gave up. "My milk not been much," Magda whispered.

From the looks of her, Magda must be approaching her due date. I wondered if the pregnancy had stopped her milk or if it had been caused by lack of food. I wet the corner of a clean cloth in milk and Magda held it to Greta's mouth. She took a few swallows. Then I gave Magda a glassful. "Drink this. Maybe it'll help you make milk."

While Magda rocked Greta, I fed Heinrich a few mouthfuls of warm bread and milk. He soon vomited them. After I got him cleaned up, I wet a cloth with cool water and sponged both children's faces, and as much of their bodies as I could manage without making them more uncomfortable. They were both so hot to the touch.

Hoofbeats and sled runners on the slushy ice were the best sounds I'd heard in a long time. The doctor opened his satchel and warmed the instrument he removed before lifting Heinrich's gown. "All the doctors back East are using this thing. Only had one of my own for a few years. It's a big help." He held it to Heinrich's chest and listened. When he listened to Greta, his expression grew even more somber. "They've both got considerable congestion in their lungs. The baby's is especially bad." Putting the instrument back into his bag, he continued, "They've both got high fevers. I've got a thing here I could use to take their temperature, but you have to hold it in place for five minutes, and I don't see any sense in putting them through that."

He took a little bottle from his bag. "This will help bring down the fever and make them feel better," he said, "but it tastes pretty terrible. You'll have to mix it with honey or jelly to get it down them."

I pulled out the cork and sniffed. "This smells like the willow bark concoction Ma used to make when we were sick."

The doctor smiled a little sheepishly. "That's what it is, all fancied up. Guess the old ways are best sometimes. Folks back East are trying to make it into a dry pill you can swallow with water, but haven't succeeded so far."

He touched little Greta's forehead again. "There's not much I can do. I pray this little one can make it." Eyes on Magda, he shook his head slightly. "You might set up a steam tent. Do you know how to do that?"

I nodded. Ma had done that for Susie's croup when she was a little mite.

"Keep bathing them with lukewarm water. They're probably not eating, sick as they are. Mix up a little sugar water and give them sips of it. Give them a little of the willow elixir every few hours, less than half a teaspoon. More like a quarter teaspoon, I guess. Mix it with honey if you have any. They'd breathe better propped up with pillows."

"I hold them," Magda said firmly. "I hold them up."

The doctor gave both children a dose of the elixir, scraping the dribbles off their chins with the spoon until he was sure they had enough to do some good. He put his hand on Magda's shoulder and said softly, "I'm sorry I can't do more, Mrs Schmidt. It looks very bad for the little girl. I'm so very sorry." Then he pulled on his coat and headed back to Choteau.

After he left, Will, Magda, and I rigged up a steam tent. Will strung a rope above the stove and we draped quilts from the rope to the bench where the babies' box and basket were placed, to trap the steam from the water boiling in my largest soup kettle. Magda and I filled the stovetop with more pans of water and moved the rocking chair under the tent, too. Magda rocked little Greta, and soon both their faces were shiny with steam.

I gave Heinrich several sips of the sugar water, and he kept it down. He fell into a deeper sleep after the doctor left. Probably the medicine was helping. We checked him often, and before long he felt cooler.

Greta seemed to breathe a little easier under the steam tent. Magda wet the cloth in the sugar water and the baby sucked it … listlessly, to be sure, but enough to get some in her body.

I kept busy topping up the kettles with water, and soon the entire cabin was moist with the steam that escaped the tent. The windows were completely fogged up, with little rivulets running down to the sills.

Magda was completely occupied with her little ones, and didn't want to eat, but I knew she needed nourishment for the unborn baby and if possible, to make milk for Greta. I dished up some of the stew that was almost crowded off the stove by pots of boiling water, buttered a slice of bread and poured a glass of milk. Then I rocked Greta for a few minutes while Magda ate. She bolted down the food, eager to get back to her baby.

During the night, Heinrich continued to improve. He fought the next dose of medicine, but Will and I won the battle … one holding the child still and one using the spoon. A little later, he ate warm bread and milk, and this time kept it down.

While I was feeding Heinrich, Greta cried more strongly than she had before. Magda called out in happy amazement. "B'Anne, look. I have milk. She pointed to the wet spot on the front of her dress. I quickly helped her lower the shoulder so she could offer Greta her breast. The look on Magda's face was blissful as her baby suckled for a few minutes.

The joy didn't last long. Greta vomited the milk. We gave her a little more sugar water and elixir, but her breathing worsened. During the rest of the night, the baby didn't vomit again, and no longer cried. She was using all the strength she had to draw labored breaths.

When dawn was turning the dripping windows gray, little Greta gave up her struggle. Magda forced breath into her mouth until at last Will said, "It's no use, Magda. She's gone."

Except for the brief times I took to nurse Hi and Maggie, Will had been taking care of them. Now he took over for Magda, too. I'm sorry to say I was too broken up to be of much help. He went out on the back porch and rang the bell for a long time, and soon Mr. Schmidt and the oldest son showed up on their sway-backed horse. Will sent the younger man to Choteau with instructions to tell the priest what had happened, and also to let the three German families the girls had worked for know.

Uncle Hiram had heard the bell, too, and rode in shortly after the Schmidt men. He went to tell the rest of their family what had happened. Then he, too, headed to Choteau, to bring back extra supplies.

Magda was grieving, but stoic until she touched the milk-stained spots on her dress. "When too late, then I have milk," she sobbed bitterly.

I was angry at my own weakness in the face of this mother who was suffering so much more. I braced myself, in order to help her. "But, Magda, she had the comfort of your breast. And you held her in your arms. She knew she was loved when she passed. Even a little baby knows what love feels like." I had managed to speak the words but started crying again as I held Magda close. I felt her nod against my shoulder.

"Yes, love. That all I could give her. It not enough." She gulped down a sob, then said, "So little time we had her. She took her first steps just a few days ago."

Heinrich woke, and Will picked him up; then changed his wet didie ... awkwardly, but he did it. Even at that awful time, I realized how lucky I was that Will and I had stuck together to work things out.

The priest arrived, followed a little later by the three German ladies. The priest did his mysterious things with holy water and Latin. The three ladies washed Greta and dressed her in the clean hand-me-down garments one of them had brought, a beautiful little white gown trimmed with handmade lace and a crocheted shawl. With her pale skin, ash-blonde hair and long lashes resting on her cherub cheeks, Greta looked like she was a baby angel, which of course she was.

Uncle Hiram drove his wagon to the Schmidt dugout and brought back the rest of the family. Konrad, Magda and little Heinrich were going to stay with us for a few days. Elsa, her oldest brother and the two youngest children were to stay with Uncle Hiram. The three German families were going to take the six remaining children.

Little Greta's funeral was held next day at the Catholic church in Choteau, and she was buried in the graveyard behind the church. The family tearfully told her, and each other, goodbye and separated to go to the different homes giving them refuge. Konrad Schmidt insisted on going back to their claim, but Magda and Heinrich would be with us until Heinrich was completely well again. As everyone drifted away from the cemetery, my heart ached for the Schmidts. All they had was each other, and now they were being parted. I hoped it would only be for a few days.

Chapter 34

Heinrich continued to improve, and Maggie and Hi miraculously stayed well. I had so quickly assured Will that our babies wouldn't catch what the Schmidt babies had, but after watching Greta die, I had lost my confidence. I knew I couldn't be as strong as Magda.

She washed and folded away Greta's little gowns and blanket, silent tears slipping down her cheeks as she did so. She lovingly took care of two-year-old Heinrich. I could tell it helped her and caused her immense pain at the same time. I offered to do it, but she quietly refused.

"Nein. He is my baby now." She didn't need to say more.

Konrad stayed on at their dugout, in case a government agent might come by and find the claim unoccupied, but Magda and the children didn't. Greta's death had evidently made quite a few people feel pity. An abandoned house on the edge of town had been standing empty for over a year; now a group of people cleaned it, patched the tarpaper roof, replaced a broken window or two, and repaired enough castoff furniture to make it livable. Just barely livable, actually, but more comfortable than the dugout.

"It's what we should've done when they drove into town," Uncle Hiram muttered as he searched his shelves to see if there was one last blanket he hadn't already donated. "It's a crying shame it took the death of an innocent baby to open people's hearts. We did the best we could, but it wasn't enough."

We helped bring what they could use from the dugout, leaving the bare minimum for Konrad to cook his simple meals. He slept rolled up in the buffalo robe Uncle Hiram had given them, so Magda was able to bring the rest of the bedding for the children. It was a pitiful amount to haul, but ladies from the Catholic church and from our community church donated what linens, kitchen items and outgrown clothing they could spare. By the time they were settled, the Schmidts had more than when they arrived at Choteau last August, except for one important thing … baby Greta.

Two days after the move was completed, one of the Schmidt boys walked from town to tell us that Magda had safely delivered a baby girl, and had named her Greta Beatrice. I was honored to have my name used, but my heart ached to think of year-old Greta being so soon replaced by another with the same name. But perhaps it was an honor for her, too. I knew that in Magda's heart, the child she lost would never be replaced.

Next day, I packed a basket with milk, butter, fresh bread, chicken and dumplings and an applesauce cake, and prepared to go see the new baby. Not wanting to offend any of the church ladies who had sewed for Hi and Maggie by giving away an item from them, I packed two of the little nightgowns Ma had made for me when I was carrying, as a gift for the new Greta.

I nursed Hi and Maggie until they fell asleep with milk running out the corners of their mouths, got in the wagon Will had hitched up for me, and left him in charge.

The weather was mild for mid-February. There was a good breeze, but it wasn't uncomfortably windy. I steered the horse over the prairie along the edge of the lane, to avoid the mud, and enjoyed the sound of the breeze through the dry, dead grass. It swished like a lady's silk skirt. I saw that the pussy-willows along the creek were starting to burst out, and told myself to ask Will to cut an armful to brighten up the cabin. I didn't lollygag along the way, though because I knew I had just four hours until the twins were hungry again and roaring to be fed.

Magda was well, and so were all the children, although they missed Konrad. He'd come in yesterday with their son, Sev, and spent the night with his family, and returned to the claim that morning. Elsa told me quietly that she knew her father didn't feel right being warm from other folks' coal and fed with their food. All the older children were saving every penny they could from their jobs, after spending the least possible for food. Fortunately, Magda knew how to feed many on a little.

The baby seemed healthy, in spite of probably not having enough nourishment in the womb. You can't call a three-day-old infant pretty, but she was beginning to lose that wrinkled, old-man look, and her redness was fading to pink.

I gave my gifts and admired the baby. Then I spent some time with Heinrich, who'd only had a short time of being the doted-on youngest child before being bumped out of place again. The full feeling in my breasts as I hugged everyone goodbye reminded me that my four hours would be up by the time I reached home, and Will would have his hands full of screaming babies.

I could hear both babies wailing when I stopped the wagon, so I looped the reins over the fence and hurried inside. Will was holding crying Maggie in one arm and using the other hand to pat Hi's back as he shrieked in the basket. He looked pathetically grateful to see me. I told myself snidely that I probably looked as good as Victoria to him right at that moment.

"Just let me warm my hands, and I'll start feeding Hi." I dipped the end of a clean rag in a little sugar water and gave it to Will to pacify Maggie until I was ready for her. Soon the settling of coal in the Kitchen Queen and the smacking and gulping of hungry Hi were the only sounds in the cabin, and Will breathed a sigh of relief.

"Did they give you a bad time?" I asked innocently.

"Oh, we managed fine until about fifteen minutes ago. Then Hi got hungry and that woke up Maggie. But I'll tell you one thing. You'd better stay healthy. I can do fine as their papa, but I just don't have the right equipment to be their mama." He leaned over and kissed me on the cheek. "How were the Schmidts?"

"They're doing well, but I feel sorry for Konrad. The man's not used to having strangers provide for his family."

"That would be hard. I can imagine how he feels." He jiggled Maggie, who was beginning to wave her arms and make complaining noises. "Is that little pig full enough to keep him quiet for a few minutes? This one's deciding sugar water isn't what she's supposed to be getting."

I always enjoyed nursing the babies, even though with twins, it seemed like a good amount of my time was spent doing it. Sitting in the rocking chair with a warm little body at my breast, while the wind whipped around the cabin and the coals settled in the stove, was for some reason so satisfying. I was glad I had plenty of milk for both of them, and for more than one reason. I hoped (and trusted) that nursing would keep me from getting pregnant. Judging from seeing the families at church it didn't always work, but still I hoped. Will was a gentle person; I didn't think he'd force it if I didn't welcome him, but that special closeness was something I treasured. It was the time I was pretty sure Victoria was the farthest thing from his mind.

I guess being in the family way was still on my mind when Bertie visited a few days later. I took one look at her sallow face and had a good idea what she was going to tell me. She wasn't too happy about it.

"We don't even have a place of our own yet," she said glumly. "Sol's ma already thinks I'm a poor excuse for a wife; imagine how it's going to be with a baby. I won't be able to do anything right!"

"Oh, you'll be in your own place by then. Soon as the ground firms up and crops are in, we'll all get together and help. There're even some things us women can do to help, like hold boards for sawing, and make shingles. We'll bring food and eat outside on sawhorse tables. It'll be fun."

"Nothing seems like much fun right now. And don't talk about food and eating."

"Oh, that'll pass in a couple of months. And just think … being a grandma might bring your ma around. After all, you'll be the first daughter having a baby, and that makes a difference."

After Bertie left, seeming a little more chipper than when she arrived, I thought about what I'd told her. Maybe it was different with a son's child, and that's why it didn't soften Will's ma any. We heard regularly from his pa, and from my family, letters that were full of questions about us and the babies, and news about life back home … enough news to make me a little homesick sometimes, thinking of my baby sister growing into a young lady, and my sweet cousin Rose planning to be married this summer in that beautiful pink dress she'd loaned me for my own wedding last April.

Will's pa's letters always said, "Ma is well," or "Ma has been ailing some from the catarrh," or "from the quinsy," but there was never a note from Mrs. Carter herself. It made me feel bad for Will, but there didn't seem anything I could do about it.

Soon, I was too busy to worry much about it. A nice Chinook wind came and melted the last of the snow. The sun and Montana wind worked to dry out the soil enough that Will could plow and harrow a big garden space for me. I'd planted seeds in boxes on the windowsills to give them a head start on growing time. Now I began planting the hardier vegetables, holding off on the tender ones until we could be pretty sure we'd had the last frost. I put Hi and Maggie in a big wicker basket close to where I worked, and they were happy to be out in the fresh air, and with wide eyes, followed the clouds scudding across the blue sky.

Even without the garden, I'd have been working every minute. As Ma used to say when she put her hands on her aching back at the end of washday, "Men may work from sun to sun, but woman's work is never done." Washing diapers and clothes for two babies was a never-ending job. I was grateful when the weather was dry and windy enough to hang them outside. Taking care of the milk from our cow... straining it, churning butter, making soft cheese ... took time. Seeing to the chickens, cleaning the house, trying to scrape meals out of the foods I'd canned and dried last summer ... my days were full. In the evening, I mended and darned and knitted for Will and the babies.

And when the mending was done, Will banked the fire and turned down the damper while I checked the babies one last time. Then we blew out the kerosene lamps and curled up under the patchwork quilt together, and the tiredness of the day disappeared. Sometimes I never even wasted a thought about whether nursing would protect me from getting in the family way again.

Chapter 35

Elsa worked full time now for a lady in town, cleaning and cooking and minding her children. Often on her half-day off she walked out to spend some time with me. We'd shared hardships and good times together, and she'd become my best friend. She usually brought sewing with her. She and her mother and sisters were busy sewing whenever she could afford to buy cloth, getting ready for the cabin that was still just a daydream. Elsa and I talked and drank rosehip tea while we worked. We'd used the last of the real tea from the caddy, but rosehips made a tart, refreshing drink.

While I dished up supper one evening after we'd spent the afternoon together, I told Will how lucky I felt to have my two best friends living nearby. "Someday our children can play with Bertie's and Elsa's. Why, we could even be in-laws someday."

"Aren't you getting a little bit ahead of yourself?" Will asked, with a laugh.

"Well, no. Once a person puts in the work to get settled here, they're not going to be in a hurry to move."

Elsa's Bernhard arrived at the end of February. Will and I decorated our cabin with pussy-willows from down by the creek for their wedding.

Elsa was beautiful in my best dress, the deep red merino trimmed with black grosgrain ribbon that she'd tried to squeeze me into the first time I went to church after the babies were born. Her long blonde braids crowned her head like a coronet. Uncle Hiram showed up in his old-fashioned best clothes, and he brought a red silk rose for Elsa to carry on top of the family's German Bible. I don't know where he'd found a silk rose in Choteau. Maybe it was something he'd given his long-dead wife Mary, and treasured for years.

After I'd helped Elsa dress, and I'd nursed the babies enough that I hoped they'd sleep through the wedding, I put on my Sunday-best brown alpaca dress. I dressed it up with an ivory colored collar and cuffs my cousin Rose had sent me. She said she no longer had anything they matched, and I certainly wasn't too proud for hand-me-downs. Elsa helped me dress my hair up fancy and fasten it with my tortoise-shell combs. My bosom filled out the bodice much more than it had done when I wore it to church back home; the babies were to thank for that. The waist nipped in nicely. My cheeks were rosy and my eyes sparkling with happiness. I wasn't as beautiful as Elsa, but that's as it should be. After all, she was the bride. But when Will raised his eyebrows at my appearance, and tucked my arm in his, I felt a special glow.

Uncle Hiram provided the ingredients for the cake I baked, and the wedding supper that went with it. We'd have been lucky to come up with turnip stew to feed that many people. The feast of Christmas was a thing of the past ... long past.

Will spoke up after the guests left. "B'Anne, that was some to-do you put together. I was proud as a peacock that we could give our friends a nice wedding. And the way you look ... oh, my!"

The kiss that finished his message tingled to my toes. The next day, Elsa and Bernhard filed a homestead claim on land beyond her family's place. What a busy spring and summer we looked forward to (or maybe, just a little bit, dreaded) with three cabins to build: the Schmidt's, Elsa and Bernhard's, and Bertie and Solomon's. Will said with a little sigh, "The older Schmidt boys will be next, soon as they find wives. There'll be Schmidt homesteads far as the eye can see." But I was just glad to look forward to having neighbors close enough to visit with, especially one like Magda that I could ask questions from. She'd never replace my ma, but what she didn't know about mothering would fit in a flea's ear ... an old saying Pa used.

Life seemed to be galloping along at a fast, but contented, pace. Then one afternoon in early March, Uncle Hiram rode over. "The telegraph office sent a boy out to my place with this," he explained, holding a piece of paper out to Will. "He wasn't sure how much farther you lived, so I said I'd see that you got it."

It was a telegram from Will's pa. His ma was real sick, it said, and begged to see him. He'd send a bank note to repay Uncle Hiram if he'd cover the steamboat fare for us to come home.

Oh, we were torn about what to do. Will said we could get one of the Schmidt boys to tend to the animals, but then I thought of the hens getting broody and hiding their nests so I had to hunt them down every day. What would happen to the delicate seedlings growing on our windowsills when the house got empty and cold? What if our good milk cow got out during the day when nobody was around, and wandered off, maybe mired down in the mud by the creek, or was attacked by a hungry wolf?

The idea of seeing my folks again made me so excited that I wanted to pack our clothes right then. But then I thought: what if we left, and a government man came out and decided we had deserted our claim? It was prime land, and we'd put enough sweat into it that we couldn't stand to lose the place.

I stiffened my spine, like Ma always instructed. "Will, you need to go, but I'll stay here and take care of the place."

He liked to have had a conniption fit. "Are you crazy? Leave you here with two babies and a herd of calves? We're not even going to talk about it!"

Well, that raised my dander a bit. "You know good and well that when you tell me we're not even going to talk about it, that means we're for sure going to talk about it."

"It's for your own good, B'Anne. Think of all the things that could happen. The babies could get sick. *You* could get sick. The calves could get sick … or get loose. You couldn't leave the babies alone to round them up." He gave me a long look, then said, "A bad person could find out there's a woman out here alone. Things could happen."

By now I was doubting my idea, too. But not only did I need to protect all our work … it was a chance to show, once and for all, that he'd made the right choice when he married me.

"Birgitta Schmidt would come and stay with me, so I wouldn't be alone. And Uncle Hiram is close if I need him. I could ring the bell, and he'd be here before you know it."

We talked until Will had to do chores while I got supper. Then we talked through supper, and our voices got loud and angry enough that it upset the babies. We quieted down, ashamed of ourselves, and discussed the question more calmly. Finally, under the patchwork quilt, we decided.

"All right," Will said. "You win. I'll go, but only if Birgitta stays with you nights, Uncle Hiram checks in on you often, and one of the Schmidt boys helps with the chores." He wrapped his arms around me. "And every day I'm gone will feel like a year."

Chapter 36

It took Will a day to make all the arrangements for leaving. He drove to Choteau and brought back another load of coal, although winter was surely finished. He also brought back two new wooden barrels and filled them with water on the porch by the back door.

"For washing and such," he explained. "I know you'll want fresh water to drink, but that won't be so much to carry up from the creek. I'll ask Sev or Franz Schmidt to do that. Wish I'd got a well dug before now."

"Will, there's no way you could have dug a well. There hasn't been time. We can do it this summer."

Uncle Hiram picked him up before daylight the next day. They were both going to ride horseback to Ft. Benton, and then Uncle Hiram would lead the extra horse home. It would be quicker than taking the stage.

The house seemed eerily empty after they left, which was silly. Will had been out in the fields or on errands to Choteau for most of the day many times, and the house hadn't seemed empty. But the thought of him being gone for so long left me with a lonely feeling in my stomach, or heart, or wherever that feeling was. The trip down the Missouri River from Ft. Benton to Sioux City would be at least ten days long. Even if he spent only a few days with his folks, he'd be gone almost a month.

I washed dishes and threw the water out on the flowers I'd planted by the back door, dressed the twins and put them in their basket while I worked in the garden planting onion sets and spinach seeds. After lunch, I scrubbed the floor and even tried to take a nap, although lying down in the daytime seemed shamefully lazy. I couldn't sleep, though. My mind was too busy imagining how far along the way Will had gotten.

Dusk was beginning to fall by the time Birgitta arrived, and I was glad to see her. Shadows were filling the little hollows of the prairie. For all my brave talk, I was glad I wouldn't be spending the night alone. When Sev Schmidt came to do the chores, we invited him to take supper with us, and he seemed glad to accept. He and two of the other older boys were staying at the dugout with Konrad, clearing land for a cabin and using Uncle Hiram's team and plow to plant a crop of oats. From the way Sev ate the stew and cornbread, he was plenty tired of his father's cooking.

Next morning Birgitta left early for her mother's helper job in town, and I was alone again. I opened the doors and windows to let the fresh air in, but the wind sighing through the grass was such a fearsome sound that I closed them again. All day I felt unsettled and on edge, like I was waiting for something awful to happen. I scolded myself … tried to tell myself what Ma would have said: *Buck up, young lady. Stiffen that backbone, B'Anne. The good Lord might give us a steep mountain to climb, but He helps us find the hand-holds.* It didn't help much. When the babies were sleeping, I went out to work in the garden. Then in the distance, I made out two men on horseback, riding across the prairie. Remembering Will's warning of what might happen if bad men learned about a woman out here alone, I hurried inside and locked the door. I felt foolish even as I did it, knowing it was probably just a couple of homesteaders on their way to Choteau.

Birgitta arrived, and it seemed like I couldn't stop talking. She must have thought I'd lost my mind, babbling like the creek in spring rush. Looked like I wasn't as good at being alone as I thought I'd be.

Next afternoon, Uncle Hiram came by. He'd seen Will off on the steamboat at Ft. Benton. He grinned at me. "Sure was one down-in-the-mouth young fellow, Will was. I know he'll be back up here soon as he can."

He had a cup of coffee, gave me the mail he'd picked up in Choteau, and went back home.

There was a letter from my good friend Minna. I could hardly wait to get the babies down to sleep so I could read it. She'd written it more than two weeks before and apologized for the delay in getting it mailed. I smiled as I read the latest news about folks in our hometown, and then I got to the sentence near the bottom that gave me a chill. "Can you believe that Victoria is gallivanting around the country when her husband's been dead such a short time? I saw her yesterday. She was coming out of the Carter's store. I never saw such widow's weeds in my life! Big black bonnet with veiling down to her shoulders, black dress with the skirt full enough and lacy enough to make curtains for the church and have some left over. Carried a black lace parasol. I hate to sound mean-spirited, but that woman wasn't mourning widowhood, she was celebrating it. And Will's ma was right beside her, chatting like old friends."

I dropped the letter in my lap and sat there shaking. Will's ma wasn't sick. Will was back home without me or the babies. Victoria was there ... a wealthy available widow now, beautiful as ever and stylishly dressed, even if it was in black. And I was here, a poor farmer's wife in a four-year-old patched, faded calico dress, in stocking feet because my mud-stained boots were drying on the porch.

The weather seemed to feel the same way I did. The wind picked up and howled around the eaves, and rain splattered fiercely against the windowpanes. One of the babies began to cry, and the other joined in. I was so exhausted I couldn't move, even to go to them. When Birgitta got home I was still sitting there with the letter in my lap while Hi and Maggie howled hungrily.

Birgitta changed the babies' wet diapers and put dry gowns on them, then brought Hi to me while she soothed Maggie. "B'Anne, what's the matter? Did Will's mama die?"

A mean part of me thought *I wish that was all that's the matter.* "No," I said, and then blubbered out the whole sorry story. I offered Birgitta the letter, but she shook her head.

"I'm trying, but I don't read English so good yet," she admitted. "Read me the part that's making you cry."

So I did. She took Hi and gave me Maggie, then said thoughtfully, "I don't blame you for being worried, B'Anne. But this letter took days to get here from Iowa and was written two weeks before that. Maybe Will's mother got sick after it was written. You don't know anything bad is happening." She patted my hand. "Will loves you and these babies, B'Anne. Surely you know that."

"You haven't seen Victoria," I wailed. Maggie dropped the nipple and wailed along with me, so I wiped my eyes on my sleeve and tried to calm down. "She's beautiful, and stylish, and knows how to charm the birds out of the trees ... or the boys off the farms."

Birgitta, wiser than her years from helping her mother with babies most of her life, looked at me like I imagined a stern older sister would. "You've got to calm yourself down or your milk will dry up. Do you have any chamomile tea?" She made me a cup, with lots of milk in it, and started supper, talking to me over her shoulder all the while. She made me another cup at bedtime, but I still cried before falling asleep.

Next day I tried to stay busy, which, of course, wasn't hard. I could always be busy. But this time I found my hands suddenly idle, as my mind went back to Iowa. He might be there by now. What is he doing right this minute? Has he discovered his mother wasn't really sick at all but had just plotted to get him back in town for Victoria's visit? Was he angry, and even now on the steamboat up the Missouri River to Ft. Benton? Or was Victoria casting the same spell over him that she had summer before last when Will's and my plans to get married went up in smoke?

Sometimes my mind didn't go to Iowa, but to the future ... to what that future would be without Will. Would I go back home and expect Ma and Pa to help me? I knew they'd take us in and make us welcome, but still, they'd raised their family. Didn't seem fair to expect them to start all over again with noisy nights and teething babies. Would I take Hi and Maggie and go to Aunt Isabel, as I'd thought about doing so long ago, before Will and I got married? Who would take care of them while Aunt Isabel and I worked? What kind of work could I do? In a factory, maybe, or as a kitchen maid in some fancy home? But a kitchen maid wouldn't earn enough to pay someone to take care of the two babies, and to feed and clothe them, as well as myself.

Then I'd look down at the beans I was sorting, or the diaper I was scrubbing on the washboard, or the milk bucket I was scouring, and force myself back to work. Taking care of the babies was the only time my mind didn't wander. I'd let them cry yesterday while I sat in shock, but that was never going to happen again. No matter what happened between us, I was going to give those babies the best life I could ... with or without Will.

Chapter 37

Uncle Hiram came by the next day to check on me. He saw that my spirits were low, but I couldn't bring myself to tell him why. "Don't know why you're so down in the mouth," he joked. "That boy'll be home before you know it." I perked up some to make him feel better and let him think loneliness was the only thing bothering me.

Each evening when Birgitta got home from work in town she chattered with news: how her mother and the other children were doing; what her father and brothers were planting; what was new and interesting on the store shelves. From the minute she walked in the door and took off her muddy boots until bedtime, the house felt almost normal. But when the kerosene lamp was blown out and Birgitta instead of Will was sharing the bed with me, I felt so awful, I didn't think I could bear it.

Even talking to God didn't seem to help. My spirit was in a hole so black and deep that I didn't think I'd ever get out. "Please, God," I prayed desperately, "please send Will back to us. Please let him choose us over Victoria." Then my final prayer gave me a little peace. "Thank you, God, for the year of happiness and for the beautiful babies you sent us. And please give me the strength to live with whatever happens to us."

I plodded along for a few days. Ma always said time made bad things better, but she was wrong about this one. Each day I looked at the calendar and tried to figure where Will was.

On the twelfth day, Uncle Hiram rode over in the early morning with another telegram. I took it with trembling fingers. I was torn. I was eager to learn what it said, but frightened to unfold it, afraid of what I'd read. If the message was what I dreaded most, that Will was staying in Iowa, I didn't want to break down in front of Uncle Hiram.

"I already read it, B'Anne. Rustle your bones. We've got things to do," he snapped.

According to the telegram, Will's mother was seriously ill and wanted to see the babies, and talk to me. Could Uncle Hiram watch our place while it was empty and buy steamboat tickets for me and a Schmidt girl to come along and help me with the babies? Pa would pay him back.

Uncle Hiram stroked his bristly chin. "Well, guess the old girl has an ounce of human kindness in her after all. Either that, or she doesn't want to meet her Maker with a guilty conscience. Don't worry about a thing. I got the re-payment for Will's trip a couple of days ago. I'll just put some with it, if we need to." He stood and slammed his hat on his head. "Get packed while I go to town and see which Schmidt girl can make the trip with you. I don't think the one younger than Birgitta is working. Helga, I think her name is. She's only ten or eleven, but all those girls are good with babies."

While he was gone, I got the babies' latest washing off the line and folded, and sorted out the best of my clothes, such as they were. I'd never been on a steamboat before. Did folks dress fancy for the trip? Well, it didn't much matter. I'd wear my church dress, and keep my very best one to change into before stepping off the boat to meet Will.

Uncle Hiram returned with Helga, her clothing in a carpet bag. Thankfully, he had stopped and got his own two bags for me to use. We made short work of packing and leaving. In Choteau, we cashed the bank note from Will's pa a few days earlier, and I ran into the general store to tell Bessie Haysom what was happening. She sent me off with a hug, a basket of hastily gathered snacks, and two clumsy looking glass nursing bottles with big, awkward rubber nipples.

"Just in case," she explained. "You've got a lot of bad things happening, and the worry of a trip with two little babies. Your milk might dry up." Then she handed me a little brown medicine bottle. "If they get to be just too much to handle, and people complain about the noise, give them each just a drop of this on their tongue. It's paregoric ... it calms babies. If you don't need it on the boat, save it for when they're teething. Just a drop rubbed on their gums." She tucked the bottle into the basket of cheese, crackers, hard sausage and dried apricots. "Just a drop, now. It's strong."

"I hope I don't have to use it, but thank you."

Uncle Hiram drove up with the buggy he had rented at the livery stable, and we were off to Ft. Benton. "This'll take longer than horseback, but horseback's no way to haul babies." Before we had gone very far, I began to think maybe we should have used horses instead. There was a road to go the seventy mile distance, but it hadn't dried out completely from the winter snow melt. To avoid treacherous-looking mud holes, Uncle Hiram often drove the team up off the road onto the prairie. We made good time on the straight stretches, though, letting the horses have their heads. He knew there was a stage stop halfway to Ft. Benton, but darkness fell long before we reached it. Uncle Hiram drove the buggy a little way off the road for the night, knowing we'd surely get bogged down if we tried to travel in the darkness. We ate from Bessie's basket, I nursed the babies, and we huddled in buffalo robes and blankets. Helga and I each nestled a baby in our arms to keep them warm.

We started again at daylight, stopped for a hot meal at the stage stop, and reached Ft. Benton very late that night. The stores, saloons and restaurants that naturally thrive around an army base made it seem like a booming place, compared to quiet Choteau. The saloons were open, but all the stores were closed, of course, as well as the steamboat office. The schedule in the window showed there'd be no departure the next day, and I was a little relieved. I was exhausted. Will's ma could wait one day longer.

Uncle Hiram got a room at the hotel for Helga and me, and one across the hall for himself. The owner heated up some stew left from the dining room's evening meal, and after washing up in the bathroom down the hall, we fell into our beds.

Next day, Uncle Hiram brought back our tickets. "Let's see what Ft. Benton has to offer," he suggested after breakfast. "I remember there's a dry goods store down the street, and I'll bet they have ready-made dresses. If ever anybody needed them, it's you two young women."

I stubbornly resisted. Every bite of food we'd purchased had slid down my throat on a worry, and the worries stayed there much longer than the taste of the food. Uncle Hiram insisted.

"Your meals are included on the boat," he argued. "When Will meets you at Sioux City and takes you to Balsamview, you won't need money. But you do need something plain, simple and comfortable to wear on the boat." He held up his hand to halt my protest. "And if you keep on arguing with me, I'll just go down there myself, look around till a I find a couple of girls about the same size as you two, and make them try on dresses until I pick something out. I'll pay for them myself, and you can feel guilty all the way down the Missouri River."

Helga and I looked at each other. I could tell the idea of a bright new dress was filling her mind, just like mine. I imagined greeting Will in something pretty. I'd never match Victoria, I knew, but maybe I could put a little spark in Will's eyes.

It was wonderful. I got a trim, dark gray serge skirt with a matching blouse, gray with little pink flowers. It wouldn't show soil badly, and with my pink Christmas shawl and only bonnet, would make a pretty outfit. Helga got a red and blue checked gingham, trimmed with ruffles and blue ribbon that matched her blue eyes.

Uncle Hiram took us to dinner in the hotel dining room in our new clothing, and we felt as good as anyone there. It was his treat, and he wouldn't let us order anything cheap and simple. Instead he ordered for us, and we finished up with Floating Island pudding. After the meal, Helga and I took turns, one caring for the babies while the other soaked in the porcelain tub in the bathroom down the hall ... a pleasure neither of us had ever experienced before.

Next morning, Uncle Hiram helped us on board and handed me the envelope with the money left over from Will's pa's bank note, and the advance Will's Pa had authorized the bank to make to him. The boat had already pulled away before I looked inside and realized that the boat tickets were the only expense he'd taken out. Clutching the envelope in my fist, I shook it at him as we noisily pulled out into the river. He grinned, waved his hat at us, and we were on our way down the Missouri River to Iowa.

Chapter 38

That trip down the Missouri River was rugged. Our steamboat wasn't a big Mississippi luxury vessel like Will's ma had once described, with a piano and stage, and a lounge for men to gamble, smoke cigars and drink whiskey. Instead, it was a parcel ship, built for hauling supplies and folks who didn't need a lot of frills. Folks joked about the Missouri River being "not deep enough to plow but too thick to drink." Our boat was especially made for shallower rivers. The engine was on the deck, taking up space that could have been used for relaxing and watching the scenery.

Our berth had two bunks, with barely enough room between them to turn around. Helga and I each slept with a baby. With space so limited, I was glad I hadn't tried to bring their basket. The meals were served at a long table and benches, and they were simple, not much better than what we'd have been cooking back home. No fancy dining room here. I was glad. It meant I could put on one of the two dresses I'd brought, and save my new skirt and shirtwaist for meeting Will.

For the most part, the babies were good. My milk didn't dry up, so I didn't have to use the glass bottles. The soft rocking of the boat seemed to soothe them, and they only had a few bouts of crying. When these happened, the little brown bottle of paregoric stayed in the basket. Helga and I wrapped Hi and Maggie warmly, climbed the narrow stairs, and walked around the deck with them. We saw the land slip by, and deer and antelope lift their heads to watch us as we watched them.

Helga and I felt like we were skimming along, never having ridden on a steamboat before, but some of the other passengers complained about the slowness. Going downstream as we were, we could easily have made the top speed of eleven or twelve miles an hour, but the river was high and swift with the snow melt.

"You'd think the company could afford to send the snag boat down more often than once a week," one man grumbled as we maneuvered delicately around an uprooted tree. "Oughta have a snag boat come down in front of every parcel boat, clear the way for us."

The boat had to edge slowly through the bad spots, and only two nights had enough moonlight to let us travel through the night. I didn't sleep well those nights, clutching Maggie to me and waiting for the crunch of the boat hitting an obstacle. On the other nights we tied up and waited for dawn. The gentle rocking of the boat felt like I imagined a cradle would, and I slept as soundly as Hi and Maggie.

Before we got to Sioux City, Helga and I carried down the bucket of hot water that one of the stokers had kindly given us. We cooled it down and gave the babies and ourselves sponge-baths with the scented soap I'd tucked in at the last minute for just this purpose. Then we donned our new dresses and put fresh nightgowns on the twins and wrapped them in their pretty shawls.

At Sioux City, the gangplank was barely in place when Will ran up on the deck and pulled me into his arms. He knocked my bonnet askew when he buried his face in my hair, but I didn't care, His arms felt so good to me that I wondered if I was glowing like a candle.

Finally, he released me, said, "Hello, Helga," and bent to look at Hi and Maggie. "They've grown!"

"Well, it's been almost three weeks since you saw them," I reminded him.

He picked up our carpet bags and helped us down the gangplank and into his pa's buggy. "Your folks are anxious to see you. I had supper there night before last and told them everything I could think of about the babies, but they want to see the real thing."

"How's your ma?" I wanted to add, "And have you seen Victoria lately?" but I didn't.

"About the same. Not good." He gave me a bleak look. "I wouldn't have asked you to make this hard trip without me, but she's determined she has to talk to you. I think she thinks she's going to die."

It took us several hours to get to Balsamview, and by the time we arrived, Helga, the babies, and I, were all exhausted. How I would have loved to go straight to my folks' house, hand Ma the twins, and climb the stairs to my old bedroom for a long nap.

Instead, we were welcomed warmly by Will's pa, greeted by his two sisters who had come to meet us, and ushered in to see Mrs. Carter.

Her bedroom was darkened, but as soon as we entered she said, "Open the curtains," and held out her arms for the babies. After examining both their faces closely, she said, "Pretty as two little pictures. They're the spitting image of their father at this stage, especially this one."

The one she meant was Hi. I bit my lip to keep silent. It sure sounded like she had to see them to make sure Will was really their father. Will squeezed my hand. He knew what I was thinking.

After a few minutes she gestured for us to take the sleeping babies. "Could I have a few minutes alone with B'Anne?" she said softly.

When the others were gone, she rubbed the edge of the patchwork quilt and stared at the wall. It was easy to see that she was finding it hard to start what she intended to say. I stayed quiet.

Finally she began. "I'm sorry for the way I've treated you, B'Anne. You didn't get in the family way to take Will away from Victoria. And even if you had … saving him from that girl was a good thing." She met my eyes at last. "Victoria came back to town a few weeks ago. Her husband had recently died." Mrs. Carter's eyes dropped to her hands, twisting against the quilt. "I'd only been sick a little while, so I got out of bed and asked her to tea at the hotel. I … I'm ashamed to say I wanted to find out what Will's chances were."

I turned on my heel to go. I didn't want to hear this. But Mrs. Carter said, "Wait. Wait, B'Anne." So I turned back around to face her.

"She asked all kinds of questions about Will and you. I think she was going to try to get him back."

I nodded. I hoped my voice would be normal when I replied, "I'm not surprised."

"Well," Mrs. Carter continued, "I finally saw how selfish and vain she is. Just buried a husband, but didn't seem to care. All gussied up, bragging about her house and servants. Eager to break up a marriage and leave two little ones fatherless." The tears in Mrs. Carter's eyes spilled down onto her pallid cheeks. "Will could never have been happy with her." She wiped her eyes and smiled, but grimly. "She was some put out when I told her Will was happy as a man could be, and loves you and his babies truly. She flounced out of the inn like her tail was on fire." This time her smile was real. "Can you forgive me, B'Anne? I'd like to make a fresh start."

I looked down at the lonely old woman who didn't want to leave life with things unsaid. How much of her illness was "woman trouble" and how much was guilty conscience? Or maybe she *was* sick, and being so upset made it worse. "Yes, I do. We can start again, as friends."

"Then I think I can sleep now," she said.

I closed the curtains and went to find Will and Helga and the babies. He raised his eyebrows when I joined them. "She said what she had to say. It's all right. We'll all make amends in time." That was all he needed to hear right now. Later, in privacy, we could talk.

We went out to my folks' for supper. They made Helga welcome, enveloped me with hugs, and acted like Hi and Maggie were the best thing since the rubber-tired buggy was invented. Tad and Susie hauled them around until Ma finally demanded that they hand them over. "I'll have little enough time with them," she reminded my sister and brother. "I don't want to waste a minute of it."

Ma and I went into the kitchen, and she peeled potatoes while I nursed the babies. I gave her the full story of the babies' births, described our house, and told her about cooking for the threshing crew. I described my friendship with Elsa and Bertie, and all the help they'd given me. Much of it I'd already told her in letters, but talking face to face was so much better.

Ma was quiet for a bit, scooping up potato peels for the pigs while I handed off the babies to Susie and Helga. When I joined her at the sink to chop an onion, she said, "Your letters sounded happy, B'Anne. You and Will are making a go of this, then, in spite of the beginning?"

"Oh, Ma, most of the time I think he loves me. I *know* he loves the babies. And then something comes along to spoil things. Will's ma and Victoria have stirred up trouble that keeps me on tenterhooks.

When I found out that Victoria showed up after Will's ma called him home, I just wanted to give up."

Ma put her arms around me. "B'Anne, I think everything is going to work out. Talk it over with Will; hear what he says. I just know he loves you. And he's always been a good boy, solid as a rock."

"We haven't had a chance to talk yet. He seemed really glad to see us. Pray that everything turns out for the best."

Giving me a tight hug, Ma said, "I will, B'Anne. I pray for you every night. Tonight I'll just pray a little longer."

Ma made potato soup and cornbread, my favorite supper. When Pa said the blessing, I felt truly back home. His deep voice made me feel like a safe little child.

"You're staying the night, of course," Ma said after we had the dishes done and the kitchen tidied. "I've lined the big laundry basket for the babies, and Helga can sleep with Susie. The two girls had already become friends, so they took that news happily. I imagine Helga was looking forward to sleeping without a baby in her arms, too. I know I was.

It felt strange to be back in my old bedroom and have Will with me. Strange but wonderful. When Hi and Maggie were fed and sleeping in their basket, Will took me in his arms.

"I've missed you so," he whispered. "I might as well tell you now before you hear it from somebody else and get all foolish about it. Victoria was back in town, and I saw her." He must have felt me tense because he stroked my hair while he continued. "We didn't have a planned meeting or anything. She came into the store and saw me, and wanted to talk. Well, we talked all right. I told her I love my wife and babies. She left for Boston the next day."

I felt a rush of joy at the thought of Will telling Victoria exactly what was in his heart and reached up to stroke his cheek. "I knew Victoria was back. Minna told me in a letter right after you left."

"Oh, B'Anne, I'm so sorry you had that on your mind, with how hard everything else was for you ... managing on your own, and then that hard trip down from Ft. Benton."

"We're together now. That's all that matters." I snuggled closer to him and gave him a kiss to show him how much I meant the words.

Will gave a deep sigh, and pulled me close to show me how much he agreed with what I'd said.

Chapter 39

We only stayed three more days in Balsamview. We let Will's ma hold the babies until she tired, and we talked. I knew that even if she got well, we'd never be close, like a mother and daughter. But at least we could visit like civilized people. She filled me with so much advice on baby-raising that my head was swimming, trying to keep it all in.

On the second day, she came out to have dinner with the rest of the family. One of Will's sisters had brought chicken fricassee and noodles, and the other brought green tomato relish and dessert, a sponge cake with tinned peaches from the Carters' store.

Between bites, Will's oldest sister remarked, "Those were beautiful dresses you and Helga had on when you arrived, B'Anne."

I sensed the hidden meaning: How could we afford two dresses? Did we use her pa's money for them? I was glad we'd soon have many miles separating us. "Uncle Hiram bought them for us," I said casually. "He insisted." I smiled broadly at her. "Uncle Hiram is a wonderful man. He's helped us more than we can ever repay him for; says that's what family's supposed to do. I love him dearly."

Mr. Carter beamed, but Will's ma and both his sisters didn't seem to share the feeling. Finally Mrs. Carter said, "Well, if I'm turning over a new leaf, maybe I'd better write a letter to Hiram."

Will nodded. "Ma, that would be a wonderful thing to do. I'm glad we went to Montana, if only so we could be close to him."

That conversation might have been partly the reason Mrs. Carter went immediately to bed after the meal. She was trying to be a new person, but it seemed to be hard.

Helga and I spent one whole day out at my folks' place before we left. I was taking wind-whipped diapers off the clothesline in the backyard when Pa hurried out of the barn to talk to me.

"Haven't had a chance to talk to you without a bunch of folks around," he said. "How is it, B'Anne? Did we make a mistake, sending you and Will out to Montana Territory? It's worried my mind something terrible, sending my little girl off by herself. You're in my prayers every day and night."

"Oh, Pa, I wasn't by myself. I was with Will. And God surely heard your prayers. We're happy. You didn't make a mistake. You did a good thing."

Pa wasn't usually a hugger, but that afternoon he was. When he turned me loose, we both had tears in our eyes.

That last day's visit was special. My aunts and cousins came for tea, and so did my good friends Minna and Pearl. It was a wonderful day, and by the time we left for Sioux City next morning we had two boxes full of hand-me-downs for the babies, along with some new garments Ma had sewn. Helga fared well, too, with dresses my cousins no longer needed. I knew some of them would go to her older sisters. The rest would all need to be taken in, but that was no problem. My sewing machine would take care of that, back home.

Yes, Montana was now back home. I hated to leave my family, and I felt sorry for Will, going away when his mother was still sick, but we were both anxious to get back. Will was fretting because we still had a garden to finish planting, and a well to dig. I was thinking about my rows of seedlings on the windowsills, and hoping Sev or Uncle Hiram had remembered to water them like they'd promised.

The steamboat trip upstream was slower than the one downstream had been. Besides the fact that the boat was running against the current, there were even more snags than before. The mountain snow-melt created rapids, and trees that had been torn out by high water had to be carefully maneuvered around.

It was near the end of April when we finally got to Choteau. After dropping Helga off, we stopped at the store for a few supplies and a welcoming hug from Bessie. Uncle Hiram was pleased to see us when we stopped at his place, but he complained that we'd let those babies grow while we were gone.

When we drove up to our little cabin, it looked more welcoming to me than a governor's mansion. It was clean inside; Uncle Hiram had seen to that. He'd left a fire laid in the cookstove, so all it took was the strike of a sulphur match to start warming the room. Sev had taken good care of the animals. My seedlings on the windowsills were straggling and leggy, past time to plant, but they were moist and healthy.

I spent the next couple of days doing laundry and planting my seedlings, with Will's help. He rode out to check fences, or so he said. I think he just wanted to admire his land, back home again.

He came in that evening from checking fences, holding one hand behind his back, like he had a surprise. I looked up from stirring the pot of stew, and he stuck his hand out to me, looking embarrassed. It held a bunch of spiky purple wild iris. "From down by the creek," he said softly. "To thank you for one year ago today."

We'd been so busy the date had slipped my mind.

"Remember? You wore that pretty pink dress, and we ended the day sitting on boxes by the campfire, drinking cocoa and talking like decent human beings for the first time in days?" He looked down at Hi and Maggie, kicking on the rag rug, playing with a tin cup and the dipper from the water bucket. His voice was husky. "We decided we'd make a fresh start, and not even think about you raising a baby with your Aunt Isabel in Des Moines, or me following Victoria to Boston."

I stepped over the babies and into his arms. Hi started to fuss, so we each picked up a baby and stood in a warm embrace. After a moment I opened my eyes and gazed over Will's shoulder at the table he'd made, the rose-painted lamp on top of it, the bright patchwork quilt covering the oak bed at the end of the room, the cradle beside it. It was like he was reading my mind when he next spoke, the breath from his words whiffing my hair.

"Everything I ever need and want and love is in this room, B'Anne."

I nodded, my lips against his neck. "I know, Will. Oh, yes … and for me, too. All in this room."

49215330R00161

Made in the USA
San Bernardino, CA
21 August 2019